W9-CAP-904

Also by Nancy Lemann

The Fiery Pantheon
Lives of the Saints
The Ritz of the Bayou
Sportsman's Paradise

To Mark Clein

Malaise

A NOVEL

Nancy Lemann

SCRIBNER

New York   London   Toronto   Sydney   Singapore

SCRIBNER
1230 Avenue of the Americas
New York, NY 10020

This book is a work of fiction. Names, characters, places, and incidents
either are products of the author's imagination or are used fictitiously.
Any resemblance to actual events or locales or persons, living or dead,
is entirely coincidental.

Copyright © 2002 by Nancy Lemann

All rights reserved, including the right of reproduction in whole
or in part in any form.

SCRIBNER and design are trademarks of Macmillan Library Reference USA, Inc.,
used under license by Simon & Schuster, the publisher of this work.

For information about special discounts for bulk purchases,
please contact Simon & Schuster Special Sales:
1-800-456-6798 or business@simonandschuster.com

"Stars Fell on Alabama," by Mitchell Parish and Frank Perkins,
©1934 (renewed EMI Mills Music, Inc.). All rights reserved. Used by permission.
Warner Bros. Publications U.S. Inc., Miami, FL 33014.

DESIGNED BY ERICH HOBBING

Text set in Granjon

Manufactured in the United States of America

1   3   5   7   9   10   8   6   4   2

Library of Congress Cataloging-in-Publication Data

Lemann, Nancy
Malaise : a novel / Nancy Lemann
p.   cm.
1. Newspaper publishers—Fiction. 2. British—United States—Fiction.
3. New York (N.Y.)—Fiction. 4. California—Fiction. I. Title.
PS3562.E4659M35   2002
813'.54—dc21   2002017584

ISBN 0-7432-1548-6

Malaise

Men who had left the port for ever would sometimes remember on a grey wet London evening the bloom and glow that faded as soon as it was seen: they would wonder why they had hated the Coast and for a space of a drink they would long to return.

—Graham Greene

Here the sun glares out of a high blue sky—a sun that can beat all sense from your brains, that can be destructive of all you have known and believed: a relentless, pounding, merciless sun.

—Carey McWilliams

1

It was the spring in New York, that uncertain season. I had just flown in from the other coast. I heard there had been snow in April in New York, followed by incessant rain, and then one of those heat waves in the high 90s that occur once in a century. There was a massive thunderstorm the night I arrived to visit the city in late May. At my hotel the security guy and the doorman discussed sports, in their common humanity, watching the tremendous storm. Maybe you have to live in the desert to really appreciate rain. The town I had just come from on the other coast, not far from the Mexican border, was very parched. Every day the sun blazed out of a clear blue sky, a sun that could be destructive of all you have known and believed. But it had not destroyed this: my loyalty to the East Coast and the green Atlantic.

The weather in New York, unlike the desert, was volatile. The next morning it cleared up completely. I headed down Fifth Avenue in the sterling spring day among the fascinating men in horn-rim glasses with achievements and bow ties. New York was suave. Men walked down the streets smoking cigars while talking on cellular telephones. But they didn't do that until I recently moved away after living there for fifteen years. Wall Street was not doing well when I lived in New York. The whole place at that time had hit a new low. Then when I left, New York suddenly achieved a pinnacle of glory: the stock market went through the roof, the Yankees won the World Series, crime plummeted, Broadway had its best season in seven decades. The Bronx botanical garden was recultivated. The Brooklyn botanical garden was renovated. Times Square was revitalized. And New York characters from opera stars to doormen were constantly celebrated in huge articles heralding the renaissance in the *New York Times,* which I read from my remote location, as I had since been exiled to a barbarous region of the world.

Some people have a song—as in, "They're Playing Our Song." I had a place. My husband and I used to go there every Saturday night when we lived in New York. It was a dive on Fifty-first Street in Hell's Kitchen, an unpretentious French bistro. I thought I would go there for old times' sake. As usual they were playing French accordion music, the kind that at first sounds exotic and elegant and reminds you of a Mediterranean port in North Africa at a Moroccan café, where Marlene Dietrich would perform in the thirties, while sun-drenched legionnaires march off toward the desert . . . but as it goes on, you suddenly realize that it's kind of grating, and they could actually play it in a torture camp to get you to confess.

As usual there were a number of empty tables. Probably their former occupants had confessed and run out screaming. I took an inconspicuous table in a corner.

The place was run by a French family who had emigrated from the Riviera. You would think they would have preferred the Riviera to Hell's Kitchen. There was an elderly grandmother who did all the cooking, and on her breaks sat chain-smoking at the bar gazing despairingly into her drink. There was a dark handsome grandson who was obsessed with the Riviera and had painted a vast and elaborate mural of the Mediterranean that was ingeniously wrapped along the walls. Assorted relatives performed the duties of proprietor, waitress, bartender—against the endless expanse of the Riviera depicted by the grandson—and lived above the restaurant, bound by the morose yet occasionally exhilarating malaise of the émigré.

A sudden glamour descended on the place, as across the room I saw someone I knew. My heart leapt up unexpectedly. I took out a card and wrote a short note. I called the waiter and asked him to deliver it.

"To Mr. Lieberman. He's that man over there in the black suit with the white hair," I said.

"Oh, I know who Mr. Lieberman is," said the waiter. "Everyone knows who Mr. Lieberman is."

So he brought Mr. Lieberman my card. "Fleming Ford"—my name was engraved—"sends regards," I wrote beneath.

Mr. Lieberman turned slowly to scan the room and signaled suavely at me, made a brief tense sign, as if he were bidding at auction. He had an air of sangfroid. A skeptical glance, a brief suave sign, an eyebrow slightly raised—this was the extent of the impact you could have on such a man. Nothing would surprise him, you felt. You could ride in on a mule and it would not surprise him. You would get the eyebrow slightly raised, the grave wry glance.

He was tall and towering, with a broad-shouldered grace, white-haired, bow-tied, the works. He could have been seventy-five. He could have been sixty. It was impossible to tell. But I knew that he had seen the last of seventy. He looked as if he would hold steady through storms, and it looked as if there had been many, for he had the quality of a gallant tortured soul. You knew instantly, when you saw him, that something sad had happened to him. But you could see the struggle: as if he had a long adversarial relationship with his grief, and had reached a sort of smooth agreement with it. It was an uneasy peace and had been hard won.

Some things are ingrained with truth, I was thinking: it

13

is never easy to learn the story of a man's life. Mr. Lieberman was a type who scented out trouble, for he had a need to try to fix things. He must mend a broken wing, protect the weak, resurrect the failure. Mr. Lieberman was a mogul. He owned newspapers, among other things, on both coasts. I had worked for him when I first came to New York fifteen years ago, in what seemed like another life. Soon after my recent remove to the other coast, I heard that he had lost his wife. It was known that he was not taking it well. For such a man to have been in love at all must have been frustrating because his way was to be a loner. Now he was alone again. But the mechanism of his heart went haywire. It would prove that he could not stay in New York, where he and his wife had lived together. Mr. Lieberman was British, and he may have wanted to go home, but he could not bring himself to do that, for some reason, and so went even farther from his home.

He suddenly turned back to stare at me across the room as if he had forgotten something. Then the skeptical glance was gone. He had the most tortured eyes that I have ever seen.

But that was for Adelaide. His deep blue eyes transmitted an electrifying sorrow. It was a pain so deep that it cast him adrift. At the same time he also had a vitality, as anyone in his still rising position would, conglomerating empires, acquiring companies, consolidating his dominions. He was a dazzling individual.

I did not know it then, but this moment was only to prolong my exile to a barbarous region of the world.

For I too would go so far—"When shall we meet again, / Dearest and best, / Thou going easterly, / I, to the West?"

2

Esperanza is a medium-sized American city on the West Coast not far from the Mexican border. This is the place of my exile. The best thing about Esperanza is it's not hard to look at. The landscape reminds me of North Africa, with the tall palms and hot flat shining sea and some dilapidated houses. The park is a raging Spanish colonial vision, and has lawn bowling played by old men in white suits and safari helmets.

Coyotes howl in the canyon at night—if not hyenas, which they sound like—among the giant eucalyptus trees, the heat, the green, the palms. The people are obsessed with the weather, as historically people there always have been, from the Spanish chroniclers of the sixteenth and seventeenth centuries to the present day. The place has always been billed as a paradise.

Paradise takes some getting used to. Paradise gives you stress, actually. That is the great crux of the place. Invalids traditionally went to California seeking restoration and good health, lost souls seeking solace. It's ironic, because once you get there, you go into a huge decline.

I am the Esperanza Chamber of Commerce's worst nightmare. This is mainly because of the heat and sun. It is as if I had moved to Africa. The African plain.

The local newspaper obsessively records the rainfall—except there is no rainfall, and they have to list it cumulatively from long years past, or discuss rain in other areas of the world.

"Here the sun glares out of a high blue sky—a sun that can beat all sense from your brains . . . a relentless, pounding, merciless sun."

I quote from one of the sociological histories of Los Angeles. You must study that metropolis to get any information at all about this region, and even then you won't find much about Esperanza. At first I kept wondering why it isn't talked about. Not only Esperanza—I can understand why Esperanza isn't talked about, because it's obscure—but this glaring sun that only one person mentioned. I'm from the South, where it's hot. In Alabama the incredible heat and humidity and adverse conditions are part of the atmosphere, and people complain of it and speak colorfully of it and it is part of the picture, but in Esperanza the adverse conditions aren't talked about. I could talk about them, though.

So another word about Esperanza. I have studied hard: "Esperanza has always been a jumping-off place. Since 1911 the suicide rate of Esperanza has been the highest in the nation; between 1911 and 1927 over 500 people killed themselves in Esperanza. Chronic invalids have always been advised to go to California, and once there, they drift to Esperanza. From Esperanza there is no place else to go; you either jump into the Pacific or disappear into Mexico."

The figures continue at that rate to the present.

There is trouble in paradise.

3

So how did I come, at the age of forty, in the middle of this journey of our life, to be set down there at the quiet limit of the world, far from correspondences to anyone or anything I know?

The answer lies in the Mojave Desert.

I have said that Esperanza is parched. It is in fact so parched that when my husband, a geologist, discovered that there was a massive unknown water plate beneath the Mojave Desert, he saw the opportunity to organize a partnership to develop a pipeline to bring water to the coast.

My husband had been employed in New York by one of the world's largest exploration and development companies. He was constantly being sent out to identify natural resources—water, oil, and natural gas. It was Mozambique one month and Siberia the next, Kuwait, the Sahara.

Contrary to what you might think, water is very political. This is why the Trans-California Pipeline decided not to base its offices in the metropolis, Los Angeles. The Mexican government was desperate to develop the area south of the border and was willing to provide a lucrative deal for the pipeline to go into the dark tortured border towns and bald hills of Mexico. So the company's base came to be at Esperanza, once the seat of a vast desert empire stretching all the way to Death Valley—the driest, hottest area to be found in North America. One of the forty-niners on his way to the goldfields first saw the possibilities of irrigation for the western deserts. It became the obsession of his life, an obsession that would descend to my husband.

4

During my trip to New York in May I had drinks with a family friend at his club: an old-fashioned historical New York men's club that is filled with white-haired gents ranging from the decrepit to the robust, but the key is, they all have white hair. And many have bow ties. And some even have seersucker suits in summer. In short it was as if I'd died and gone to heaven. Where everyone has white hair and looks as if they just stepped out of a band box. Where age and formality are prized.

The family friend, George Bellamore, had hair white enough to thrill me and was moving thrillingly toward decrepitude. If there is one thing I love in a man it is decrepitude. If only I could love it in myself.

It developed that George Bellamore had recently had what he called a puzzling lunch with Mr. Lieberman. He said that Mr. Lieberman was "lost." Somehow even in the circumstances it was inconceivable to me—a man of his illustrious accomplishments being lost.

But even before his wife died, Mr. Lieberman had that quality of melancholy. Maybe that is why I came to love him so. I thought I loved him for his achievements, but maybe it turns out I loved him because he was lost. If you asked me what I thought distinguished him, I would have immediately said: a devotion to excellence. By that I mean standards of excellence he expected of himself at all times. This to me is the definition of heroism. He also expected it of others. This is the sure road to disillusionment.

Mr. Lieberman's grandfather, Lord Northwood, controlled a vast chain of newspapers and periodicals including the *Daily Herald, Sporting Life,* the *Tatler,* and *Horse and Hound.* He started life in Frankfurt as a poor Jewish errand boy and became one of the most powerful press barons. Lacking any formal education, Lord Northwood had a remarkable genius for business. He was the first Jew of humble birth to be created a peer, in 1910. His capacity for finance was probably never eclipsed in England. His descendants were raised in a way totally alien to his own origins.

The man rose to heights that would be spectacular from any origin. He had emigrated to England in 1859 at the age of twenty-one. He became the mastermind of the British acquisition of the Suez Canal, the financier of the regeneration of Egypt, and the inventor of the French Riviera as a British retreat. His legacy was long. His descendants lived mostly in its shadow. You'd have to be a strong character to wear the mantle of Lord Northwood and not just spend your life hanging around at European racetracks and estates. With an inheritance of that magnitude, both in finance and achievement, it would be hard to measure up to its creator. Only one of his descendants came close.

George Bellamore claimed that Mr. Lieberman had affairs, during his marriage. This did not coincide with my belief in his standards of excellence. Furthermore it was astounding to me because he had been almost unnaturally devoted to Adelaide. To Adelaide he was so overpoweringly devoted that it caused certain somewhat weird elements in their relationship. They were reclusive. They didn't have close friends. They saw no one, which for a mogul in New

York was unusual. They stayed home doting on each other. Or rather Mr. Lieberman stayed home doting on Adelaide. She entertained a notion at one time of being a concert pianist, of which he was very proud. She played the piano for him at night. She was perhaps the reclusive one. She was actually quite a bit older than Mr. Lieberman, although she was very beautiful and retained her youthful looks. It was said by some that he had not known, when he married her, just how much older than him she actually was. Also that neither had he known it when she died.

The truth is, Mr. Lieberman idolized his wife. After she died he could not stay in New York. During the six months that had passed since her death he had moved around a lot. He did return to England at first. He went to cheap holiday resorts out of season. February is not the time for which depressing British seaside resorts, the dreary and loathsome towns of Hastings, Torquay, and Broadstairs, are famed. He went to seedy ruined places of seaside retreat, Menton, Biarritz. In the summer he would go, also out of season, to the arid deserts of the American West—Death Valley, Palm Springs. He became obsessed with Scottish glens and Norwegian fjords. Then it was the Riviera. But wherever he went, he went at the worst time, with a haplessness, or perhaps a perversity, that was soon to overpower his character. He searched for something, maybe penance to Adelaide. If it were true that he did have affairs while she lived, I could see that remorse would consume him now. But to me that remained a mystery. He careened from coast to coast and continent to continent. There was a basic aimlessness to his plans. The mechanism had been broken, the spring had gone haywire. There was a violence in what would become his decline.

I didn't imagine I would run into him again during my short visit to New York in May, but I did, and the disintegrating British mogul was soon to play an overpowering role in my life.

5

New York always had a We're-All-in-This-Together air. Everyone was always doing the exact same thing at the exact same time, like taking the train to Long Island on a summer Friday afternoon, or coping with the once-in-a-century heat wave while struggling through midtown to the office, experiencing the same thing in the same way. Or everyone would decide to stay home, and midtown would be deserted. Everyone always did the same thing. It was your common humanity.

The weather continued to be volatile during my trip in May. In my hotel lobby the security guys continued to discuss sports. A nanny provided by the hotel had been looking after my little children that day while I attempted to revisit the scenes of my lost youth. The weather had just turned fine; the nanny would take the children to the zoo. My little children, aged two and three, had learned better than to cast aspersions on a person who would take them to the zoo. I could advise them, teach them, love them, but I could not take them to massive children's emporiums while hopelessly contriving to carry them and the various elaborate contraptions that comprise their equipment. Why? In a nutshell, I was too old. Yet despite my age, forty, I had a suspicion of pregnancy. This scared me, for I am a coward. The world stopped, I got off, and contemplated the nine months of ailments before me. The vast decline, the untold worry. The world was fraught with risk. As Boswell said when his son was born, "When I saw the little man I knew I should never again have an easy hour."

You give your atomic particles to make these children, to compose another soul, so you're literally not all there anymore. A part of you is missing—your reason, perhaps.

Or maybe I had lost my reason on the job. In New York years ago I had started as a reporter on the metro desk of Mr. Lieberman's newspaper but that was not how I formed an acquaintance with him. My acquaintance with him was through Adelaide. But more on that later. And as to the newspaper, he had sold it during the course of my tenure there. I had moved around from cultural affairs to the architecture beat and historic preservation to the travel section, and ultimately, about six months before I left New York, I was elated to be promoted to a shimmering realm known as "New Perspectives."

It was a plum assignment. I would not be out doing the daily grind of reporting with deadlines and late hours. I would be dreaming up New Perspectives and working at home, drinking extra coffee in my pajamas, conducting my own personalized think tank.

But it turned out that New Perspectives was sort of like being transferred to Antarctica. It was like being stationed in sub-Saharan Africa. It was like being at a dinner party where one end of the table is hilarious with the clink of glasses and revelry and funny stories, while the other end is subsumed by darkness, silence, the deep freeze, and can't keep the conversation going.

For instance, what do you actually do all day in New Perspectives? Do you have to think up the New Perspectives yourself or does your editor come up with them? Actually the weight of New Perspectives was a heavy one to bear. You set up your new office and immerse yourself in Perspectives so amorphous, plans so vague, that of course in the end you are doomed. You are in a dark wood where the straight way is lost. You are wearing your pajamas at twelve noon. Sooner or later the chilling knowledge comes that your Perspectives are not really that New. The prospect of taking the afternoon off no longer obsesses you with broken hopes because a meteoric rise in New Perspectives no longer seems so sure.

New Perspectives began to cause me various neuroses. I would have giddy fits, followed by malaise. I had comatic ideas. Sometimes I had visions. New Perspectives danced vainly before my eyes, giving me headaches and inner-ear disturbances. My nerves were shot. Pretty soon the men with butterfly nets would be coming to take me away.

You come to a point in your life, age forty for instance, when you might reasonably decide to try to figure out who you are. You try to find yourself when you are twenty. It would not be too unreasonable to try to figure out who you are when you are forty. I had given fifteen years of service on the paper. Maybe I was burnt-out. Maybe I should try to find out who I really am. Not to mention what we are all doing here. Who planned it that our humanity should grow on this green earth for its finite term? These must be worthy New Perspectives.

My editor saw which way the wind was blowing and assigned me to the "Metro Special Perspectives Team"— being too kind-hearted just to call it going back on the metro desk. First he subtly changed the name. After all, "New Perspectives" sounds like a meaningless presidential campaign slogan. So then it was the somewhat Soviet-sounding "Special Perspectives," later briefly streamlined to the equally vague but simpler "Special Projects." Meanwhile I went back to covering some huge disaster like a water-main break depriving thousands of heat and hot water in Chelsea, disrupting the IRT for two days at rush hour, and similar events that enabled me to regain that We're-All-in-This-Together air of which Special Perspectives was the antithesis.

Then I found out that I was moving to the West Coast. I had long ago formed a close relationship with my editor, and it was with the vague promise of more Special Projects and a freelance contract that I left for Esperanza.

6

When my husband first lured me out there to look the place over, it did not seem so bad. I contemplated the blizzard raging in New York as we flew over the Grand Canyon, and Esperanza began to look pretty good.

The plane ride to Esperanza tends to get kind of turbulent somewhere over Iowa, where they have twisters. Also over Salt Lake City, where they tend to have incapacitating snowstorms well into late spring. But you finally get past the snow-capped mountains back to the desert, and the California coast laden with palms. Soon I was sitting beside a sheath of palms outside my hotel room, it was 80 degrees in the middle of December, and I had seen the vast Pacific Ocean.

Actually it was a little too vast. The Pacific is a bit much. There is something pitiless and barbaric about it.

On the other hand you could practically be on the Amalfi coast, the Mediterranean, even North Africa, what with the gardens—bougainvillea, jacaranda, palms—and the views of the water and the hills.

You can love a place if it has correspondences to other places that you love. Possibly I was desperately trying to correspond it to places that I love.

I am a southerner, so my inescapable first impression of California was that you wouldn't have the Civil War out there to brood about. The Civil War does not loom large in California. I would have to find something new to be haunted by. Maybe I could be haunted by the Mexican War. That looms pretty large in California. But I don't think California people tend to brood about it. Not too much brooding goes on in California.

But a word about southern California. "Transport a man to a remote wilderness and what happens? No matter how a transplanted man may thrive in his possessions, his life is to some extent impoverished, even though he may be quite unconscious of the deprivation, though he may have disliked the old and may like the new: he once had a close and vital tie with the world about him, and now he has little or none."

Take me, for instance. Sometimes driving home to Esperanza from the north coast towns along the sea I would be ravished by the lights of the Mediterranean-like coastline in the night. Beautiful? Yes. But can you even understand its beauty? It would take twenty years' familiarity to understand its meaning. I keep thinking, if it were Florida, say, which it resembles in spirit (place to take it easy in), I would understand its meaning from familiarity, for I belong to it and it belongs to me, because when you're from the Alabama coast, Florida is a second skin to you. I know what's going on in Florida. It's a green old frivolous place where you take it easy. People take it easy in California too. But there are many subtle differences. For one thing you're allowed to complain in Florida. Then too, in California there is often a blood-thinning chill at night from the desert that you never get in Florida. There is not that gentle climate the mid-westerners longed for when they first came to California to live in little bungalows beside the palms. They expected to sit on the porch as night fell on the Tropics—whereas desert weather comprises first the intolerable sun, then as night falls, a blood-chilling cold. It is enough to drive you mad. But the truth is that I must begrudge the beauty of the other coast—even the stars, the vast Pacific in the night—out of loyalty to my other loves. I must begrudge the blue Pacific out of loyalty to the green Atlantic. So I had come back to visit the East Coast.

7

Having returned from his haphazard travels after the death of his wife, Mr. Lieberman was apparently back in New York for the moment. His attempts to retrace the steps of his previous travels with her or to search for his own lost youth in England had not turned out well. The Yorkshire Dales are not noted to allure in February. Seaside resorts do not present their least depressing aspect in winter. He had it all mixed up. Without Adelaide he was too free. Domesticity had been his cage for fifty years. One likes being in a cage. In the cage you are free, ironically.

Before his wife died, he had generally walked through Central Park every day to his office in midtown. He was prone to lengthy episodic walks. He lived in one of the last large private houses on Fifth Avenue, where Adelaide had presided over his dominions. But he liked the cavernous gritty beauty of Times Square, as it once was, and the breezy American chaos cast there. He also liked the green hope of the park on his long walk every day to the office. No doubt such a man keeps his trim grace by taking his long walks every day. My hotel, the Century, was in a central location between the park and midtown on his old route. So I ran into him again near there during my trip in May.

This was my first visit to New York since we had moved to Esperanza. My husband was somewhere in the Mojave Desert. I marveled at all the weather changes in New York. I had become a weather freak like the Esperanzans. Any deviation from the perfect sun makes them demented. Every day the sun glares out of a pure blue sky—etc. You get used to it.

I was taking a stroll in the park. The leaves were blowing around in a fresh dark wind as if it might soon rain again. The park was like a stage set of metropolitan glamour. A couple of blocks from the hotel, I saw Mr. Lieberman. He recognized me and gave the same little sign, enigmatic, grave, tipping an imaginary hat.

It happens that I myself had been quite close to his late wife. She and I were from the same crumbling but ornate old social town on the Alabama coast, Fort Defiance. It was rather Proustian there, with aging figures of distinction or pretension depending on how you looked at it, and a taste for debauchery. In her day, Adelaide had been a southern socialite hostess type in New York, until in later years she secluded herself. Mr. Lieberman would have placed me as one of the few people she still let into her circle. I used to have lunch with her once or twice a year in New York, where we would reminisce about Fort Defiance. We did not see each other often, but that does not account for all the time I spent in her company. Her spirit always seemed to travel with me. We had a lot in common.

Fort Defiance is the type of town that is still living on its memories of being the state capital from 1830 to 1831. This brief status of renown was quickly shifted to Montgomery but Fort Defiance would never forget its moment of glory, would in fact bask thereafter in its moment of glory, like a football star in college who goes downhill from there. In Fort Defiance you generally spent your life doing what your father told you to do. You worked for your father, you went into your father's business, you lived on the same street as your father, you would swing your children on the same oak tree that your father swung you on. Your father was the world's most towering figure, just as the year 1830 when your town was the state capital was the world's most shining moment.

Fort Defiance had a somewhat hapless history. It kept wishing for a chance to illustrate its nature of defiance, which it never actually fulfilled. It was founded by the French in the sixteenth century, taken over by the Spanish in the seventeenth, and the British in the eighteenth. In each instance the population was defiant, but defeated nevertheless. The people waited defiantly for an attack, which would give them a chance to show their mettle. But when the attack came their mettle showed to less advantage than they'd planned. At this point the spirit of defiance still reigned and thrived, but there were fewer opportunities for rebellion. In the nineteenth century the city took a bitter stand against Napoléon, and the fort was built in open challenge. But of course Napoléon never got that far. In the War of 1812 the fort again was ready and enraged with hate, heavily manned against the British, hoping for attack. But the British chose to attack elsewhere (see the Battle of New Orleans) and so another chance for glory was denied. Finally, in the Civil War, it seemed the time at last had come for victory. But when immediately and gleefully the fort was manned, it was instantaneously captured by Union troops during the opening months of the conflict.

Adelaide and I escaped the destiny of Fort Defiance, with its taste for debauchery, perhaps brought on by its disappointed hopes. Secretly you would realize that Alabama depressed you. But you would defend it till your dying day. So Adelaide and I had a lot to talk about when we met, such as reminiscing about our fathers, the world's two most towering figures. When I moved to the West Coast in December, she told me she had a trip to Los Angeles planned for June and we would have lunch there then. This date was still pending when she died.

Mr. Lieberman was standing there regarding me curiously in Central Park. I thought he would have walked on but he stopped. "June twenty-first for lunch, I know you're free, Miss Ford," he said. He gave me that tortured look again. "In Los Angeles. So how about having lunch with me there on that day?"

Obviously he had track of all her appointments and meant to fulfill them. It was a bit as if he were shadowing her ghost. Searching for his sign of her, or to do his penance for her.

"You don't quarter a filly like Fleming Ford in Esperanza," said Mr. Lieberman, looking at me closely. How strange to get a compliment from him. "Now if it were one of the Abernathy girls," he continued, referring to an old social name in Fort Defiance, "then it would be fine. They would fade in quietly to whatever culture they were taken to without complaint, and cook dinner every night."

"That sounds very gallant of them," I suggested.

"But not very interesting."

"Maybe."

"That's their reality, Miss Ford. The reality of the Abernathy girls is to cook dinner every night without complaint. There is no actual reality," he said calmly. "There is only what you see. And that is reality for you."

The impact of his somewhat curious philosophy had an electrifying effect on me.

"What are you doing with yourself out there?" he inquired.

"I'm working on Special Projects for the paper."

"It sounds a little vague."

"You've just hit the nail on the head."

"How are they coming along?"

"My dream of Special Projects has not worked out."

"So your dream got shot down? There's plenty more dreams where that one came from, kid."

I found him electrifying. With his towering grace and stern glamour.

"Do you like the West Coast, generally?" I asked. I was only trying to prolong the conversation.

"Very much. It's the last frontier."

"And do you like Fort Defiance?" I asked him.

"Very much. It has an indefinable air of civic failure."

That definitely wraps up Fort Defiance, and its bemusing lost hopes for grandeur.

With his tall commanding presence, an upright posture forever unbent despite his grief, his decline—he seemed a man from an earlier era. It was the last year of the twentieth century and somehow you couldn't quite picture him in the next one.

"So it's Los Angeles next week. Same place, same time," he concluded. "Good-bye, Miss Ford."

"You don't have to call me Miss Ford."

"Right. I'll see you in Hollywood, Miss Ford," he persisted, staring me down, but somehow oblivious and aloof—his trademark regard. He was wearing a seersucker suit, which looked as if it had seen better days. He mopped his brow in the heat, and departed.

"Please don't call me Miss Ford!" I mentioned to his

now receding figure. But he only looked back briefly and tipped the imaginary hat. Then he walked on.

8

New York was suave yet dilapidated—like Mr. Lieberman. A characteristic of world metropolises: they're dilapidated. That gives them humanity. The Beaux Arts buildings glittered darkly in the afternoon, the angels carved on architraves laden with the reassuring dust of time. You don't get the reassuring dust of time in California. It doesn't seem old. At the hour of twilight there was a tremendous rainstorm. I watched, in a moment of happiness at its beauty, elated by the novelty. It was rare that I was able to dawdle at a café past twilight, what with the children—and another, I thought, on the way.

Bulgarian violins were playing in the tea room when I walked into the Century. The bar was another world— people smoked and drank in a darkly poignant atmosphere of decadence. It was the opposite of California, where everyone was in a health craze.

Upstairs I dismissed the nanny. This was a mistake. The children were strung out. My three-year-old daughter had a tantrum. I fixed her cheese and crackers, which fell on the floor, so I picked them up but this had betokened a tragedy whose like the world could never bear. She lay down on the floor in despair and cried bitterly. I tried to talk reason. A gracious discourse was given to instill Alabama manners. This seemed to calm her down. She artfully arranged her hands into a tepee under her chin like she does when she is about to impart very detailed information such as that the boy across the street taught her how to spit. This of course degenerated into both children illustrating with increasing hilarity the art of spitting, while I contemplated the momentarily forgotten fact of my future demise.

It seems when you have children you tend to look at them and suddenly see years down the road when they will shake their head and shed a tear to remember you. In other words there is a constant reference to your mortality. Pretty soon you're picturing your own demise, then embroidering it, until you are virtually planning it.

Maybe this is partly the effect that California has on you. Where in paradise you can't stop thinking of decline and decay. Take me, for instance. I can't stop thinking of decline and decay. And it's not only me. The gorgeous bridge to Santa Maria from Esperanza is copiously posted with suicide counseling hotlines and pleas not to end it all. There is a beautiful train to Los Angeles called the *Starlight* that goes along the coast; there are often suicides at the most bucolic oceanside spot.

There is trouble in paradise.

My two-year-old son is going through a soldierly phase. He wants to murder the sea and kill the government. In between staring contests my daughter and I discussed subtle gradations in the art of spitting. I searched ceaselessly for order, in an effort to cope, by incessantly cleaning up. Maybe being a mother after all makes you brave: I was so tired I didn't care if I died. But I sailed through the storm. I met what came.

What came was staring contests, spitting contests, and piteous pleas in tortured voices for water at all hours during the night, as if we were crawling through the desert.

In the morning we were still strung out. I had to avert

danger, avenge injustice, create diversions, figure out how to procure and serve food, correct disobedience and the failure to cooperate, try not to use curse words, and in fact realize that I must set an example of grace, for if I am kind and calm, then it would be contagious to them.

Or if you're too kind and calm they'll walk all over you. Yes dear, coming dear, right away dear—I've been down that street and it's the wrong route.

With very small children, you can't have pristine order. Things are instead in chaos. This in turn leads to squalor. No doubt the fact that I even try to constantly restore pristine order in the face of the overwhelming odds contributes to my painful knowledge of futility. If I let things go a bit it would be easier, but then I might be like the man who gives up his routine and the next thing you know he's in his bathrobe all day and has lost his grip on reality.

So I go to the opposite extreme. Like the Englishman who built a vast estate in the middle of nowhere in Africa at the end of the British Empire, and insisted on being served by attendants wearing scarlet uniforms and fezzes at a vast dinner table even when he was alone. His aide tried to tell him he was overdoing it. But he received the reply, "The moment one gives up the niceties is when one stops being an Englishman." Every night the guy dresses for dinner in white tie and tails in the middle of nowhere in Africa on his madman estate. The aide gets upset again and tells the master that he's not in England anymore. "Yes and that's all the more reason to maintain one's standards."

I felt that way about maintaining order amid the chaos of the children, though I knew it was excessive, like the guy in Africa creating pomp and circumstance on the Equator. I felt a bond with him and his quixotic quest.

Or maybe he reminded me of Mr. Lieberman.

9

I followed the complicated instructions for reaching my
husband, Mac, at his remote drilling outpost in the Mojave
Desert.

"Today is our anniversary, an event that tends to escape
your notice," I informed him. I had an appointment that
morning, my last in New York, with my old obstetrician to
confirm my suspicion of pregnancy. I can always tell when
I am pregnant for in the early stages I am filled with *angst*
and revenge. Not toward the little stranger, of course. Just
toward the world at large and especially my husband. After
the early stages, an overwhelming interest in knickknacks
takes over. As in, decorating the house with huge amounts of
knickknacks. Wicker baskets. Tea towels. That type of thing.

After the knickknacks phase, there is the phase where I
can only read cataclysmic books about World War I.

But I didn't tell my husband all this on the phone. Having engaged the nanny for one last morning I walked east to
Madison Avenue and stopped in at a café. Inside there was
a sudden warmth. It had just begun to rain again and was
quite chilly. This café had an atmosphere of the North. It
had an Adirondacks theme. There was an old song playing;
it dated from the time I first left Alabama for the North,
which filled me with intolerable nostalgia. Six months ago
I had left a home again, this time to go West. The struggle
between the North and the South was something I had

always understood. To add the West to the equation was something more than I could as yet comprehend. I felt somewhat fondly for the West, with its wide spaces, palms, and desert, but—then again, after the novelty wears off, malaise sets in. Sometimes you get a malaise for places, you drive up and down the same avenues too many times, you turn a corner and suddenly become demented with despair. Even in the old beauty-haunted East Coast the malaise pursues you. Even in that beauty on the green Atlantic. It can pursue you anywhere.

My obstetrician received a phone call in the examination room during my appointment. He listened into the receiver for a moment. Then he flew into a rage. "Put her on, put her on, put her on the phone!" he yelled. He was a man with a large mustache and a large paunch. You would have called him robust. There was something jolly about him, despite the rage. "Go straight upstairs to your room!" he yelled into the phone.

"Go to your room immediately!" he continued. It was mesmerizing. "GO TO YOUR ROOM, DO IT NOW!" He was yelling at his little kid.

He held the wire. "She's just a very annoying child," he said with pride.

He confirmed the pregnancy. He sent me to a pathologist on Park Avenue because of some sort of bacteria or infection he had found, but this did not unnerve me, because it was part and parcel of the nine months of ailments and worry before me. It was no more unnerving than the whole experience, which is fraught with excessive amounts of worry and ailments throughout. My maker is standing near through those nine months, until I finally meet him in the delivery room. I've gotten two solid glimpses of my maker so far. I'm practically dating him. Our relationship revolves purely around life and death. It is a matter of that each time.

35

10

So I returned to the West. Westward the course of empire
takes its way. The Spaniards first laid eyes on Esperanza in
1602: a wasteland in a bowl of sagebrush amid cactus-dotted
hills. But wishful thinking goes a long way. Hence, the
name. In the 1850s as the pioneers made their way across
the desert, Esperanza became a ranching village. Drought in
the 1860s decimated rancho herds and there was no money
for irrigation canals and water lines. Geographical location
was a drawback (though the boosters called it paradise)
because of the isolation—hemmed in by impassable mountain ranges, deserts, and Mexico. The boosters said the town
was poised for greatness when a railroad was proposed to
link Esperanza to the East. Such a line was under consideration when the Civil War broke out and the plans were
dropped. The town was poised for greatness once again after
the war when the railroad was proposed anew. But the boom
went bust in the financial panic of 1873. The Southern
Pacific moguls thereafter hoarded Los Angeles as the West
Coast metropolis and would crush Esperanza if they could,
which they did when the railroad finally came through—to
Los Angeles, bypassing Esperanza and relegating it forever
to the sidelines as a dusty border town.

As time went on and water was diverted from the Colorado River to irrigate the place, the desert was transformed

into a garden. The Agua Caliente Racetrack in Tijuana became popular with the silent screen stars who came down from Hollywood in the 1920s and stopped at watering spots in Esperanza along the way. But World War II was the real boon for Esperanza. The military came out in a big way, destroyers cruising on the sunlit harbor, battleships galore, munitions factories, naval academies, and later, retired admirals drinking vodka tonics in the blistering sun of the endless evenings on the sea.

Great things were expected for Esperanza that never quite materialized. In that way it shared a part with Fort Defiance. Adverse conditions defined both places: suffocating heat and humidity and torrential flooding in Fort Defiance; in Esperanza dangerous aridity and isolation. In the South adversity developed the soul. In the Wild West adversity made cowboys.

Some say that Fort Defiance has lost its luster. But Fort Defiance has been losing its luster since 1831. Whereas Esperanza has come into its own. A California resort sensibility now defines it. Wellness has sprung from the Wild West town. Transformed into a paradise from a wasteland, it may once have been a struggling dustblown ranching village, but now it is an idyll.

While traveling on a plane for six hours with two small children you must preface all your remarks with the phrase "Under no circumstances." My son is in the process of learning not to throw knives. Not throwing knives, not spitting, not using curse words and not having a major American nervous breakdown was the basic program for six hours. We finally got back to Esperanza. I tried to Think Positive. Esperanza is what you would call a destination, not a pit stop on the way to somewhere else. It is the end of the line. The end of the rainbow and all that. It is itself at the end of the world, the quiet limit of the world. The landscape looks foreign, as ever like North Africa or the French Riviera.

Pilots love flying into Esperanza. The airport is in the middle of town. It is wedged into a daring strip of land between Main Street and the azure Pacific harbor. So you fly in spectacularly through the hills lined by palms and old parks and churches to the sea. This is the quaint part of town. The vast preponderance of Esperanza sprawls up and down the coast as well as east into the desert with new development. What propels a man to seek an escape from the old history-haunted East Coast, even to these bland precincts? You would be hard-pressed all in all to comprehend that it is California's oldest city.

Take Costa Verde. This is an extremely sybaritic Esperanzan community directly on the vast and after all quite glamorous Pacific. There is a racetrack founded by Bing Crosby in the thirties. You take Jimmy Durante Boulevard to get there. A fabulous hotel was recently built to reproduce the one from the thirties. They don't let things get very old here before they have to make them new again. You take long walks and look at the vistas of the vast and glamorous Pacific. If you live there the message is: "I live in this incredibly sybaritic California paradise, I see the ocean constantly, I take it easy, and basically my ceaseless plea in life is to relax." As if you were so tortured, so spent, that you had to go to the end of the earth, the quiet limit of the world, and stare at the vast Pacific to get a shred of peace.

They have some sort of exaggerated phobia of stress, even though there is meant to be no stress here to begin with, and it's meant to be the least stressful city in the U.S.A.

Every day in the local paper the stories are always about the following topics:

Surfing
Panda Bears
Baby Whales
Trouble at the Border
Obsessive Record of Rainfall Accumulation (lack thereof)

Once the impossible happened: it got cloudy. At first I rejoiced, while the Esperanzans contemplated forms of suicide. Actually it was cloudy for about ten minutes. Then it cleared up.

But I am awaiting the Santa Ana. That is when a hot wind blows through in September and it gives you a nervous breakdown.

The fact is, in L.A. you may get a nervous breakdown but not in Esperanza—reputed as paradise, noted for perfection, considered by experts to comprise the ideal climate. The entire cosmos of meteorological conditions comes to a screeching halt at Esperanza, in this apocalyptic holding pattern of the ideal. But actually the ideal standard of perfection exists only in the imagination, or as Mr. Lieberman would say, in each person's individual reality.

I had a friend who lived in Monte Carlo for a time but had to leave; he couldn't take the sun every day. He wanted shade. He wanted rain. The ideal climate for a vacation is different from the ideal climate for the ordinary work of every day. If you confuse the two, then you get Brain Swirl— an ecstatic effect produced by the vivid colors rendered of the green palms and dark red bougainvillea, as if in an African paradise, with sheets of dry heat hissing in the windows like a radiator.

In a normal climate it would rain maybe half the time and you would prize the lovely days. Here every day is lovely. That is the main cliché of the place. The rustling of the leaves, ecstatic fair skies, being by the azure sea, and the eucalyptus trees making the terrain look like Africa. It's lovely, all right—as long as you're wearing sunglasses well into the evening past seven o'clock. If not, flee the area immediately.

Due east of Costa Verde is the incredibly ritzy Rancho Santa Rosa. It is composed of polo grounds and horse farms raising thoroughbreds to race at Costa Verde, beside the views of Tuscan-seeming hills laden with the bougainvillea. The whole place used to be Douglas Fairbanks Sr.'s ranch. History here is the ranchers, the Spanish missionaries, the Hollywood stars. It is another community whose attitude is: "I have arrived in paradise. I want to relax." But what does prolonged contact with such a place do to you?

One night I went to see a movie about racial tensions in the South. I was so affected to see the South and all its anguish and defeat depicted. I kept wondering what the Esperanzans in the audience would think of all this passion and hate and violence. I have a feeling they would think: "I want to go boating. And I want to wear shorts. I want to wear shorts 365 days a year."

Once in a while the headline screams in panic: WE MAY GET A LITTLE RAIN! and then everyone goes to pieces and gets phobic.

It is very esoteric trying to observe the seasons here since there are few identifying changes in the weather throughout the year. September is hotter than August. October is hotter than September. I don't suppose you have much of a fall. There is supposed to be a rainy season but usually it doesn't pan out. You prepare and batten down the hatches, and then find the rainy season means that you get about five days of light rain over three months.

Some have tried to deny the aridity issue by claiming that Esperanza gets the same amount of rain as the French Riviera. This claim is tremendously false. Esperanza gets about five inches a year, give or take. Nice gets thirty-one. Not a drop falls in Esperanza for at least six months of the year (summer and fall). El Centro, what some call the hottest place on earth, inland at the Mexican border, gets two inches. Death Valley gets one. Palm Springs gets five, this relative luxuriance being the source of the oasis. Whereas Seville (Esperanza is often compared to the Andalusian region) gets twenty-three, Tangier and Algiers respectively (North Africa also frequently figures in the comparison) thirty-four and twenty-nine. And finally, New Orleans, representing the Gulf Coast including Alabama, gets sixty, taking the grand prize.

For some reason Los Angeles, only a few hours to the north, gets a very elaborate rainy season.

The city of Esperanza incorporates the ritzy towns up the coast as well as the most humble villages on the Mexican border. The solid middle class resides in the communities of Homeville, Normalville, and Normal Heights. One detects a rage for normality.

Nileville, Cairoville, and Alexandria stretch east to the desert. One detects a certain Egyptian craze—quite natural in a desert metropolis.

The last town on the California side before the border, San Jamillo, whose main industry was breeding thoroughbreds for the horse track in Costa Verde, used to be very charming. Its downfall came when Esperanza forced these rustic villages to incorporate into its bland American sprawl. Then San Jamillo, for one, went to pieces—urban renewal, crime sprees, freeways cutting it down the middle.

San Jamillo comes to an abrupt stop at the hills. There is a crumbling mission with tangled gardens and a fat monk in an old brown habit tied at the waist by a rope. He is holding a bright umbrella for the shade, next to a cactus and the bald hills beyond. If you drive on to the border from there, it will remind you of the Gulf Coast, almost of Fort Defiance. You will pass through a very pretty area of rolling fields, a bit parched of course, but with horses and old ranches down to the actual border, which is guarded by a chain-link fence and two distinctly unintimidating girls in a Border Patrol car putting on lipstick while watching the fence to check for people trying to escape and come over. An old-time stadium for bullfights heralds the Tijuana side. There is a Border Patrol car posted every mile or so along this fence with a man watching the hills. When you go to the north towns, Costa Verde, Rancho Santa Rosa, you get these incredibly ritzy sybaritic California towns, but when you go to the south, you approach the incredible, uncapturable, ominous squalor of Mexico.

My husband hoped to relieve the parched hills of Mexico with his water plate. He had grandiose engineering schemes to do for Mexico what William Mulholland had done for Los Angeles, which without his work would have remained a dusty desert town. The bald hills would bloom and the border would become a garden paradise.

The Mexican border was fixed by the Treaty of Guadalupe in 1848. Someone must have hiccupped while drawing the map, otherwise Esperanza would be in Mexico. It takes ten minutes to get to Tijuana from my front door. Aside from the Mexican flavor—mariachi bands loom large in Esperanza—there is no mistaking the American side for its gleaming air of prosperity as you head up the coast.

But Esperanza has an identity crisis. It's meant to be the last frontier with cowboys and a raw-boned integrity; instead it is proliferating with luxuriant subdivisions called Andalusia. Somehow the modern version of the cowboy has made his homestead in a luxuriant subdivision trying to recall the old world, the one it was meant to escape.

11

When we first got out here we lived at the Marriott Residence Inn. In a certain way it was exhilarating to be among a sea of gleaming new subdivisions built to resemble vaguely modernistic Spanish haciendas—it was deeply thrilling to be somewhere so nameless. But that only lasts for a week or so. Then it wears off, and you must ask yourself, Do I really want to live in a subdivision carved into the bald hills about five minutes ago that has a name like Vita Eterna? Or Lakeside but there is no sign of a lake. River View and there is no river for miles. The Crest at Mountain Laurel. No sign of a mountain. Or a crest. To get directions is difficult. All the streets have the same name. Take Sea Crest View. To Sea Crest Point. Turn on Sea Crest Lane. Go left on Sea Crest. No sign of the sea, of course—the developments are carved into the bald hills of the Inland Empire.

The burnished golden stucco is occasionally relieved by a bougainvillea brought in by an enterprising matron, but since these places have all been carved into the bald hills about five minutes ago, the planting is not mature, and there is the relentless North African–like sun.

I've moved around a lot since I got here. After the Marriott Residence Inn we moved to the old part of town, where we lived for a time in the Nile Apartments and the Twilight Club. Then we had several rented houses.

Once we got settled in our first house we didn't really

mean to move again. But we got kicked out. It's pioneer land—every man for himself. California people don't go in for overt yelling like in New York, but they're much more subtly twisted.

Take my real estate broker. In New York the real estate brokers are sharks. It's straightforward. It's out in the open. Everyone yells. Whereas in Esperanza, real estate brokers say things like "This house is a hug." "This house is a hug from the street." "Give yourself a hug."

Prepare to evacuate. You're doomed. When they start talking about hugs, flee the area immediately.

When we moved into our first house, brokers would show up periodically to try to sell it to prospective buyers. I would always try to be gruff and put them off. But there was one broker I could not put off. She wore a green velour leisure suit and a large medallion in the shape of a dragon. She invited herself over for afternoon tea. She gazed deeply into my eyes and told me she only wanted to protect me. She tried to talk me into buying her boat. She told me to give myself a hug.

I was doomed.

The California bungalow was actually derived from the British Empire—built for temporary use in tropical countries. This broker wanted to sell us a house. She was relentless. So one day we gave in and asked her to show us some California bungalows.

The first house she showed us was an ornate Spanish Mediterranean fantasy.

"We wanted to see a California bungalow," I said.

"This *could* be a California bungalow," she said. "It just needs some landscaping."

Finally professing to understand our desire to look at a historic Craftsman house, she took us to another property while constantly repeating the phrase in an almost autistic manner, "It's a *period* piece."

"What period?"

She stared blankly.

Then she took us to a neighborhood which she kept saying was for "the little people." It was comprised of adorable bungalows built for "the little people."

"The little people," I mused. "Do you mean the common man?"

It turned out she meant dwarfs. The Hollywood Midgets Union. Something about refugees from the old set of *Cleopatra*.

She kept talking about her anxiety. So she took me to a massage therapist who offers foot reflexology, facelift massage, lymph drainage, and other zany California treatments. In New York, brokers take a straightforward approach: they show you real estate. In southern California they take you to lymph drainage massage parlors.

Everyone keeps talking about vitamins, hand massages, foot massages, and getting their eyebrows waxed. They bring out strange pieces of wood to trace for relaxation. They are on strange diets called Zone and can't eat any food outside of their own homes because they must stick to their esoteric diets and concoctions. It all seems to key into the mortality and decline obsession—trying obsessively to fight those things.

At first it was simply so unfamiliar that it made me hysterical, paranoid, and vulnerable. Then I suddenly became more adjusted and started making an impact on people. For instance my real estate broker took me to a yoga class and whispered, "I'm very excited about your quadriceps."

I was really making an impact. My real estate broker kept calling me to say, "There's something I need to share with you." Pregnant silence. "I'm very drawn to you." Significant pregnant silence. "We need to talk."

"Yes?"

"I feel very protective about your spirit."

"That's nice."

"You're very spiritual."

"I am?"

Then she would go on in this vein and I had no idea what she was trying to say. My husband explained to me she was trying to say, "I'm selling your house out from under you and I want you to buy my other listing."

I kept telling her that I would prefer to just stay in our rented house for a while until I got my bearings. She kept saying she understood and felt very protective about me. "Give yourself a nice big hug."

The next evening our house was lit by Los Angeles–style searchlights with flags flying and balloons and huge signs emblazoned with the legend OPEN HOUSE. This is where a million prospective buyers come trooping through your house—no matter how spiritual you are. So of course we got kicked out of the house after that. My real estate broker sold it. We had sixty days to vacate the premises.

I found another rental house. The broker dropped off candy. She took me to Loehmann's. She tried to get me to buy a boat. Finally she lost interest. I am not a California real estate broker's dream, I am her nightmare. Every time I see a sign that says FOR RENT, my pulse quickens, my heart beats, and I know I am home: just renting, just passing through.

12

Now when you move around as much as I do, a certain derangement of the mind sets in pertaining to all the different houses you have lived in. You pine for your other houses. You reminisce about them. You compare them incessantly to each other. Nostalgia works in a relentless continuum, always for the thing just past.

You evaluate each epoch of your life and pine for each. Pretty soon you're walking down the street and are seized with nostalgia for five minutes ago. If only life could be like it was five minutes ago. You pine for time to stop. Or rather to rewind.

The odd thing is that it is always the epoch just previous that seems most alluring. In the evening I sometimes walk past my previous houses and neighborhoods, thinking happiness was more proximate there, as after a long summer day I stand transfixed in relief to see a deep twilight, resembling the concept of shade.

Ours is now an ancient house for Esperanza, built in 1914. Two giant palm trees line the entrance. There is a balcony on the bedroom where you can sit and stare at the two giant palms. The house has an air of dark dreaming rest which is welcome in this land of barbaric sun. It is on a sloping street, in a hamlet with blue awnings on the other early California bungalows, and a view to the lights coming on in the smashing palm-laden twilight on the Mediterranean-like coast.

Paradise? Perhaps. When I see the beauty of the lights on the harbor in the night as the street slopes down, indeed there is always hope.

Our house looks like a Swiss chalet, a Germanic farm, among the California bungalows. Of course our house used to be a California bungalow—someone changed it into a Swiss chalet. Probably later someone will change it into a Spanish Mediterranean fantasy.

There is a subtle difference between our present neighborhood and that of our first house, which was like plain America—bake sales, skateboards, mothers taking children to the orthodontist. Our current neighborhood is more eccentric. It has a dark side.

An incredibly handsome eighty-year-old man lives across the street with his dog. The mismatched couple on the other side have exciting quarrels and drunken brawls. Then there is the misfit neighbor. His house looks as if it is inhabited by ax murderers. His lawn is choked with weeds surrounded by a barren desert garden. His house, unpainted, unloved, and unrestored, looms darkly. His phone constantly rings at two in the morning. He has a demented barking dog. But it's exciting living next door to a weirdo. He also watches *Tarzan* on TV at excruciating volume at all hours. The local cable television channel seems to be having a *Tarzan* festival. But maybe it's permanent since they've been having it ever since I got here. *Tarzan* is somehow especially fitting for Esperanza. Coyotes howl in the canyon at night, making a fitting accompaniment to Tarzan hollering among the banyans.

The view from my dining room is to an exotic boulevard of proud palms. I could be in the British Empire, posted to Malaysia. It is an exotic view. From the street you can see the harbor, which looks like Monte Carlo. The blue bay, the boats, the hills and stars. The immense Pacific in the night, along the vast highways and palms toward the desert.

You can hear the train whistle blow at night, which reminds me of an old green town in Alabama.

The Alabama coast is known for hurricanes, torrential rains, and flooding. When my husband was one year old his parents had to send him off to relatives in Chicago for six months as they feared for their lives in the flood of 1955. How ironic after growing up in such conditions that he should become obsessed with the desert.

Moonlight is brighter in the desert. I noticed this on visiting Mac's base camp. Only ten minutes out of Esperanza the back roads are lined with date palm groves. Soon the roads are lined with orange groves, which give off an exquisite fragrance. The whole place used to be nothing but orange groves from the Mexican border to Hollywood.

Although he also came from Fort Defiance, my husband shares the ideal of a California person. That is to say, his dream is The Outdoors. He ought to be out taming broncos on the plains. Or climbing out from under avalanches in the mountains. Or subduing rattlesnakes with his bare hands. All of which he does.

He stays out in the desert for weeks at a time. It's like being married to Lawrence of Arabia.

The Mojave, unlike the Sahara, is rocky. At the last stop before the actual drilling area for the water plate, the base camp is to be found in a date fan palm oasis that looks exactly like the old set for *Tarzan*. There is an old cabin from prospecting days which bears the legend Dolly's Last Chance Café and is now converted to a series of camp beds and an office.

I find the desert very enervating. When I go there I am overcome by apathy and even when I return to Esperanza I am so dazed that I can't unpack for weeks.

The Santa Anas originate in the Mojave—the hot winds that blow through in September and give you a nervous breakdown. But down at the coast in Esperanza, they're not very nerve-wracking. Their main manifestation at the coast is actually nothing but an exquisite clarity and stillness, an exaggerated visibility with a pristine blue sky. On the other hand if you happen to take a commuter plane to Los Angeles that gets tangled up in a Santa Ana, it is not a pretty picture at all. I wouldn't advise it. I wouldn't advise taking a commuter plane to Palm Springs. I can see getting a nervous breakdown in the desert. The desert is kind of grating. The atmosphere is intolerable until five o'clock, when a brief illusory rehabilitation occurs at twilight.

When I last brought Lawrence of Arabia to the daring Esperanza airport—he would fly to Vegas and drive on to the drilling post from that point—there was a hole in my heart to preview his absence. Sure, you don't quarter a filly like Fleming Ford at the quiet limit of the world. But I'm supposed to be feisty. I'm supposed to be fine when he's not around. Maybe it was the pregnancy. But I could not bring myself to tell him yet. We were not the kind of couple who, when we were apart, called each other every day. His absences for his work had always been protracted and we had adjusted to it. It is not for me to interfere with his dreams. And now his dream is being Lawrence of Arabia.

I always know the moment of conception for each one of my children because his absences are long and our time together is pronounced. Our youth in Fort Defiance was spent looking to a tropic sea and being inundated by storms and floods. It may be I was dazed on last returning from the desert for this reason: a conception in the desert moonlight, in a tent in a drilling camp among the quacks and cowboys searching for redemption.

13

Being married to the companion of your childhood and youth is like living in a Proustian flashback. In this world of exile from your home and instability it was a point of continuity. The way his clothes fit or the peculiarities of his drawl would remind you of your farthest past. But now that I'm married to Lawrence of Arabia, I'm not sure it's quite the same. Can you hold on to that sharp sense of place out here at the quiet limit of the world, where the sun is destructive of all you have known and believed?

When you get married you are like a person getting off a train in a strange place not knowing where to go from the station or what to expect from the town. You only know that it is time for decadence to end—the decadence of youth. We were very decadent in Fort Defiance. Debauchery was very big. Now of course I seek for equanimity—not to be unduly elated by success or depressed by failure. I seek regularity of purpose.

It used to be that he transported me to Proustian flashbacks of my youth on the Gulf Coast, hurricanes, tropical depressions, debauchery. Some say that decadence is the last ensign of a fading empire. So it was with ours. Debauchery is actually the pleasure I always liked best, but you can't be debauched when you're a mother. So you would have Proustian flashbacks of the windows blowing in during a hurricane when you were a little kid. On the Gulf Coast you get used to the prediction of hurricanes. Everyone gets Sterno and fills the bathtub with water in case the water shuts off and the electricity goes out which it always does, everyone stays home from work, the air turns green, the leaves swirl around in the wind, then everything becomes very still, the golf course looks like a ballroom, there is a sensation of nameless excitement, you evacuate to your mother's house, or flee to Jackson, Mississippi (high land), and then at the last minute the hurricane diverts and goes somewhere else, usually to Biloxi.

Or Proustian flashbacks of your great-grandmother, Muz, a silent and diminutive dame of ninety wearing antebellum dresses out of *Gone With the Wind,* chain-smoking and drinking whiskey.

Or of your father, the world's most towering figure, standing among the azaleas in front of his mansion while his many children wrought havoc around him in an incredible tableau. Wearing a seersucker suit after the day's work in Mobile, smoking a cigar in the evening, always in the same pose surveying the scene, with a worldly air, a stately and towering figure presiding over his dominions. When your father died you never got over it, just as in Mississippi no one ever gets over it when their mothers go. In Mississippi your mother is bedridden for thirty-five years and then one day she goes and you never get over it. But in Alabama your father was the world's most towering figure and you never got over him.

It is the life that you know best, or most familiarly, something about the way it is on a weekday morning going downtown, driving across the causeway to Mobile, so like the deepest part of regular life.

In Fort Defiance you were married in the same church that your parents were married in. There you would be eulogized as well. Your parents would be born in the same hospital that they would one day die in. Towering figure as my father was, the first man who was kind to me, there was another figure equally towering, and I had lost her also. For a time one half of the beloved picture remained. Being so accustomed to my mother's towering personality, I could not delineate between it and true physical frailty; I thought that she would live to a great age. I'm quite certain that this too is what Mr. Lieberman had felt for Adelaide, who also never seemed old. Is it the same world, the same palms and bougainvillea in such exacting colors, without them?

My earliest memory is of walking to the corner with a nurse when I was two years old. All we did was walk to the corner but the atmosphere of the thing encompassed an intense excitement, optimism, and happiness. So when you're a kid it doesn't take much. The crisp day, the air of mystery that you would seek to penetrate, the desertion of everything around nearby, a quietude in which a curious gaiety could be found at the heart. The hope, the promise, of getting past the corner to the avenue was extreme. Maybe this was why I had to flee from Fort Defiance or why it could not hold me later. The intense sense of promise could not be met or satisfied in later life but by a farther road.

But there is a part of your heart forever trapped in Fort Defiance. "God gave all men all earth to love, / But since our hearts are small, / Ordained for each one spot should prove, / Beloved over all."

14

On my return to the West I received a note from Mr. Lieberman, formulating his hope that I had achieved a safe trip home. For its sweetness this missive glinted radiantly in a patch of sun on the hall table. It was written on a sumptuous card engraved with a heraldic motto: *Forward, Kind Heart.* Below that was his crest. It seemed to be the work of the old-world Englishman of my imagination. His note sat on the hall table radiating glamour and igniting certain visions.

I used to drive up the Hudson on spring and summer days in the greensward with opera music playing on the radio. Then floating back to town with *La Traviata* blaring in the car the first thing I would sometimes see when swinging back up Ninety-sixth Street was Harry Lieberman, a vision on West End Avenue in a dapper black suit with his shocking white hair and a cigar, striding along on his episodic walks throughout the city, cutting a certain memorable figure.

I liked his looks. I liked his atmosphere. I liked his ties. In his dapper black suit, his old-fashioned suspenders, and overstarched white shirt like a southerner, and that furrow in his brow that reminded me of *War and Peace.*

On the night that I received his note in Esperanza I had a vision of the moment when he steamed into New York Harbor on a hazy afternoon in 1949 and passed the Statue of Liberty. It was his first transatlantic crossing. You couldn't know what was in his heart, for he guarded that secret. Few who knew him could ever guess it. He guarded it well with a crisp mannered wit.

I knew his basic history. When he arrived in New York in 1949 it was with an inheritance of five million dollars from his grandfather that he founded the Syndicate Trading Company, which is to be found on Madison Avenue at Thirty-seventh Street across from the Morgan Library, a Greek Revival building of limestone with the name engraved into the pediment. It's still there, you may have seen it. Later its offices occupied half of a modern skyscraper in midtown. The company traded commodities, then insurance companies, Caribbean utilities, newspapers, venture capital investments, and eventually natural resources. He made his name on the Street right away. He became a reclusive American tycoon who controlled parts of the American economy for decades. Yet no one could be less obtrusive or pretentious.

You will note the anonymous name he gave to his American enterprise: the Syndicate Trading Company. He also insisted on anonymity for his philanthropic work. But everyone knew who he was. The Lieberman star glittered still.

Lord Northwood's family had mystical beginnings in Baghdad and biblical associations across the strait from Africa to Europe. Professing his faith in England in the nineteenth century was not a help to the later lord, and Queen Victoria, although she doted on Disraeli, did not confer the peerage, after the matter was pressed on her every year; her successor, the raffish Edward VII, later obliged. There were those who felt that Lieberman should have declined. If it had been my Mr. Lieberman he would have certainly declined. But Lord Northwood felt he had a way to pave. At any rate he paved a way for his grandson to be raised in various luxurious hotels and retreats at the Riviera, Bellagio, Biarritz.

I kept having visions of his early history. The French

Mediterranean cornice roads of the Esterel, the Negresco in Nice. The Villa Serbelloni in the Savoy Alps, the green playing fields of Harrow. I had visions of his childhood on the French Riviera and other old world resorts. The corniche roads between Nice and Monte Carlo, the deep calanques of the Mediterranean, the lost quiddity of Biarritz.

Nice work if you can get any. Wandering around in an ecstatic trance.

Each vision was like a photographic memory of his youth. It seemed so realistic. I had some sort of subterranean connection with him. The main emotion of the thing was bliss.

From California he represented a glittering older world I missed. For I was at the other end of the world, under the bright sky of America and the last frontier.

15

It's quite dangerous in the desert. Death Valley, not far from Mac's drilling site, is the hottest place on earth, taking the record of 134 degrees in summer from the Sahara.

Engineers in the desert are always demonically trying to see what will explode at high temperatures. The military is very big in the desert, experimenting in off-limits bombing areas. There seems to be a lot of leftover napalm floating around that they don't know what to do with, and sometimes they have to blow things up to get rid of it. You hear a lot about the loneliness of the American West. You really see it in the desert. Maybe making the desert bloom will assuage the loneliness of the American West.

But things were looking bad for Mac. The legendary water plate, once they actually started drilling for it, proved elusive and the investors were growing skeptical. Science had determined the site: geology and seismic analysis. But something more mysterious, like art, was required to put all the pieces together and drill at the exact spot to make the direct hit. He had staked a lot on this and also, he did not know of the new developments at home, the result of our last meeting in the desert among the quacks and cowboys searching for redemption. While I am thinking about pregnancy and life and death he may be in the desert thinking about pre-stressed concrete, but I love the guy and I could not spare a child of his. Still it's not necessarily something you would be ecstatic to hear when you've got a shaky business enterprise in the middle of the desert that could go up in smoke like hot tires on the asphalt.

When I got back from New York I got a call from the complicated satellite hookup at the drilling post, where a cellular beneath the vast stars could never find a signal.

"Mac, I love you," I said, "but we haven't seen you for six weeks. I love you, the children love you, we have two children, and—"

Maybe this would be the time to tell him about the pregnancy. But no.

"I love you too, Fleming dear."

"Most girls in my position, I mean, with the husband never around, would be mad."

"It's an economic reality."

"I too make a contribution to that reality."

"True. But this is a project that has more potential than anything I've ever worked on. And we have an equity position."

In other words a man has to do what a man has to do. He's done it before. He'll do it again. It's not the result that matters—the equity position and what would come of it. It's not your destination, but your conduct as you go down the road.

"Yes, but most people in my situation here would still be mad. I just have to find a way to adapt, and be more like the Abernathy girls."

"How's that?"

"The Abernathy girls fix dinner every night and don't complain. That's their reality."

Mac's reality is in the desert among the quacks and cowboys searching for redemption.

I could not seem to find the right time to tell him about the pregnancy. I would have to build up to it.

"It's a little difficult adjusting out here, Mac."

"You've adjusted before. You adjusted in New York. Why is it different here?"

"It's pioneer land out here. It's the Wild West. I'm not a cowboy. It's like those old movies of the desert where they keep panning to the sun beating down with annoying freak-out music of the bow ripping across the violin in screeches."

"Old movies. Violins. Screeches."

"That's my reality."

Mac's reality, when not in the desert, is roaming around the Pacific and staring at it in a trance, probably trying to figure out how to get the salt out of it so it can make the desert bloom. Hydraulics, engineering, science, geology, those are the types of things Mac thinks about. How to get a trove of oil from the Arctic Circle to New York. The canyons being formed by the continents slamming together in the Ice Age. He can always keep things in perspective, since three million years is a very short span in geologic time. His reality is in his engineering brilliance: designs for high-tech canals and pipelines formulated from some ultramodernistic and impenetrable materials twisting through the fault lines of the

Imperial Valley down through the border and Baja California.

My reality is in being the emotional shock absorber for the family, or more accurately, for Mac, while he thinks about things like prestressed concrete. He keeps telling me that since the desert has shattered the beliefs that I cherish, all I once understood and held dear, that maybe I am now in a position to reevaluate them, my beliefs.

But where would that leave him? In exactly the same place. It had not shattered my belief in him.

16

I have a certain amount of time on my hands due to my career slump and my stunning remove to the other side of the world at age forty in the middle of the journey of our life. I'm supposed to be working on Special Perspectives, which I attempt to dream up at my office in the garage overlooking a canyon. Canyons are weird. I saw a coyote once come up from the canyon: it looks like a rangy berserk sort of wolfhound. No telling what else is down there: foxes, monitors, hyenas going mad.

Special Perspectives—it sounds so official, like some sort of evil Soviet enterprise, some sort of daunting euphemistic committee to winnow out people who should be executed. Or at least who should be airbrushed out of existing photographs. It's like something out of the Politboro. My editor would soon create a new and even more euphemistic title for me: West Coast Special Perspectives Team Coordinator.

The insubstantial nature of the endeavor was betrayed by its vague and redundant title, which continued to go through various changes, in the end returning by a circuitous route to the blandly cheery New Perspectives, in the meanwhile persisting with the perhaps more nebulous Special ones.

In time I did come up with several thought-provoking Special Perspectives pieces on such vague subjects as Optimism, Pessimism, and Nostalgia. But then my Special Perspectives tended to get too apocalyptic. The universe being so vast, who planned it that our green earth and humanity should grow, why are we here, what is before and after, the span before and after life being so immeasurably longer than the span of life itself. I grew seedy hanging out in my pajamas all day trying to figure out the universe.

I kept thinking about atomic particles. Because we are made up of them. And consciousness resides in some of them, and they are never destroyed. And if you look at your television set when a channel is not operating properly and see little white things, those are photons left over from the big bang sixteen billion years ago. You may ask how I know all this. It is because there are a lot of nuclear physicists in Esperanza. There is an emphasis on science. Science nerds. That's quite distinct in this part of California. Most of the nuclear physicists are Russian, and are the parents of my daughter's friends. So at children's birthday parties I take them aside and interrogate them about our atomic particles.

Then I dutifully go to my office in the garage and wallow in nothingness, trying to figure out the central mystery of our finite existence.

I also spend a lot of time with a group of squirming three-year-olds dressed up as ladybugs in a series of incredibly long and complex rehearsals for my daughter's ballet recital. Intrigues ran high among the ladybugs. They formed cliques. They had tantrums. They were heartless. Their mothers snapped. I stayed backstage during the rehearsals marshaling kaleidoscopic varieties of ladybug trauma.

At the actual performance the audience was packed to bursting. The ladybugs were supposed to form a big ring on the stage holding hands, then skip around. Naturally they went too fast and one ladybug got caught in a spinning vortex causing the circle to snap like an electric cord pulled abruptly out of the socket. One ladybug ran to the edge of the stage all alone and started twirling around. Others were madly jumping up and down like human pogo sticks. One ladybug sobbed quietly and inconsolably in a corner— thank God not my daughter. Several ladybugs stared vacantly ahead, paralyzed.

My daughter was the last to leave the stage—trapped in the spotlight like a deer in the headlights. Finally, thank God, she turned a broad smile directly on the audience and scampered toward the wings with her awkward grace amid thunderous applause.

I was so relieved my daughter had not been scarred by the experience that I was walking on cloud nine. But I was crushed with guilt. For once they wheel you out of the delivery room, you carry out of it forever a mother's guilt, no matter how good a mother you are, or how many ladybug rehearsals you attend.

After soothing the frayed nerves of a fifty-year-old man dressed as a giant duck who arrived in a souped-up Corvette to perform at my son's birthday party, I realized I'm not the only one in a career slump.

Somehow when you hire a man over the phone to dress up as a giant duck at your son's birthday party, you expect him to be maybe an enthusiastic college kid or a wholesome young camp counselor. Seeing as he never took off his costume, you might wonder how I even knew that he wasn't a wholesome young camp counselor. It was the frail rasping voice and the delicate fumes of scotch that emboldened me to ask, in the course of making polite conversation, how old he was. Pretty soon the next thing I know he's telling me how his wife left him, he lost his job, he's broke, and if it weren't for the napalm factory in Chicata closing down, he wouldn't be dressed up like a children's fairy tale character sweating his brains out because it was hotter than hell in there.

In the costume.

That's another thing about Esperanza. It's supposed to be idyllic avocado farms and Mexican-style villages and orange groves, and then suddenly you find out there's a napalm bomb factory just down the road with escaping napalm that they have to shut down. AVOCADO FESTIVAL NOT MARRED BY NAPALM LEAK the local headline will decry.

I guess it's the dark side of paradise.

17

At night I lie awake unnerved by every single noise, as if in an Alfred Hitchcock movie, until I am ultimately able to trace most of them to the misfit neighbor hacking away at the canyon with his golf club, accompanied by his bloodthirsty German shepherd, or having conversations conducted at the top of his lungs. The misfit neighbor has a lot of conversations conducted at the top of his lungs. At first I thought he was carrying on these screaming conversations with imaginary people. I have since learned that he lives with his mother, and yells at her a lot.

As I lie in bed I hear his strange doings. Often he plays at excruciatingly loud volume episodes of *Ozzie and Harriet*-type family shows emphasizing normality—ironically. Otherwise *Tarzan*.

I'm in tune with the misfit neighbor's entire life as I hear the whole thing going on throughout the day and night. This afternoon the usual screams and grunts and sounds of hauling things out to the Dumpster. No telling what's in the Dumpster. He may be dismantling his house piece by piece. He may be dismantling his mother piece by piece.

I wonder where he fits in in terms of the phobia of stress. On every page of the newspaper there are ads for Wellness things. Get Counseling! scream the headlines. Now! Stop the Overwhelm! Plan and map your mental well-being. Resolve your most pressing issues. Rejuvenate your relationships! Get intuitive counseling and healing.

I should give a copy of these ads immediately to the misfit neighbor.

His relationship with his mother definitely needs to be rejuvenated.

The irony always is that in a place like New York where there is a lot of stress, no one bats an eyelash. Whereas here in paradise—but there is obviously trouble in paradise—we have the pronounced phobia of stress. That is the crux of the place.

Take me, for instance. After six months here I had a botanist, a facialist, a physical therapist, a yoga teacher, a hair colorist, an entity from a mid-causal plane, a driving instructor, and a visceral manipulator. Since I never had a visceral manipulator before I never knew that once you get one, you're doomed. You have to keep going to him or your viscera are doomed. The same is true of yoga. If you stop going you get a back injury every five minutes. Then of course it's back to the physical therapist.

I met someone who had an ailment just being discovered in California based on stress. Esperanza is too frenzied for her. Something in her sinus is connected to her brain and it gives her "overt panic." She kept saying things like "Something extraordinarily painful and shocking happened while I was in graduate school that I can't really talk about. I've thought about it every day of my life and it gives me overt panic. I'd prefer not to talk about it."

But she kept bringing it up. She kept talking about it incessantly.

She kept nonchalantly tossing off terms like Anger Management Counseling. She was sending her husband for that.

I made a sardonic comment about Wellness.

"You're venting," she said. "It's OK to vent."

So I gave up and got a massage down the street.

"Your legs feel empty," said the masseuse. "They feel dead."

"I wonder what that means," I asked.

More probing.

"Your solar plexus, it feels dead. It feels leaden," she observed.

"What does that mean? Am I OK?"

She moved to the head-scalp massage.

"Your cranium is empty."

"Really. So I've lost my brains. What exactly do I have inside my body that is actually still alive?"

She felt around.

"The base of your skull feels active," she remarked hopefully.

"Oh, great. The base of my skull is active. What the hell does that mean?"

"I don't know."

More probing.

"What are you doing?" I screamed.

"I'm massaging your gallbladder."

"Leave my gallbladder alone!"

"Just accept the moment," she advised.

She tried to ask me some personal questions. Then she started telling me about massage school. Healing training. Energy work.

"Isn't that a little embarrassing?" I asked.

"What do you mean, embarrassing?"

It had to do with getting a complete stranger to tell you his innermost personal problems while probing his solar plexus and instigating intercranial sacral manipulation. In short, it had to do with exactly what was happening to me at that moment.

So I really shouldn't cast stones, for I'm a quack now myself. The perfect quack in southern California in the palm trees and desert sun subsumed by ailments spending hoards of dough on quacks. Quack treatments.

"Have you tried magnets?" she asked.

"For what?"

"They restore your magnetism."

"How do I know I've lost my magnetism?"

"We've been losing our magnetism over thousands of years. Thousands of years ago, we used to go barefoot. Modern life has lost its magnetism."

She went on to expound that the earth itself is losing its magnetism.

"I couldn't walk without magnets," she claimed. "My feet have lost their magnetism."

"Don't you have gravity?"

That stopped her. But it didn't stop me. Instead of working dutifully on Special Perspectives and figuring out the galaxies I went to the mall. The malls here are laden with burnished terra-cotta pots of bougainvillea and fountains and outside cafés. Then they're always getting redone to become even more a burnished Italianate paradise of cafés and cosmetics and it is mesmerizing to inexorably spend hours there. At the Erno Laszlo counter I was taken with an allergic fit. But at forty you can't resist ceaseless women's moisturizers. I can't breathe when I'm wearing it but that doesn't matter, Erno Laszlo is worth getting asthma for.

18

Since I became a mother I wake up every night at midnight or three in the morning, in order to do some studious worrying. Some of the best worrying on earth is done at two in the morning. Conditions for worrying at that time are optimum: fright, phobia, solitude, darkness. Not to mention the deranged howling of the misfit neighbor's dog, the hollering of Tarzan among the banyans in the misfit neighbor's bedroom, and the coyotes going mad in the canyon.

It is a good time to wander down into the garden and reevaluate your beliefs. I have a garden of bougainvillea and camellia and gardenia. A senseless desert beauty—because nothing was meant to grow here save for chaparral and sagebrush. Cowboy stuff.

At first gardening bored me to tears. It still does but with a gradual lessening. No doubt I'll end up a fanatical gardener with a Latin flower named after me. Meanwhile my garden is so complicated that I had to hire a professional botanist. This guy, his whole life is geraniums. There was a front-page article about him in the local paper. If you intend to sacrifice your entire life to geraniums, he says, which he recommends, you have to be willing to have tattered furniture and drive a beat-up car. It's worth it—to spend every last cent you have on geraniums. Also, you get to wear shorts all day. If you work with geraniums. But everyone in Esperanza already wears shorts all day, I would note.

This guy is just one of the many mad horticulturalists around town—and believe me, there are many, and they rate front-page headlines in the paper. I was getting kind of excited about geraniums from reading the article, and I thought I would try to go to the next meeting of the Esperanza Geranium Club, meeting studiously at 7:05 Tuesday in a room at the park. What could you say about geraniums for an entire hour? I wondered.

I soon found out. This guy's passion for geraniums began when he was three years old. His nanny took him to a nursery and he was seized, transfixed by the sight of a red geranium. The world stopped. He got off. His whole life suddenly had meaning. As soon as he was old enough to haul a shovel, a planting of geraniums took over his parents' house, gradually subsuming it in a tangle of weeds, until his mother tactfully suggested college.

After graduating from college he moved around aimlessly trying to grow tropical plants in nontropical climates, trying to plant bromeliads in inhospitable regions, seeing if gardenias would grow in the desert, and other hapless quests, until finally one day he called his mother (he's a bachelor, it may not surprise you to find out) and said, I'm depressed, something's missing in my life, and I think I know what it is—geraniums.

His mother tactfully decided to invest in a geranium nursery that he could operate. His mother is certainly tactful.

Ironically, the popularity of geraniums was just beginning a slide at that moment. Also the climate was inhospitable to geraniums. Adversity kept in his way. But with determination, it's all worked out. Now he says "For as far back as I can remember my life has revolved around geraniums. And I have no doubt that it always will. How many people can say that they are truly living their dream?"

This guy is not in a career slump.

It is said that the learned people here are horticulturalists. So I went to a horticulture lecture at the park, seeking scholars. The hall was filled with horticulture nerds of every age, size, color, and description. A numbing series of announcements was read out. The Bromeliad Study Group; Palm Club; Delphinium Society, Succulents Club, People for Plants, Plants for People, Bougainvillea Society, Orchid Group, Rare Fuchsia Association, Derelict Begonia Society, and the Cascading Mums Group—meeting studiously every third Wednesday at 8:01.

I used to think the biggest difference between New York and Esperanza was that the atmosphere in New York is: "I want to achieve something"; whereas the atmosphere in Esperanza is: "I want to relax." Now I think the attitude in Esperanza is: "I want to garden, I want to be a horticulture nerd, and I want to belong to obscure and insensible gardening societies."

In the newspaper's list of local cultural events, the events are always things like:

Ornamental Pear Trees Are Bursting into Bloom
Acorn Dropping Reaches a Crescendo
Clark's and Western Grebes, Crested Grebes, and Cactus
   Wrens Are Sighted
Esperanza Flood Control Channel Opens

You get the drift. Last week they had an exciting cover story on Dust Motes.

Sometimes at two in the morning while listening to Tarzan screeching through the banyans I study in bemusement the Events section of the local paper:

Windswept Vegetation
The Planet Mars
Raptor Watch
Thin Green Flash
The Moon Abhors the Day

I find myself worrying a lot about starved birds, after poring over articles in the local paper about them. But this may be due to the pregnancy. I tend to worry a lot about starved birds when I'm pregnant. Though I didn't worry about starved birds in New York. It's an Esperanza thing. Starved birds and beached baby whales—they have a lot of those in Esperanza, and they rate daily front-page headlines so you can't escape worrying about them. Actually I'm not really that worried about them. Why can't they just evolve with the ecosystem, like everyone else. I don't really know what the ecosystem is, but you can't escape it in Esperanza. I find myself poring over books about things like Wind, Dust, or the Arctic. Maybe you worry about that type of thing more when you're pregnant. Actually you worry about that type of thing when you live in California.

I also have an insatiable craving, destined to be unfulfilled, for Eggs Sardou from Galatoire's.

I was irresistibly drawn to amass little knickknacks, then to furiously arrange them at strategic points. I couldn't walk down a street without getting irresistibly drawn into a store that sold knickknacks, which are ordinarily deeply annoying. But when you are pregnant you are inexorably drawn in to dote on and marvel at them.

Matronhood makes you a tad lame, at least in my case. All that incessant nattering about knickknacks. It used to be I didn't know how to get curtains. And was proud of not knowing! Now I know how to get curtains, coat racks, foot stools, knickknacks, cable TVs, and God knows what else.

Also when pregnant I can only read books about people going through vast declines. Dante's *Inferno, Anna Karenina, All Quiet on the Western Front, Testament of Youth, Goodbye to All That.* This segues neatly into only being able to read books about World War I. In turn, this leads to being obsessed with declining empires and atomic particles, the battlefields of Europe.

It is an issue in this situation of controlling your nerves: to constantly act sensible because you're a mother, even though you're actually crazed.

The tasks are infinite, the journey long. When it comes to serving the ceaseless needs of small children. You should square your Alabama shoulders and perform your duties uncomplainingly. Like the Abernathy girls. But you could be noble and still crack.

19

I received another message from Mr. Lieberman. It was handwritten on another sumptuous card. Engraved was the heraldic motto *Faithful but Unfortunate*. In the stark formality of an old-world r.s.v.p., his note was written in the third person with no signature: "Mr. Lieberman seeks to remind Miss Ford of their engagement for lunch on June 21 at the Alexandria Hotel in Los Angeles." There was nothing so alien, so foreign to California as Mr. Lieberman and his trademark formality and his old-world European antecedents. It would be a shocking juxtaposition to see him in L.A.

That night I had a curious vision. I kept having visions after I heard from him. At three in the morning I was up worrying—the kids, the husband always out in the Mojave—when to my surprise the next thing I knew I was in a breathtakingly consoling dream of the French Riviera—it was green, gorgeous, thrilling; there was a glamorous old hotel: Mr. Lieberman was a boy with his father there and felt the joy of heaven.

After that, my reality wasn't so bad. Even if it was at the other end of the world from his, under the bright sky of America and the last frontier. At twilight the glittering harbor lined by palms was like the Mediterranean coast of my vision.

The coyotes were going mad in the canyon. I got up and

71

watched *Tarzan,* which always makes me feel better. Take Jane—as comfortable in the jungle among lions and elephants as in the drawing rooms of Mayfair.

I kept picturing the formal enigmatic figure I took Mr. Lieberman to be, wearing a black suit in the sunshine among the palms and the modernity that I would soon meet with in L.A.—a picture encompassing a certain incongruity—a man at odds with his surroundings. I found this picture to be profoundly consoling. Here I am in the new world and all I can do is think about the old one. I have the same identity crisis as Esperanzan real estate developers: I pine for the old world.

In the late afternoon I walked to the Presidio, which is the most ancient site not only in Esperanza but in the entire state of California. I stopped in at El Pico, a Mexican dive with an outside café where the usual people sit staring vacantly. You get a lot of vacant stares in Esperanza. A mariachi band was playing. A mariachi band is always playing in Esperanza, usually at an inopportune time, like when you have a throbbing toothache or a hangover. And the sun never stops shining. I was reading the local paper. There is the occasional jubilant headline: LEAKING NAPALM BOMB FACTORY MOVED TO OREGON or ESPERANZA NUCLEAR WASTE DUMPED ON ARIZONA. Later I noticed the mood became less jubilant. But the saga wore on. NAPALM QUIETLY MOVED TO TEXAS ran the latest headline. Apparently we have more napalm than we know what to do with.

I was thinking about the span of a pregnancy and birth, which often coincides with the span of disintegration and death. That's the kind of thing you incessantly think about in southern California, usually while a mariachi band is playing. It's that whole trouble in paradise thing. It's too bright, the sky is too big, and we're always trying to foist our napalm off on Arizona.

In the not too distant future they would have the gall to try to foist their napalm off on Alabama. But Alabama wasn't having any. Neither was Arizona, Oregon, or Texas. So the saga wore on.

I have found that when you worry enough about something, like world annihilation, it generally turns out all right. So I try to pack in as much worry as admissible within the scope of human comprehension and endurance when it comes to my children and pregnancies. I've often noticed the conception of a child coincides with the death of someone dear. I've often wondered if the outgoing and incoming souls are somehow related.

Meanwhile I awaited the return of my husband from the desert, or my meeting in Los Angeles with Mr. Lieberman, whichever came first.

A succession of enigmatic gardeners, obsessed botanists, loquacious tree specialists, and pitying horticulturalists came by to analyze my garden. Each one showed what he could do. It must be admitted that they had indeed transformed my garden into a thing of mesmerizing beauty. In fact when I see my garden, I don't mind as much that my life appeared to be falling in ruins around me: collapsing business enterprise in the Mojave, secret unplanned pregnancy, career slump, failure to adjust to new surroundings.

At three o'clock in the morning I awoke to worry, or perhaps to dream, sometimes of Mac. From time to time I heard from him. How had the desert come to separate us so? He called from the complicated satellite hookup in the base camp when they weren't having meteoric interferences or other esoteric obstacles to cellular communication. "How's your malaise level?" he asked.

"Medium," I lied.

20

The geranium horticulturalist came over to preview my garden. He won my heart from the first. He was wearing a pith helmet and nattered on about his hangovers. On successive occasions he seemed to be crumbling into debauchery. I am sure he is the only botanist in Esperanza who works on Saturday night, ever armed with the *National Rose Society Rule Book,* just in case. As noted, he's a little crazed. But I like him that way.

Then he showed up Sunday morning. "We need to fertilize!" he yelled madly. He discussed his latest hangover. Something about accidentally mixing the fertilizer in with the cocktails. Sometimes he doesn't entirely inspire my confidence as a botanist. What they didn't tell you in the newspaper is that his past life before geraniums involves many career changes and shocking deviations from horticulture including aerobics instructor, catering, and journalism.

I was telling him about the skunk trapped under our house. It turned out that skunk removal strategy is one of his major hobbies and future career options. Usually he likes to kill them with an ax. I requested something more benign.

So he duly returned at night to strategize about the skunk, bringing flowers, potted plants, and his insensible horticultural report, of which he is the sole contributor. At night we went outside to perform skunk treatment, the benign version, as requested, which involves large amounts of cayenne pepper.

As we chatted about caterpillars in the foxglove and white fly disease in the hibiscus I was looking at the *New York Times*. I kept staring at it and recalling how you go out on the subway and then walk in midtown to Sixth Avenue in your trench coat in the late winter which presages spring and anything could happen—you could achieve something, you could merit the attention of moguls, you could run into your old flames (not new ones since you're married and a matron, even if your anniversary is an event that tends to escape your husband's notice)—whereas in Esperanza anything could not happen. You could instead have strategy sessions about skunks and obsessional rages over geraniums.

However, my botanist kept staring at me adoringly during the skunk strategy session, so that was a plus.

As for the misfit neighbor, whose unintelligible screams punctured half the afternoons from my office, as long as he's not dangerous I don't really mind, but it's only that he is the type of person that after he suddenly comes out with a gun one day and murders everyone on the block, everyone interviewed for the newspaper says, He was always a problem.

Skunks walk nonchalantly up and down the street in the evening. Sometimes they walk nonchalantly under your house to form a domestic establishment there, and then you have to confer heavily on skunk removal strategy with a drunken botanist.

The phone rang.

"Can you feel it?" said a man at the other end of the line.

"Who is this?"

It was my botanist.

75

"Go to the window," he said. "Look at the shadows. Can you see it?"

"What?"

"It's the Santa Ana."

So a Santa Ana had come to the coast. The day was spellbindingly gorgeous. In a Santa Ana at the coast in Esperanza everything becomes so pristinely clear, so crystalline, so clarified, that there is an elation to the thing.

My botanist is taking over my life. "Did you do anything about caterpillars in the foxglove?" he asks heatedly. "Drop everything! We need to fertilize." His conversation is quite esoteric. It has to do with spider mites and mealybugs and "supreme OK-ness." He wants you to do your gardening at night, because he says it's more therapeutic that way. If he's not staring at you adoringly, he's inviting you to the Geranium Getaway held at his farm. But it's nice to have someone adoring me, considering the ever-lengthening absences of my husband in the Mojave Desert.

Some people, I think, have children so that they can have someone to adore them. I deplore that. I don't ask my children to automatically adore me. I have to earn their love. Besides, in my day I had a lot of people who adored me who didn't have to be my own children. But when I moved to Esperanza I basically hit a midlife crisis plus career slump at the same time so right now I'm in double jeopardy, not to mention the pregnancy.

As the pregnancy increased, so did the adoring looks from my botanist. Some men are like that. It was strictly amazing to me that he could find my decaying forty-year-old washed-up self attractive. But he did. And he wasn't the only one. Then there's the guy who rings the bell for the Salvation Army outside of the grocery store. He likes me. My botanist had gotten to the point where he called me every five minutes. We need to fertilize. We need to stipple. Whatever that is. I could also tell he had a crush on me because he kept bringing inordinate amounts of flowers, in large containers, giving my garden a crazed appearance.

The mail brought still another note from Mr. Lieberman, written on the card with the heraldic motto. But he had a new one this time: *And I Desire.*

What was Harry Lieberman's motivation in contacting me? I wondered. Maybe he was collecting people from Fort Defiance, to bring him something of Adelaide. Some people thought he would get over it, but I knew better, as later I studied his face in L.A. when he spoke of her.

A brilliant and sublime outburst of opera in the night accompanied these considerations. The misfit neighbor suddenly played an old recording of *Don Giovanni.* If his vice was to play *Don Giovanni* all night I'd be in ecstasy. But that only happened for about ten elegiac minutes. Then back to *Tarzan.* In this one some old beaux of Jane's from England come out to Africa to try and fetch her back. They try to lure her back with evening gowns and gramophones. So she puts on evening gowns and listens to jazz but Tarzan gets mad and carries her off to their hut madly swinging through the banyan trees. But it's OK because she prefers that to the drawing rooms of Mayfair.

One of the old beaux declaims to Tarzan, "Do you know who I am? I am the head trader of Leopold Loeb Securities in Paris and London."

"That won't help you here," says Tarzan.

It's really about the British Empire. It's the juxtaposition of the British Empire and the untamed jungle.

It's also sort of like my life in Esperanza.

So my thoughts in California strayed to a world of the British in white ducks and topees playing bridge and drinking gin at the club and being overpowered by love affairs in remote outposts in the twilight of the British Empire.

In the same year that Mr. Lieberman's grandfather received his peerage, when the British Empire was at its height, out here it was outlaws holding up Wells Fargo trains in the Wild West. The empires would soon shift, but there was always a connection. A British horticulturalist came out to Esperanza at the turn of the last century and went bananas, madly planting it with palm trees that had just achieved a worldwide vogue on the French Riviera, bringing on the rage for horticulture. California had the same appeal for the British as the Riviera: health resort, tropical climate, a love of gardens, and the desire to flee. But you're trapped between the desire for civilization and the desire to flee from it.

21

Days turned into weeks. May became June. I developed a phobia of the freeways, so I had to take driving lessons. Now if you have a phobia of the freeways in southern California, you're in a pretty tight spot. Back roads and trains can take you only just so far. But I took them as far as they would take me.

My driving instructor does have some emotional problems. Right when you get on the freeway and are scared out of your wits, he starts telling you all about his emotional problems and how if it weren't for losing his job at the nuclear reactor plant, he wouldn't be forced to be a broken-down driving instructor, plus his wife left him. It seems as if your wife leaves you more often in Esperanza than in other places. Also, another career slump. And another bomb-related job opportunity lost.

When I got home the City Water Department was here with their gigantic water trucks to work on my water meter leak. In a regular city the infinitesimal rivulet escaping from the iron grid at the edge of the lawn would be just something to notice like the oak trees and the dusk. But in the desert metropolis it's an emergency. Calls from the landlord, calls from the City Water Supervisor. They keep trying to repair it, they're here every day, they can't seem to get on top of it. Even though they can't actually repair it, they have taken it one step forward: by crushing the pipe to cut off my water to prevent a catastrophe—and then they had to hook me up to the misfit neighbor's house's water.

So I started telling them, look, he's sort of a nut and when he sees it he might go mad. He might go berserk or something and I have small children coming in.

Just then an explosion was heard from the street.

"What's that?" I asked.

"That would be Leonard," said a nearby matron with a doom in her voice.

The misfit neighbor rolled up the street in what appears to be a German tank. It's actually his car. He spends a lot of time in it parked on the curb incessantly revving the motor, or making backfire explosions, and when at some long and desperately hoped for moment he finally turns it off the silence is like a euphoric paradise.

Then he went off to drive his motorcycle in the backyard. If you've ever seen a canyon you know that driving a motorcycle in it is not the first thing that pops into your mind when you consider what to do with it. Maybe water it. Maybe avoid it. Not drive a motorcycle in it.

For a time I just stood staring at his house, transfixed.

His lawn is choked with weeds surrounded by a dying garden. His bedroom is directly across from mine, separated only by a narrow alley. Thus his screams and curses permeate the night.

As noted, he lives with his mother. Which is extremely comforting, considering that at first I thought he could be dangerous or at least disgusting. I pictured orgies. There would probably not be orgies, if he lives with his mother.

I told his mother that she might want to get her son a muffler, for the car. It doesn't look like a car, but it is a car. Then she winked at me in a cornball way as if to indicate, "We're all just putting up with his adorable wastrel youth."

Actually it's not that adorable. It might be adorable if he were fifteen. But he's thirty-five if he's a day. On the other hand I am after all drawn to people like that—demented botanists, wastrel youths, and weirdos. I guess in a certain way I admire him. At least he's not a conformist. At least he is troubled. Disturbed. At least he's not bland.

As I turned to go back home it was not too difficult to notice that there was a gigantic catastrophic water leak in front of my house gushing like an oil well.

The misfit neighbor was now doing something with his boat that involved loud torturous grinding and pouring huge amounts of gasoline through torturously grinding motors obliviously. To him I'm sure the gushing oil well of water in front of my house was just some normally fiendish occurrence in the course of my madcap experiments.

22

I went inside to call the Water Department and who should be there but my husband, Mac MacMoreland, staring darkly from a window at the catastrophic water leak. I know what's going through his mind. It's what he wants to come up with underneath the Mojave Desert.

He came from a place that is inundated with water and so he is obsessed with finding water in the desert. And he's not only searching for water there to service the parched towns of Mexico. He's trying to make the desert bloom, an undertaking that is beginning to take on *Citizen Kane*–type proportions.

I saw it in his wiry frame, crazed with devotion, and in his dark stare. "Agriculture is the basis of civilization," he says about making the desert bloom, staring darkly in a trance.

He snapped out of it to kiss me and the kids and went outside to fix the water leak. The city engineers might not be able to fix it, but Mac could.

After that he came back in and started fixing everything in the house that was broken, rigging up trolleys in the icebox, building a pantry, rearranging the shelves. Rewiring the floor lamps, repairing a child's broken drawer. Refinancing the mortgage and mowing the lawn. Lassitude is not a word I would use to describe his atmosphere.

He's a fireball all right. He's the king of Home Improvement. He has a lot of things going on in the garage—experiments, home improvements. Once I had to give him an ultimatum: It's either me or the garage. Soon I'll have to tell him it's either me or the Mojave.

He wears short-sleeved seersucker shirts and khaki pants and white bucks and has an Alabama drawl. Wherever he goes he brings the entire state of Alabama with him, with his drawl and his seersucker short sleeves. It's like getting a personal visit from a haywire southern governor.

He's the type of person who not only fixes his own house, but also everyone else's. If he's your neighbor, give thanks. He can be seen calmly mowing the lawns of the neighbors, sometimes eccentrically at night, walking around on their roofs to fix leaks, getting them gadgets and going to obscure electrical stores to get wiring to fix their floor lamps. He drives a beat-up pale green truck from the 1930s filled with tools and wears Hawaiian shirts on the weekend. And is the nicest guy in the world. So it's hard for me to fault him even through the strain. He's a nutty character and I love the guy. His is an airy burdenless love that never stifles you. To say the least.

Before we were married we used to fight more. I remember fighting in the gardens of Palermo, packing my suitcase at midnight and storming out of our hotel. Only of course to meekly walk back in five minutes later, having gotten no farther than the elevator, the lobby, or the pay phone on the corner. He had won my heart years ago in Fort Defiance, when I was but a dreaming youth.

It may not have escaped your notice that the most brilliant men are often absentminded. This is true of Mac. If he has to catch a plane to Timbuktu, he will have your car keys in his pocket, or your house keys. He would leave confidential documents in strange hotel rooms. Show up for important dates on the wrong day. A courier to Kennedy is always speeding through the night to bring Mac's passport, for he could never make an international departure without forgetting it.

My father was at one time a professor of mathematics. One night there was a meeting at our house for high school students with an aptitude in that department. The following evening the doorbell rang after dinner. My father answered in his bathrobe. It was Mac dressed in a suit and tie, holding a briefcase. "I'm here for the meeting," he said, taking in the bathrobe and the empty house. "That was last night," said my father, but invited him in anyway, and they sat talking for some hours.

The forced politeness, the goodwill, his mild and bemused yet unflappable demeanor touched my heart. When he left I saw him to the door. It was then that I had my epiphany. There he stood in his suit and tie, so mild-mannered and polite and bemused, holding his briefcase. The world stopped, I got off, and saw far into the future. There was a calm amusement in his face, looking at me, and a stalwart kindness. There were all our future children in his mild blue eyes, even at our young age then, just as now there is the glinting memory of that moment when our future course together was determined.

"Mac, there is something we need to discuss."

"What is it, Fleming dear?"

This would doubtless be the time to tell him about the pregnancy. But I lost my nerve.

"I'm trying to be more like the Abernathy girls."

"Remind me about that again."

"They don't complain. That's their reality."

"You? Complain? What a joke. You would never complain."

Sarcasm.

He drifted off to the icemaker. Soon he was under the compartment checking the wiring.

"Your reality is trying to make the desert bloom," I called.

"The potential, Fleming dear, with this project in the Mojave, is worth my time."

He was now drifting toward the garage.

"My reality is that screeching freak-out thing with the sun."

"The violins. The old movies. Have I got it?"

"Yes."

"You had a message from Mr. Lieberman just now," said Mac.

"What did he want?"

"Just to see that you had arrived here safely from New York. And to remind you of your meeting next week in L.A. He's staying at the Alexandria and will book you a room for the night."

"Don't you want to know who he is?"

"I know who he is. He's an international tycoon."

It was a little annoying that he was so mild-mannered about my going to a hotel in L.A. to meet with another man.

"I gave him my condolences for Adelaide. I remember her," he continued. "Who could forget her?" he mused. It may be that her atomic particles were careening past.

"As I was saying, this thing in the Mojave, if I can just get to the water, then I can get the investors, the support, and the pressure will be off."

But I could always tell when things were looking bad for him and when he was becoming slightly desperate, because he would always travel more incessantly at those times, his absences would be more protracted, his appearances ever more fleeting—unnecessarily, fruitlessly. He was playing a desperate game. So I thought.

If anyone could make the desert bloom, it would be Mac. But secretly I was starting to lose hope of making the desert bloom. Not being a geologist I can't feature the reality of the water crisis. It doesn't seem like such a crisis to the layman, who is brainwashed by the bougainvillea and the fanatic gardens to forget that they are artificial.

But the history of the West is the history of the search for water in a desert.

The financial prospectus for the project was staggering. It would take twenty million to find the water plate, whose exact location was not yet determined. The drilling, further seismic analyses of the geology, and construction of the consequent aqueduct and pipelines would cost another four hundred million. The investors had assembled a syndicate for the first twenty million: five million each from the Mexican National Energy Corp., South Texas Power and Light, and a French oil company. The remaining five million would come from venture capital investors and certain individuals in Texas who wanted to see the water go to the panhandle. The Texas panhandle had completely dried up. Some people wanted to see the water go toward the agricultural uses Mac favored, in his worldwide campaign to save agriculture.

Geological and engineering work in the desert is not sophisticated in a technological sense. If you want to get rid of something you have to blow it up. If you want to find something you have to drill for it. Once you find it you have to construct an elaborate system of conduits, based on gravity, to get it where you want it to go—whether to the parched panhandle or the bald hills of Mexico. And the Metropolitan Water District in L.A. would be jealous, for as mentioned, water is very political, and the Metropolitan Water District is as shady now as it was in Mulholland's day. Obstacles were many.

Mac said he would stay with the children when I went to L.A. to meet Mr. Lieberman. Then he would go back to the Mojave. I would have to find a way to adjust my heart and house as ever to his absence.

I had the curious sensation that I was about to throw myself into the arms of another man. But the nature of my commitment to the father of my children lent impossibility to that ridiculous scenario.

Before I left I took the kids to various hideous children's emporiums that can have no interest for a sane adult. There I ordered lunch.

"We'll have the Happy FunTown Sunshine Special Meals," I said.

It was the children's version of Special Perspectives West Coast Coordination Team.

"I just want normal french fries," said my daughter, Josie.

"That includes normal french fries."

At home I had to endlessly read aloud a book about a character called Little Sal who has a thing for blueberries. My daughter had a thing for Little Sal.

"What's so great about Little Sal?" I asked my daughter.

"She's very sweet and very very lovely."

"OK. Fair enough. I guess she is. Now do you want pancakes or waffles?"

"Pancakes. Because they're very very sweet and lovely."

After the kids were in bed, dreaming endlessly of the sweet and lovely Little Sal and other sweet and lovely things, I tried to talk to Mac about the pregnancy.

I had reached the stage of pregnancy where I can only read books about the execution of the Romanovs. If Mac were observant he would know this about me and so I put the heavy and dramatic tome in a prominent place where he would see it.

But he didn't notice. So at dinner I put the book next to his plate. Still he noticed nothing. During dinner he took his plate into the living room to watch the ball game. So after dinner I got mad.

He keeps watching this thing called *Home Run Derby*.

Home Run Derby takes place in 1952. They play it on the Classics Sports Channel, which is a cable outlet devoted to airing old games from the past when current sports are too upsetting to endure. In *Home Run Derby* some cornball announcer dreams up a way for one baseball player to see how many home runs he can hit in an empty baseball stadium, and consists predominantly of forced awkward conversations where the sports announcer tries desperately to keep the banter going between himself and Gil Hodges, a taciturn power hitter. A nameless pitcher and some guy loping around the outfield catching balls complete the strangely hollow cast. Gil Hodges is the sole batter in nine innings where he gets three pitches twelve times. After each inning he has to go talk about it to the announcer in the press box.

"Well, you didn't really get too much to hit that time, Gil," says the announcer.

"Nope."

Gil Hodges doesn't really do his part to keep the banter going.

Or maybe one time Gil Hodges gets a home run.

"Wow! You really blasted that one, Gil. And you've just won FIVE HUNDRED DOLLARS! How do you feel about that, Gil?"

"Good."

I forgot to mention that every time Gil Hodges gets a home run he gets five hundred dollars.

"This is really exciting!" says the announcer desperately.

"Yep."

It is incredibly boring and yet Mac is completely spellbound by it. He can watch it for hours on end. He watches it every time they replay it on another slow sports day. He's glued to the screen. You can't talk to him about anything when *Home Run Derby* is on.

But I would try.

"Mac, how are you really? How are you feeling? Let's take your emotional temperature. Let's take a reading psychically, emotionally, mentally."

His eyes strayed to *Home Run Derby*, where Gil Hodges was battling an incredibly unexciting series of foul balls.

"I do have a neck crick, now that you mention it."

"Look, Mac. You're going to be all right. We're going to check your emotional temperature. You're going to be OK."

"It's not like you have to talk me down from the bridge, Fleming dear."

"But what about your emotions?" I tried again.

"Your expectations for each day are too epic, too grand, Fleming. They always were."

In Fort Defiance when we were growing up, no one was regular and calm—except perhaps Mac, who retained those qualities through it all. Most were dissolute, idle, and errant. Some say that Mobile, Alabama, is an exact microcosm of New Orleans except without the depravity. Fort Defiance is an exact microcosm of New Orleans including the depravity. New Orleans was your incessant destination anyway, driving along the coast at all hours toward society and late nights and jazz and decrepit black torch singers. The bluer Mac's eyes got the more I remembered, for he was there.

At that time usually you got home around four in the morning. That was good because I couldn't go to bed until four in the morning. I was too hedonistic, did not follow my duty, and too often did not even recognize where my duty lay, and in what it consisted. Now of course with all these small maniacal people—the kids—I do. You don't have to be Albert Einstein to discern your duty there. It pins you down.

But the next day I left for my rare night out, with the uneasy peace of a woman who was leaving her children behind, and whose love and gratitude for her husband could only be expressed, it seemed, through sourness and sarcasm.

Instead I'd meet the old-world Englishman of my imagination at a sumptuous Los Angeles hotel. It's probable I would prefer what I would find in my imagination to the reality. But you never can tell.

23

I drive but I don't merge. It's a threshold phobia. So I generally took the train when I went to Los Angeles. I should say the suicide train. The daily train to L.A. that is called the *Starlight,* which goes up along the coast, and has the frequent suicides.

There was an abrupt delay after passing the three palms signifying Costa Verde, with its velvet green lawns and palms and the spires of the racetrack rising on the sunlit slanting sea. It is just north of La Dolcita, another one of those ritzy neighborhoods on the coast. I stared out at the pitiless Pacific Ocean.

There was the usual lack of information. We were eventually told that it was a fatality. A suicide. It reminded me, as always, of *Anna Karenina,* and I mentioned this several times to passengers, receiving blank looks, of course.

A mariachi band was playing remorselessly at a nearby café. One irony of mariachi bands is that if life is sweet at a nice café and a mariachi band is playing, it's great; but if you're depressed, or have just virtually witnessed a suicide, there is nothing like a mariachi band to make a mockery of you. It happens a lot in Esperanza. You can't escape mariachi bands here. It's like being trapped year-round in a glaring Mexican resort.

The other passengers, however, did not appear to feel that way and started playing cards, rolling up their sleeves, loosening their ties, and drinking beer.

"We have a fatality," the conductor reported periodically into his cellular phone while walking up and down the aisle. The train had been going ninety miles an hour at the time of the accident. They had to get cleared of liability, as the victim was considered a suicide. I kept asking for a profile of the victim but could not extract any information.

You would think that if someone wanted to commit suicide they would do it near the oppressive environs of Los Angeles, not in the café-laden twilight on the blue Pacific, but the suicide mania has as its backdrop the bland untroubled paradise of Esperanza. You would think that having escaped from the hideous ugliness of their urban environment the people here would revel in the beauty of the undeveloped coast. But the blue Pacific seems to have the opposite effect on them.

After an hour we got rolling to San Juan Capistrano. As in the swallows. We passed a gorgeous situation of gardens and historic cottages, long boulevards to the mountains lined with palms and the occasional Spanish spire.

There was another delay at Santa Ana. An unaccountable spot of rain caused a crisis. The slightest note of adversity causes overwhelming desperation. In general the *Starlight* does not have the vitality of the more viable East Coast route. Back east along the coast there is a grim history of toil, the hardy seafarers, whaling, wrecking, adventure. There's no industry to the sea here, no toil, it's not grim. And yet everyone is in a major panic.

24

I took a cab to West Hollywood. I stayed at the Alexandria Hotel, a strange respite in the metropolis which shows what a paradise the whole place used to be. It is as if you suddenly stepped into the Italian Riviera. A rambling ornate place with courtyards and cafés and bougainvillea and couches outside in the garden. The astounding thing is that the whole town used to be such a paradise as that. Sunset Boulevard was a vast array of gardens and bungalows and garden courts. There are still some decaying mansions that are French châteaux or Moorish palaces or southern-style plantations, built by demented stars and exiles from another world, for they wished to bring their old world with them. We're talking about the twentieth century, and yet its relics here seem like the vanished haunting of an ancient civilization.

In the 1920s there was in southern California a Mediterranean craze, or you might say an Italian Riviera craze. The Mediterranean craze was based on the weather, the foliage (imported bougainvillea and palm), and the coastline. Also a Spanish Colonial craze, when people suddenly remembered the Spanish heritage of southern California and decided to feel nostalgic about it. So they created a Spanish-style architecture based on a nostalgic idea, a sudden remembrance, perhaps even a swift burst of scholarship. Then there was also a Moorish craze, an Egyptian craze, and in Hollywood, starting with the old set of *Intolerance* by D. W. Griffith, a Babylonian craze.

There was a garden at the Alexandria with a European vaulted ceiling along a colonnade—hibiscus, camellia, night-blooming jasmine, and palm—among Italian wicker chairs and tables ranged about, and the occasional disheveled tortured young person coming in, for the metropolis lures the aspirant, by ambition and art.

The benign ghosts of old stars did haunt the hotel. I got a guide to Hollywood about the old stars. They were always doing things like building aviaries and archery ranges on their estates and growing seven thousand orange dahlias. They hanged themselves with bright silk sashes, they dressed up in elegant gowns and wrote elaborate suicide notes to several people explaining various things. Usually they were stars from silent pictures who couldn't make the transition to talkies. They were matinee idols in their (and the century's) twenties and washed-up has-beens in the thirties. They stabbed themselves with sewing scissors or leapt off the roof of hotels, first writing elaborate suicide notes apologizing to the other guests. A director attempted suicide when a silent-picture star refused to marry him; later he achieved suicide after being married to Jean Harlow for six weeks. The first girl died of heavy drinking and fast living, after being celebrated as the most beautiful girl in the world in silent pictures and then having a nervous breakdown at age thirty. They died of alcoholism, surrounded by scotch bottles and their dog. They died broke and forgotten and a drug addict in a small apartment. A silent-picture idol who became a has-been was reduced to selling hot dogs outside of the Paramount lot.

The man who started the whole show, D. W. Griffith, was by the 1930s "used up and finished, doomed to lonely hotel rooms, whiskey, and brooding resentment that the Hollywood he had founded had now cynically rejected him."

So the achievement came at a cost. But here is the exact spot where humanity made an astounding contribution to civilization. You must search for signs of it. Each relic, each corner, each green area and grove has its drama, and each drama bears some relation to this astounding contribution. Unlike Esperanza, this town has aspiration and longing and failure and exiles and art. Humanity tried to achieve something there.

Hollywood has an air of mystery that allures me. Why is it all in ruins, like relics of ancient Rome?—"And suddenly the streets were filled with something one could only speak of as remembrance."

The weather was intolerably hot and glaring. It would have been troubling to walk out, even to sit in the garden. The old neon signs in the cooling evening were more promising.

All afternoon you could not go out, the sun and heat being too barbaric. You would not bear to go out unless you wanted the sun to beat all sense from your brains. What a difference it must be especially to the expatriated Englishmen traditionally populating Los Angeles, a difference from their damp drenched moors.

Parched. The hills are very parched.

By evening I was restless and strolled down into the lobby, where I saw some television cameras rolling and the white glare of film lights. An interview was being conducted with an intriguing white-haired gent wearing a bathrobe and expensive alligator slippers and dark sunglasses. Various people appeared to be hanging on his words. Even in his curious wardrobe he lent an air to the place, a vitality that made the city seem cosmopolitan in the waning twilight as I looked on from the vaulted colonnade of the European garden.

It was Mr. Lieberman, the international tycoon.

It seemed a little strange that he should be in his bathrobe, though he looked curiously debonair in it. But I'd only ever seen him in a crisp suit and bow tie looking like he'd just stepped out of a bandbox. Perhaps he had disintegrated in some way or was ailing. The robe gave him a certain air of decline. Though tall and towering as ever he seemed older and foreign and intriguing. His bathrobe was the kind that matinee idols used to wear in movies in the 1930s—like a smoking jacket, in a rich vermilion brocade. The sunglasses appeared to be a Hollywood touch, considering it was almost night. That was it, in fact, the whole thing was Hollywood. The whole thing was California. He had arrived at a place that he loved quite dearly, I was to discover, strangely enough. He wanted to be the perfect Californian. But despite himself, perhaps, he had a refined or cultivated air, as of someone juxtaposed from the old world to the new.

I did not interrupt the scene or say hello. Our lunch was set for the next day. I hung back in a corner, for some reason cowed. Then the television cameras left and he ambled slowly in his bathrobe and expensive slippers down the hall to the elevator. Only then could you perceive some air of sadness as a memory that he carried with him. It must have been the ghost of Adelaide.

Suddenly I had a vision of the place where I had last seen her. It was in Florida. An old couple at the Biltmore were walking on a verdant path up from the sea, he dressed in a brilliant green jacket (the brilliant green jacket that men wear in the deep South, which Mr. Lieberman had long ago adopted for certain occasions when visiting the old haunts of his wife on the Gulf Coast), she pale but dapper in a black dress. She looked sort of ethereal. There was something about her. You had a feeling that if you hitched your star to hers it would bring to you great benefit. So I could see how he must have felt at losing her. It wasn't mysterious. She was someone I rarely saw but who meant that much to me, and had a ring of fate or benefaction about her. She used the address Dearest once (Dearest Fleming) to me in a letter, which I cherished as a treasure. There was a kind of heroic beleaguered presence about them, as if they were stoically waiting for deliverance from pain. Maybe Mr. Lieberman didn't really want to put on this bright green jacket anymore, maybe he was sick of coming up the path in his silly southern sportswear, not commensurate to the imminent occasion they both awaited; maybe they were tired even of these verdant paths up from the sea. I had that vision of them suddenly. It was actually a kind of consolation for mortality, that they seemed so world-weary and disgusted. They seemed ready to move on. You could tell she was sick and you could tell she didn't want to get well. It would be a deliverance to move on. To the next world.

25

It was a beautiful night in Los Angeles at the Alexandria. Tortured disheveled young people ranged in the Italian wicker furniture in the vaulted garden, among camellia, hibiscus, and palm, in that respite off Sunset Boulevard heralded by the green-and-white striped awning just beyond the winding road.

The televised white-haired gent of the evening, Mr.

Lieberman, still in this world, came down the next morning and pottered around the lobby in his bathrobe again, and expensive alligator slippers, with his mixed air of vitality and sadness. Again I did not accost him. Somehow I did not want to meet him in his bathrobe. It's only one step from constantly hanging around in your bathrobe to losing your entire sense of reality.

Only someone very debonair, or very confident, or very tired, could pull it off—constantly hang around in their bathrobe looking natural and suave. Nevertheless at hotels you don't ordinarily go down to the lobby in your bathrobe. You don't ordinarily conduct interviews for television in your bathrobe. It formed a conflict with his meticulous British reserve and alignment with decorum, the crisp figure striding up West End Avenue in New York in the wintry weather, the brief and enigmatic appearance in New York in May.

When I went back upstairs I received a phone call from him in my room.

"You're still free, Miss Ford?"

"Yes, yes, of course. Please don't call me Miss Ford."

I notice he didn't ask me to call him Harry.

"Come to my suite then, Miss Ford. Number seven. I will await your arrival."

Strange. Here I was at forty, in the middle of the journey of our life, in a strange place where I knew no one, and where I could not get anyone in the entire state to pay me any mind, except for a debauched botanist, yet suddenly I was meeting with a towering international tycoon crazed with grief who made eccentric public appearances in his bathrobe at a storied Hollywood hotel.

When I knocked on his door, it was answered instantaneously, as if he had been standing in attendance directly behind the door waiting. He was still wearing the robe.

Maybe he had jet lag. Or maybe it had something to do with California. People hang around in their robes a lot in California.

Standing behind him was a fifty-year-old Spanish man called Alberto, known as Albert, whom apparently Mr. Lieberman had hired in Los Angeles to be his secretary, steward, chauffeur, and general factotum on the West Coast. Then Mr. Lieberman received a phone call and excused himself. He disappeared into the recesses of the suite.

On a table in the living room I noticed three clocks set up side by side, two thermometers giving the outside temperature, and two altimeters. Beside the clocks lay a complicated set of instructions, explaining that they were controlled by a long-wave radio signal from the German time transmitter for Central European Time based on an atomic clock in Frankfurt. This elaborate setup somehow caused them to be set automatically on the correct international time as you traveled through successive time zones.

Albert had tactfully removed to the kitchen, where he began to iron Mr. Lieberman's ties.

I realized that the clocks were emitting a very faint but discernible series of high-pitched sounds that reminded me of the old RKO Pictures trademark: the tower with the beacon at the top of the world flashing Morse code.

Albert returned bearing a tray of lunch. Apparently he was also a cook. He set down the tray and remarked, "Do you find it chilly in here? I'm very chilled. Here. Feel my face." He bent down to where I was sitting.

"She'll take your word for it," said Mr. Lieberman crisply; he had just reappeared. Albert was overly familiar.

Albert retired to the kitchen, unfazed.

"What is the purpose of these three international clocks?" I inquired. Apparently he had to keep the European time. He also seemed to be obsessed with the altitude: he kept checking the two altimeters, as if the altitude might change while we were sitting there.

"The frequency is different for the U.S.," he said vaguely. He bore a sharp physical resemblance to someone I could not quite place. Then it hit me: Fred Astaire. With Astaire there's a kind of a frailty, which may be misleading, because there's an overwhelming agility. In his expression is a knowing gaiety and understanding. When he puts on white tie and tails and saunters toward the dance floor then the world is filled with glamour. Also Mr. Lieberman was an older man and he had the frailty of an older man that touches my heart.

He asked me how I liked Esperanza. I told him.

"You have a pitiless glare," he said. He kept talking about my pitiless glare—maybe getting it confused with the sun. I said my view of Esperanza seemed awfully dark. He said it was more like the dark side of paradise.

Esperanzans generally hold an attitude of boosterism. A scathing diatribe from an awkward outcast would not sit well with them. I had the feeling that L.A. on the other hand would get a kick out of a scathing diatribe of itself, being populated, like any great metropolis, by many other awkward outcasts. Boosterism implies a lack of sophistication, an inability to see or admit to the dark side. Always boosterism, no self-loathing or darkness, just as the sun always shines.

"But the darkness is your reality, Miss Ford," he said as if reading my mind, "and you had better hold on to it tightly indeed. That is the test for you here, to hold on to what you are, be it dark and neurotic, and remain what you are defiantly in the face of all that sunshine and the Technicolor paradise. You must never give in."

He knew nothing about me, really, but he displayed an unaccountable and electrifying knowledge of my circumstances and past history that he seemed to formulate through a conjectural study of my soul.

"Now then, Miss Ford." He sat across from me at the table.

"Fleming. Please."

"I am not a young man, Miss Ford. Allow me the expression of the habits of a lifetime." He studied my face carefully. Then he wrote something in his notes. "Now your father had the breakdown, when? Before you were born."

It was a declaration, not a question.

"There were recurrences."

If I had been wearing a necktie I would have loosened it at this moment. These were not things that I would have told Adelaide who could have told him. She hadn't lived in Fort Defiance for fifty years and would not have heard these things from other sources, for my family was not a public one.

He shuffled some papers at the side of his plate, as if consulting notes. He searched my face for clues. "Your husband has the five brothers. Healthy family. Your mother was very strong. So we come back to your father. A nervous illness."

I began to wonder whether the notes on the table comprised some sort of dossier he had collected on my history—my chart—as if he were a pathologist trying to determine what was wrong with me. And yet he seemed to be getting his information just by studying my soul.

"Your mother took him to be treated in New York. It was when they were both very young."

It was as if he were a gypsy fortune-teller.

"So there is the history of melancholy in your family. Whether it may be hereditary is yet to say. In your father's case, an abnormal aptitude for mathematics was the original source of the anxiety. There's a fine line between genius and insanity, of course."

Mathematicians tend to be crazy. And mathematics often have no practical utility for the world, at least to start out with, being of purely intellectual interest. Then later they tend to have utility for things like the composition of atomic bombs and world annihilation.

My father was at one time a mathematician for the National Security Council, so his work was not known to the public. But apparently it was known to Mr. Lieberman.

"He was working on something big at the time. And it was this discovery that upset him."

In other words he went crazy making bombs for the American government. After that he went back to his elegant formulas of probability theory and code-breaking.

"He was better off in another area of research. Your mother almost lost him."

"How is it you know all this?" I asked. "Were you there? Did you know them?"

"In my business you learn to read the history of a person in his face, Miss Ford."

"In natural resources you learn that?" For that was his corner on the financial markets.

He brushed this aside.

"In the mogul business, Miss Ford."

A joke.

"I believe you were named for your mother's family. She was a very strong person. You take after her. But you have your father's nervous streak also. In fact you're nervous as a cat. Jumpy."

It was all very odd. Yet the elegance descended, the curtain of glamour, the light returned that had been lacking, someone could understand me, someone could get me, and it was Mr. Lieberman.

I noticed for the first time during this queer conversation that he had a sort of almost rude sexuality about him. Maybe it was the bathrobe. He didn't look bad in it. He didn't look exactly good in it. He just looked natural. It was unnerving. I wondered if it were true that he had had affairs while Adelaide lived. But what of his famous devotion? It wasn't that he was looking at me lecherously or leering at me or anything like that. It was just an air about the man, and his bold pronouncements, his assured vision.

"I think you'll have another child in California, Miss Ford. It must be all this sunshine. And it will mean much more to you than you can begin to realize now."

That stopped me.

"At my age?"

I just wanted to test how he knew so much.

"It could only happen here. In the desert. It's the sunny atmosphere. The expanse of the sky. It's quite healthy, you know. You'll look as young as your daughter."

Flattery.

"Now you have three main points of trouble. You're in a strange place, your husband's venture is a little questionable at this juncture, and as you may know, the stock market will crash."

He stopped his amazing recital of everyone's circumstances for a moment. "But I myself may be able to help."

He knew all about my husband's work in the Mojave. It was not I who had told him. When you're a mogul you have ways of discovering everyone's business enterprises.

Natural resources being among Mr. Lieberman's closely held interests, there would prove to be a link to my husband's work in the Mojave Desert.

Mr. Lieberman had originated the vast increase of the fortune he inherited by betting on the most common commodity, coal, whose day had supposedly past. When nuclear power came in and oil was plentiful Mr. Lieberman had taken up a contrarian position in the majority of old British coal mines; he had expanded into West Virginia and Colorado. Nuclear power became too dangerous to be put into wide use, oil became scarce, and in short, coal made Mr. Lieberman a fortune.

So what could be more basic than water? My husband's water plate in the Mojave would be, thought Mr. Lieberman, another gold mine.

His interest was opportune. My husband's investors had grown somewhat skeptical. After our meeting it looked like Mr. Lieberman might have an interest in financing the project. Perhaps it appeared that I had gone up there to pitch the idea on my husband's behalf. But it was not that way at all. I think Mr. Lieberman was fascinated by a woman who in some way reminded him of Adelaide. I don't think he ever really separated that interest from the project in his mind. He had lost his wife, and here he was now searching in the desert for water, as if crazed by thirst.

"I expect you can't count on people here," he remarked. "They're not bound by decorum. But you don't come here for society."

This was a penetratingly true observation.

"You may count on me, however. And the desert will look as green as an Oxford quadrangle."

But I was not so keen on that as he and Mac. It seemed to violate some natural immutable law. He was very keen on it, though. "This is your husband's dream and it is in danger of being shot down. So we'll resurrect it. There's plenty more dreams where that one came from, as I told you, kid."

I saw that he meant to fulfill his reputation as fixer. He meant to ease our way.

"When you get old it's one thing after another until you check out," he said suddenly. He said it in a distant way. He seemed very hard-boiled about it. "How does it feel getting older? Sometimes you can't feel it. It's still the same blue sky I see every morning from my window. I change. It doesn't."

"How do you reconcile yourself?"

"By planting forty-five palm trees on my property in Florida."

"But how can you reconcile to saying good-bye to them?"

"I have a theory," he said. "The Lord gives you what you can tolerate." He stopped. "That was always my theory before. But that's not true anymore, Miss Ford," he said. "Because the Lord took Adelaide and I can't tolerate that. It was Adelaide and me against the world."

"Who won?"

"The world is winning now."

26

At lunch he talked obsessively of Adelaide. I think her ghost accompanied him wherever he went. I could not quite discern whether this was a comfort or a trial.

Just for the record, I kind of idolized Adelaide too, but from afar. She looked like Greta Garbo. She came from another era. Even her name was from another era. But we all have names like that in Fort Defiance—Fleming Ford, Mac MacMoreland, Adelaide Ames.

She had had another life before she met Mr. Lieberman, being so much older. She had gone from Alabama to New York as a girl in the 1940s. She married another British aristocrat before Mr. Lieberman. Maybe for Adelaide there was some connection between that atmosphere and our ornate though crumbling Fort Defiance, where there were a lot of doddering aristocrats, who probably thought they had titles. The British Empire had crumbled; so had Fort Defiance. In

England you got the title from an ancient king or from making a political contribution or some achievement. In Fort Defiance you were self-ordained. Adelaide's first husband took her to live in London. They frequented New York, which was where she met Mr. Lieberman, while still married.

It is true that there had been something a little weird in the age difference between Mr. Lieberman and Adelaide. She was a figure whom he had guarded and defended, through what was her old age. When she died, Mr. Lieberman was turning seventy and Adelaide was well into her eighties. But you would not have guessed her age. You would have put her at sixty or seventy. She was quite equal to her husband in every form of deportment and countenance, which belied her actual age. But her actual age was not belied to God, who took her back at the usual time. I still don't know if Mr. Lieberman knew her actual age at the time of her death. She did have the coquettish streak—she was a southerner, after all—her age was not a subject for heralding to the rooftops. You might reason that Mr. Lieberman needed a mother and so had married a woman that much older.

And maybe it was so. He had been farmed out almost immediately from birth and rarely lived under the same roof as his parents for more than a month at a time. He was born when his father was fifty. He had numerous brothers all vastly older. He barely knew his father; the patriarchs in the family tended to die of sudden heart attacks at fifty-five. But Mr. Lieberman said that he had a dim memory of one or two family dinners in London. His father wore white tie and had a rule: No talking at the dinner table. He also had a dim but ecstatic memory of his father taking him to Antibes on the French Riviera. So my vision was an accurate photographic memory from his youth as I had thought, with its accurate emotion of bliss. Having Proustian flashbacks to your childhood is one thing but to someone else's is another. Strange.

It would have been the Hôtel du Cap in Antibes. It would have been the Meurice in Paris, or the Lotti. It would have been the Aquitania or the Blue Train. I had photographic memories of someone else's life, a study of that person's nostalgias, of an old and glamorous and storied world I'd never myself known. Not only that, but it meant more to me than it did to him. He liked the Wild West.

Mr. Lieberman had already lost his numerous older brothers one by one, leaving him with a solitary air, which he had actually always had, being so much younger than everyone else. Perhaps this made him feel comfortable being so much younger than Adelaide. As a very small child he was sent to live with various overbearing aunts—one in Paris who lived on the Place de la Concorde; he remembered the lights at night driving up to the house. There were others at the Riviera, Biarritz, and Bellagio, where Lord Northwood had died at his Lake Como retreat.

Among the many legends associated with Lord Northwood's name, one was his discovery of the French Riviera as a British retreat in the nineteenth century. Actually the British liked it for the same reasons that a British person would like California: health resort, tropical climate, a love of gardens, and the desire to flee—*la maladie du siècle*. After World War I, as Lord Northwood did not live to see, it was populated by exiled White Russians, fleeing kings and princes, conquering Americans, now deposed British, but was then still a fairly quiet place, and the Americans in those early days sometimes missed the clamor of empire. Theirs was the empire now.

It was decreed that Mr. Lieberman would go to Harrow, loathed by boys from Byron to Churchill. While he was there his mother died. One day at Harrow he saw a picture of a palm tree in Los Angeles and had an epiphany. The world stopped, he got off, and vowed to light out to a newer point, one with that climate and that broad unending sky and those trees such as are not found in England, as are the diametric opposite of England. At this time he was embarrassingly chauffered to Harrow every day from an overbearing aunt's house in London after his mother's death. He realized he had had enough of England and his relatives and the mantle of Lord Northwood. He didn't get as far as California, but he went to America, and had lived in New York for the forty years since.

He said that he and Adelaide had planned to retire to California. I found this strange. To me they were too worldly for California. But then I didn't have an epiphany about the light in Los Angeles when I was fifteen on the damp playing fields of Harrow. I would imagine him retiring to some place like the Italian Riviera or the Tuscan hills or Lord Northwood's villa on Lake Como. But then he never would do that. He rejected all that. In favor of the new world. In his grandfather's day it was the Riviera. In his, California. Each time for the light.

But there is a more normal climate on the Riviera, light or no light. It is no desert there. Still in another time it was a tonic climate for people suffering esoteric diseases, just as California was advertised for invalids at the turn of the last century in the origin of its reputation as paradise.

It was after the death of Adelaide that he traveled to England, attempting to recapture the scenes of his early life— but he couldn't make sense of it—he had deliberately left it too far behind. He had lived in America longer than he had lived in England, after all. He was more English to me than he was to himself. But he was the one and only American Lieberman, for Lord Northwood's single strategic mistake in finance was in not bringing his business to the U.S., a mistake which his grandson rectified. Then the one and only American Lieberman tried to go back. He embarked on a

Scottish idyll, inhabiting wild bleak moors, he rambled across the fells. The Mediterranean would have been too gay. Sometimes he retraced the steps of the travels he had taken with his wife. Obsessed with seeking cool climates, he went on to depressing British seaside resorts, ruined resorts in a driving rain, decaying palaces out on the pier at Brighton made of wrought iron and glass, the ravishing road to Rottingdean. Toward the end of his term on the English coast all other travelers had departed. It was out of season. For him it was a most uncertain season. He became somewhat accustomed to the atmosphere. But in the end it was no good. He could not find what he had sought in it. Instead in the end he finally achieved his boyhood dream of the light in Los Angeles, a light which to me was completely overbearing. As it turned out he would never leave this region. It was where the Englishman once came out of hope, "ruined peers seeking redemption among the orange groves." He moved around a lot in the area. Arcadia, Bel Air, Hollywood, Idyllwild, Palm Springs, Riverside, San Bernardino, Santa Monica, Silver Lake, the Mojave, and Esperanza, living the rest of his life in hotel suites and rented quarters, spending a good deal of it in his bathrobe, like some ruined matinee idol. A man who had left his home so far behind—I guess I could understand why that man would go to California. The place may have been a paradise before the First World War. But Mr. Lieberman liked it now with only remnants of its former state, while the coyotes howling in the canyon transfixed him all night. New York held for him a promise unbearable to look back on now that it had been fulfilled. Still in California he was a solitary traveler pursued by malaise. When he got somewhere new, he felt he must be gone, and would make arrangements to depart, for what was beautiful suddenly turned sour, then as he was leaving he might find he was mistaken, it became beautiful again, and he wanted to go back.

27

Maybe it was his ancestral antecedent, this desire to flee. He had intended to stay in California for a month, a season, a year. But of course the seasons never changed. "I can't keep track of time out here," he said. Maybe that was why he needed all the clocks. I think it's hard to keep track of the seasons when you live in a place that doesn't really have them. That happens on the Gulf Coast too, as he had noticed on his trips there to visit Adelaide's family.

Adelaide's father, Standard Ames, had been one of the five men who ran New Orleans. Now just as if you're from the Mississippi Delta, Memphis is really your town, in a similar way if you are from the Gulf Coast, New Orleans is also home to you. There used to be five men who ran the town, strictly from behind the scenes, from the backseats of limousines gliding along the Gulf Coast to New Orleans, and from back rooms and clubs. They weren't senators or governors but they were the men behind the scenes in politics. They didn't want to be senators or governors. The campaign trail is arduous. You have to go to Bogalusa when it's 90 degrees. Adelaide's father was one of them. The fortieth senator, they called him. But he was crafty, this old gent, Standard Ames, who ran things. So Adelaide had your prototypical towering father in the South. She had that connection to the powerful, which Mr. Lieberman also had, from his grandfather. Her people were as powerful as his, in a smaller world. The people in that world were dynamic and they were sentimental. You got the feeling that they didn't need to leave. But then where else would they have such power? Some people wondered how Mr. Lieberman could have walked away from his privileges in England. But he was not sentimental; he just walked away. In fact there are not that many opportunities in England. You have to be born to them. Which he was, but he also walked away from that.

Despite some similarities between Lord Northwood and Standard Ames, the distant gods, nothing could have been further from Mr. Lieberman's personal experience than the situation of Fort Defiance: sons following fathers into a family business, never leaving their small world, never departing from their circumscribed existence, never deprived of their moorings, always following a predetermined path to maintain a certain social standard.

Mr. Lieberman did not have a father to emulate in his work. His father had not been strong enough to withstand the temptations of his massive inheritance. So what did his father do? Nothing, of course. He occupied that world of swank to which Lord Northwood had created his entrée. It was the way he'd meant to pave. It was the way Mr. Lieberman did not choose to follow.

He had some traits endemic to entrepreneurs although he was not strictly speaking a self-made man. For one thing he didn't fit in. Some say New York is a city made up of people who didn't fit in in their hometowns. So that was his first adopted home. He hated rules. He wanted to make his own rules. He thrived on uncertainty, yet was the consummate optimist. An entrepreneur has to be that.

He was a sort of double outsider. In America he was distinctly European, though he would have it otherwise. In England he was not, like his grandfather before him, totally accepted in society due to his faith.

In the Wild West you wouldn't have to reckon with the mantle of Lord Northwood. The same had been true in New York. The mantle of Lord Northwood was not heavy in New York, where after all it actually meant nothing. It would seem that most British people who come to America would seek to escape a class system that they detest. I don't think Mr. Lieberman detested it. He just had no interest in it. He would have spurned the family title had it come his way, to assert his independence and his acceptance of his more humble antecedents. He insisted on distancing himself from the storied figure, never realizing how much they had in common.

There was something in his life that gave him a handicap, despite his privileged upbringing, which he had to overcome. He had something to struggle against. I could not figure out entirely what it was, but I could see it was there. Like his grandfather before him, he was an outsider no matter what success he attained. He felt more like the grandson of the Jewish ghetto than the grandson of the British lord. He never for a moment took his own or his grandfather's storied success for granted, and he had meant to land in paradise among the palms and bougainvillea and desert moonlight with Adelaide on his own steam and initiative and achievement. The only trouble was that this paradise had come too late.

28

Everyone has their moment of epiphany—that is when the world stops and they get off and realize what is most dear to them to pursue. For Mr. Lieberman it was the photograph of the palm at Harrow. For my botanist the sight of a geranium at age three—they found him staring at a seed rack in a trance. For my father it was the realization that the ratio between the circumference and diameter of a circle is always constant. The moment is a joy. Maybe it is the idea of elegance. It may be an event that leads you to your life's work, showing what quantity to you is most important to distill, as for Mac it was the flood of '55. Or it may be the revelation of the place that makes you feel at home, or the realization of the place that you must flee from. But where did the palm at Harrow lead Mr. Lieberman if not to the end of the road, the end of the rainbow and all that? In a way it was the same for Mac. This obsession in the desert, the light, the palm oasis, the water trapped beneath it—I had the feeling that this would not end well.

Various assistants in Mr. Lieberman's entourage started swarming all over the hotel suite after lunch. An army of gardeners came to work on the courtyard. Other assistants walked in and out with clipboards and laptops and consulted Mr. Lieberman on various things. He appeared to have a vast staff. Albert would come in every so often and start raving about what appeared to be various obstacles and household disasters. He was in charge of the domestic staff. Mr. Lieberman received a phone call and attached a gadget to his head, an apparatus small and luminous, encompassing communication. "O'Hara wants out," he said briskly into the mouthpiece. That was pretty much it. A short conversation. All of his conversation was clipped.

He took off the apparatus.

"Don't make any sudden movements, Miss Ford."

"Sudden movements? Why not?"

"The A/C is off. You'll perspire."

Then he asked me to wait while he went into the recesses of the suite somewhere. There was a din in the place. The A/C people came in wearing utility belts. I wandered around for a while. Albert was having a tremendous bonding experience with the housekeeper. Every time I went into the kitchen he would be sitting at the table staring deeply into the housekeeper's eyes saying things like "And then I lived in San Antone," later progressing to include complicated family sagas. Then he went back to yelling at his relatives on the phone. Later he seemed to calm down. But maybe not. "If you don't bring her back right now I'm going to come down there and rearrange your face," he said very quietly into the phone, emitting vast waves of danger. Soon he came into the living room where I was sitting.

"They're killing me," he said.

"Who?"

"My children."

It had something to do with fighting, jail, drugs.

I made sounds of sympathy.

"I'm a diabetic," he continued.

I gave condolences.

"I think I'm getting a migraine. When you get old no one really loves you but your dog."

After an ominous silence he got up and starting rifling

through drawers mumbling about some monkey business, then disappeared in the courtyard.

I waited around some more. Albert was telling his life story to the gardener. I could hear the conversation going on from the kitchen. It had something to do with collapsing in the parking lot that morning. It had something to do with the kids.

Mr. Lieberman had not materialized. So I asked Albert, "Do you think I'm supposed to stick around, or do you think maybe I should go?"

"Stick around. I'll go and see."

He disappeared, which was OK by me because there was a hole in his heart where quiet dignity should be. Mr. L. soon reappeared, stage left. He was finally wearing regular clothes. These consisted of a somewhat odd assortment of what he may have felt was California garb: a sort of safari outfit—khaki trousers—jodhpurs, really—and a khaki shirt with flaps and pockets all over it. Again for me it was jarring, having only seen him before in his bandbox mode—a white summer suit and pink shirt and green tie, say, dramatic outfits of the kind that Adelaide would have decreed. Or the bathrobe. Now suddenly he was Gary Cooper at high noon. Maybe Cecil B. DeMille—with the jodhpurs. His hair was so white that it had an almost yellow cast. At times he seemed frail but his frailty was belied by his agility and endurance, displayed during his long episodic walks in strange cities.

I couldn't really figure him out. After lunch he made me walk from West Hollywood to Santa Monica, which is a distance of some twelve or fifteen miles. We arrived there after dark. Apparently you had to be in Olympic training to hang around with him. So the frailty was misleading.

*   *   *

We walked out to Sunset Boulevard. Sunset Boulevard laden with sleaze can be very oppressive but on my long walk with Mr. Lieberman the sleaze gave a negative pressure that was darkly beguiling, like the French Quarter in New Orleans, which is the type of place where people are drinking beer at ten o'clock in the morning, and the trash has not been picked up from the night before, and the whole place basically has the air of a bordello, and the view from your hotel room is to the brick wall of the Holiday Inn next door. But it is home, of course, and that makes all the difference, for in that there is redemption. So you're picking your way among the tourists and the trash and yet if it's home, then anything could happen, and every situation is a stage set, every bar or lounge. All the ghosts of those you most have loved are there, and it is overpowering. The whole place peopled with ghosts, and maybe one or two who accompany you everywhere you go. Just as it is for me in Alabama. Or New York—it was home, although I did not know that at the time. I only know it now.

Is it the torture of California that screws up your head in such a remove from your home? But it is human nature to adapt, and it is American to feel fondly for whatever spot your car is parked in. Then there are those who feel the desire to flee. Just as I fled from Fort Defiance, while my father remained there to defend it.

"If you actually lived out here," I asked Mr. Lieberman, "what would you feel?"

"Rootless," he said with the greatest satisfaction.

"Outlandish commercial establishments," he pointed out ecstatically on Sunset Boulevard. "The real California."

The combination of the heat and oppression and sleaze was interesting due to the teeming humanity and vast world metropolis with more history and architecture and intrigue than you would ever find in Esperanza. Off Sunset you would see a crumbling ornate ruin in the hills, hidden in the palms, just as you would see in Nassau or Havana, remains of what was once a grand hotel or mansion. Now ruined, haunting, still beautiful, with overgrown gardens, everything falling apart, but at least a vivid remnant of history. For some reason the architectural style that touched my heart the most in L.A. was the Italianate, or as they would say in Esperanza, Italianesque, getting it wrong, for a subdivision called Venezia built five minutes ago. In Esperanza there would be a subdivision mistakenly called Triage, which means emergency room treatment, because it sounds French. And everything would be strictly new. But in L.A. there would be actual decay—the torn awnings, the encrusted corinthian columns, fading palazzos in the palms.

At Doheny in Beverly Hills the decay comes abruptly to a sudden end, replaced by an oversized fantastical landscape of towering palms in symmetrical rows, gauche unapproachable mansions, green boulevards, and leafy walkways. But with no one walking on them. Because they're all driving.

Every so often a dark blue limousine driven by Albert would pull up Jeeves-like miraculously not causing accidents at our side and a door would open for us when, as sometimes happened, there were no sidewalks. Then he would just as sleekly drop us off again when the sidewalk reappeared.

Mr. Lieberman was pointing out the foliage, the old-world palms and peppers, imported from another place: Australian eucalyptus, Caribbean hibiscus, bougainvillea from South America.

"How did you learn so much about gardening?" I asked.

"From being in a garden for thirty years."

"What exactly do you mean by that remark?"

He vaguely gestured with his hand, as if encompassing the trees.

"It's really kind of overripe and decadent here," I noted.

"I like it that way. I like things that are overripe and decadent."

We passed the Beverly Hills Hotel, oversized and sybaritic and luxuriant, the gigantic palms looming, everything on a fantastical scale. It's California just being so big. The biggest state in the country. The sky is too big.

But Mr. Lieberman liked it.

He pointed out a king palm and eucalyptus grove, remarking that it was "accurate" because both species came from Australia. None of the vegetation was indigenous except for the Hollywood juniper—the local scrub, he noted, and the chaparral bowling down the barren hills above. The whole place was nothing but bald hills in 1910, the same year that Lord Northwood had received his peerage; the only thing around was Pickfair at that time, with winding rows along the roads of very small palms that had just been planted, which now rage to a fantastical and improbable height.

He identified a rare orchid tree from Hong Kong. This led to a rumination on orchids. "They're so forgiving, you can neglect them," he mused.

There was a dear and familiar scent. "The gardenia—it can grow here but the dry air will always be its enemy." The gardenia required attention. You couldn't neglect it. The same was true of certain women.

He kept making philosophical remarks about the foliage. Discussing the palm trees he explained that palms have thin roots, not like the vast roots of oaks in the South. Palms will grow anywhere—from desert to shopping mall. They transplant easily. That is the story of palms. Maybe that's why he liked them. He transplanted easily too.

He mentioned that he had been thinking of taking a controlling interest in one of the picture studios, which was what he was being interviewed about last night at the

Alexandria for the news reports. Now he foresaw a spectacular Mexican Water Power deal in which I did not like to feel I played a part in case it was not so spectacular. It worried me. Could I really play such a part in his dominions? It didn't really add up. He rhapsodized about the construction of a tunnel through rugged and remote country from the water plate in the Mojave.

"The desert is kind of an acquired taste, you know," I mentioned. "It's better in Egypt."

I was raving about the bald hills being parched.

"The parched earth is your theme."

How uncanny to see the endless avenues in L.A. stretching interminably and blazing away, even in the deepening twilight. Maybe in some occasional districts there is shade—but it's rare; you can see how the whole place was meant to be a desert. Mac ought to discover his aquifer directly beneath L.A.

"Don't worry, kid. I'll fix that," said Mr. Lieberman.

The road was now very leafy and winding and almost like regular life—a winding leafy green road—but not quite like real life, no, not out West.

He explained that he and Adelaide had planned a trip to the West Coast to scout locations for their retirement; she had planned the lunch date with me to coincide with this, and he was now fulfilling the date. "I would have been here with Adelaide now," he said. "I would have arrived to meet her today. So I have decided to start my memoirs instead," he said.

"Will your memoirs begin in 1927?" which I assumed to be the year of his birth.

"It's not organized that way. It's organized by subject."

"Your grandfather, your family, England."

"Yes, to start with. But that's a chapter like the others, and these are the other subjects."

He took out a small leather book and showed me a page under the index with a list:

Gardens
Floods
Foibles
Theology
Theories
Trees
Music
Cigars
Temperatures
Bugs
Cool Weather
Lakes
Rivers
Fjords
Scottish Glens
Bestiality
Salesmen
Reality
Decadence

"It's really an index of life," he announced. "This list is not conclusive."

I was enthralled.

"I'm looking forward to the chapter on Theories," I said. "Can you give an example of one?"

"Some long for their land, Miss Ford, some leave it behind. I'm in the latter category."

"What about Bestiality? That doesn't seem to fit in."

"I'm not using it in the sexual sense. I'm using it as in brutish or beastly behavior."

"Why Salesmen?"

"Americans get a lot of calls from salesmen in their homes. It's intrusive, but it's the American way."

"And Decadence?"

"Oh yes. Decadence. Very significant. Quite right."

"What about Bugs? Why bugs?"

"What a question. Why not bugs?"

I was beginning to get the picture. He was nuts.

The dark gleaming precincts of Bel Air gave way to Pacific Palisades, where he made me walk up a mountain on Will Rogers' Ranch. There was a pleasing old house and stables and a dignified polo field surrounded by eucalyptus trees. From this mountain you could actually understand California. You could see all the way to the ocean. In the other direction you were surrounded by the foothills and they were not bald but green. The leaves rustled in the wind, they glittered in the pristine air. A sign was posted to beware of mountain lions. Some people rode past on horseback. By this time the light was more endurable; sometime in the evening a curtain of glamour always descends with the twilight.

So we had walked on Sunset Boulevard the whole way to Pacific Palisades. We reached the end in the oncoming night among the huge palms and overpowering blue Pacific where he suddenly spoke of himself as a figure of failure in his own surmise, though not necessarily in the world's surmise. It was only through self-loathing, he remarked, that I could understand anything. I felt with regret that he would wear out soon—not from the walk to Santa Monica, though the mogul had taken too many long walks in too many cities, he'd worked far too hard, and maybe he had loathed himself too much.

"The best kind of love is the one you don't have to pursue," he remarked.

Life stirred. You would think that walking up a mountain and twelve miles would not be the thing for a woman in my delicate condition. But it was the first time I had felt the new life stir. The baby liked it. We had walked slowly but for her protection I would not walk quite that far again, though he did on other occasions make me walk up a mountain in the middle of Hollywood called Runyon Canyon, which was the most sublime sight I ever saw excepting the one he showed me then in Santa Monica.

It was thankfully cloudy in Santa Monica, like a normal place. The sea was more majestic than it is in Esperanza where it is usually just flat and endless and plastic with no personality. But in Santa Monica it was majestic and moody like the Hudson and noted for its famed resemblance to the Mediterranean. The sky was gray and the sea was cobalt and the hills and mountains were green unlike in Esperanza, where they are bald. The gigantic and lustrous palms lined the boulevard of the sea. We came to a curve, a turn, which was even more a paradise, for it just became quieter and quieter, with ever the Mediterranean memory. The turn in the road led up one last street before going back down to the Pacific Coast Highway. There was sort of a mysterious enclave with a few old white wood bungalows, their roofs laden with bougainvillea, situated on this magnificent perch looking out to the sweet gray sea. I looked at the street sign and found it to be called Adelaide. That's what he wanted to show me, this quietude in that relief-laden dark blue beauty of the winding coastline, and then to see it was called Adelaide, this treasure—that was the end of the line.

But life stirred.

29

There was a hotel near the spot; he immediately decided to move there. He suggested that I do the same. It was late. He would call Albert and have him arrange it and bring over our things. I found that I couldn't protest.

I would have been perfectly happy taking a cab back to the Alexandria and watching the tortured disheveled young people in the garden. I would revel in the air of aspiration and longing and failure and art. But somehow I couldn't protest. Life is a dance; sometimes you lead, sometimes you follow. So I let him lead the way.

This hotel only had suites. It was small and suave. Mr. Lieberman took over the ground floor. There was a two-bedroom suite that he allotted to me. I wished my children were there in the vast extra rooms of my quarters. Mr. Lieberman said that Albert would soon arrive with my things and would take me to the train station the next morning. Then he disappeared.

So I repaired with some dread to my vast two-bedroom suite. I watched an old Bette Davis movie. It took place somewhere in the South, the Hollywood 1930s version of the South. In this version of the South the streets are made of mud, instead of sidewalks, and everyone is always racing off in motorcars at night to roadhouses in the country with risqué black jazz bands and an air of debauchery; everyone lives with their parents even after they are grown, like Bette

Davis flouncing around in her room and being decadent, nervously playing jazz records and rushing out to roadhouses, and her bedridden mother just down the hall and her duty-bound father standing at the bedside and her evil uncle paying frequent calls and her sister Olivia de Havilland getting walked all over by Bette Davis. Those who were up to it (Bette Davis was up to it) attempted a drawl. It actually had a sort of subterranean accuracy, recalling my decadent youth.

I called home.

"What did you do at school?" I asked my daughter.

She gave the universal answer required by law for all children to respond to this question: "Nothing."

A short tragic silence ensued—required by law.

"I painted a jingle bell," she admitted.

"Good, dear."

"I'm going to South America and I'm taking Boopsie" (her doll). "Boopsie doesn't understand me," she added.

"Then maybe she's not the one you ought to bring."

"But it's OK because no one understands me. Raggedy Ann doesn't understand me, Kitten doesn't understand me, Boopsie doesn't understand me . . ." The list of her dolls was long.

My son got on and gave a garbled account of his weapons. I don't worry about him for I know that as long as he has weapons, he's ecstatic.

I did have the smallest one with me, however. She stirred.

Mac came on and described the many Home Improvement projects he had going in the garage. I would soon have to tell him the news.

Albert arrived with my bags. He made a point of shaking my hand, which he held a little too long. A little too lovingly. Then he sank down into an armchair and sighed heavily. He started talking about his dog again. "It's a proven fact that you'll live longer if you have a dog. Why? Because they're true blue. When you get old no one loves you but your dog."

Albert was obsessed with his dog. He was also obsessed with Francis X. Bushman's dog. Albert had been the butler and housekeeper for Francis X. Bushman, a film star of the 1920s, for the last thirty years of his dotage. He rambled on for some time about the sad and noble qualities of Francis X. Bushman and his dog and their various ailments.

Albert had an almost unbelievable number of relatives, most of whom appeared to live in his house. They were looking after Lucille while he went to his job. He was obviously accustomed to spending time with inordinate amounts of people and talking to them incessantly. Albert's daughter had just dropped off another grandchild to live with them; the daughter also dropped off four chihuahuas. Albert invited his sister to come live with them; a son dropped off his newborn infant.

"They're killing me," he said.

He rambled on. Eventually I made a few gracious remarks indicating I would shortly retire. But nothing sank in. I picked up the newspaper and actually started reading it. But he just kept talking. Finally I simply edged out of the room, all the while making the appropriate comments to his tragic soliloquy—"Hmmmm" or "How terrible" or "So sorry." At this point I was in another room. I wondered if maybe the Spanish temperament was prone to crisis. Maybe Spaniards are like Italians. Basically if an Italian isn't throwing a plate of fruit at you while cursing you out, you should have his pulse checked. I would rather have had a clipped conversation with my host than this endless soliloquy from Albert. But for me Albert felt a subterranean bond of classless California kinship that apparently he did not feel for his boss. He tested my humanity. Eventually I heard him let himself out and I locked the door.

Albert wore a stifling perfume. It stayed behind when he had left.

30

The phone rang in the middle of the night. It was my host. He said he was going to visit a sick friend; would I like to come? I looked at the clock. It wasn't the middle of the night after all; it was 9 P.M.

We met in the lobby and Albert drove in the limo.

Mr. Lieberman explained that there was a tradition in his family of visiting the sick. He still remembered, when he was with his family in England, being taken every Sunday to visit the sick—in institutions, resorts, nursing homes, or family seats. A sort of competition even arose in the family: who could visit more sick, forgotten, and pathetic people. Hospitals, heart attacks, wheelchairs—this was the stuff of the Sundays of his childhood and youth. It was one tradition he carried with him to America. In Adelaide's family in Fort Defiance it went down well—there were many invalids in the South. People tended to be bedridden for thirty years. They formed tremendous bonds with their gardeners and chauffeurs and in fact not many people visited them. But Mr. Lieberman always did.

The person we were visiting was also British, and a Lord something or other or the Duke of something. You can't keep it straight. He was a childhood friend of Mr. Lieberman. He was quite close to his childhood and school friends, though most were so far away.

"This person, does he have friends here?" I asked.

"He prefers having enemies," said Mr. Lieberman.

The sick friend was staying at the Beverly Hills Hotel and we were back on Sunset driving through the greenery. I noticed that Albert was curiously silent. But that's how he was with his boss, showing normal human respect. While we went in Albert stayed with the car and had tremendous bonding experiences with the doormen and the other chauffeurs.

The sick friend didn't look very sick. Although it is true that he had had all his teeth removed and a complicated process of regrowing them had been instilled. It made him look like an aging British actor who has second-rate parts. He was planning to write a book about his Cold War experiences, which were very overpowering. But apparently instead he went through other troubles that were more overpowering, like becoming an alcoholic. Somehow he ended up in L.A. Just kind of washed up on the beach one day, more or less. He was attired, of course, in a robe. He was about Mr. Lieberman's age. Neither one of them ever wore a suit and tie again, once they hit California. The sick friend rambled on about his three houses, their gardens and lawns, which house he was leaving to which of his children and his nieces and nephews, life insurance for senility, his trips to San Remo, London, and Egypt. He had vast amounts of storage space where he had masses of things, but was very bitter about the few things he didn't have. Family heirlooms. But he was quite a gay blade. He constantly threw parties. He appeared to be drinking himself silly at that very moment.

When Mr. Lieberman wandered out to admire the view the sick Duke took me aside.

"It's not going well with Harry," he said. "See if you can help. He's gone around like a zombie for months. And be careful," he added. "No woman is safe with him."

That was odd. I had nothing to fear on that score. One heard rumors. But they never added up.

The sick Duke remarked that he had noticed at the hairdresser they were offering Botox—this is where they inject botulism into your forehead so you won't frown for three months.

"What if you were forced to witness a mass killing?" said Mr. Lieberman. "You'd be smiling."

"In California frowning is considered a very bad thing."

"So you'd be smiling nonstop for three months."

"No. You're just not frowning. You have a placid expression."

"That wouldn't do at all. You don't want to be relaxed and happy all the time. Especially you, Miss Ford."

"Of course not."

"You see the dark side."

"Maybe I'm just making mischief."

"Someone has to. Otherwise life would be boring."

"The maid here has a mania for rearranging my stuff. It takes gall."

"But it shows their concern. At dinner the other night at that town in Big Sur the waiter asked if his shadow was disturbing us. Where else but California would a waiter be so concerned?"

"Yes, and he told us all about that town. The town has a population of fourteen thousand, but seven thousand of them are in prison. Rather disquieting. Better than having them roaming the streets, though."

They kept having this kind of disjointed clipped British conversation. British people are kind of decadent and jaded, I notice.

When you watch British Parliament on C-SPAN, the members of Parliament are always howling with laughter during someone's speech, or making witty rejoinders or raucous remarks, catcalls, telling dirty stories, and basically acting like a bunch of drunken sailors, whereas in the House of Representatives everyone is sedate, earnest, and self-righteous, saying "I yield two minutes to the gentleman from Virginia" or "I disagree with the gentleman from Illinois." I wonder why that is. I guess it is because the institution of Parliament is about five hundred years older than the House of Representatives and the people are more exhausted and jaded and cynical, living in a dying twilight empire. Or maybe it just looks that way from California.

And why do they like it so much here? It reminds them of their old empire. They're travelers. They want to live in a bungalow under the palm trees. They want to live on a frontier.

Soon we took our leave. Visiting the sick had a very exact etiquette. You didn't want to stay too long. It might tire them.

31

As if on cue from the sick friend's remark, in the car going back Mr. Lieberman said, "I'm very fond of you, Miss Ford."

"Then maybe you can stop calling me Miss Ford."

"You worry me, Miss Ford," he went on.

Actually I wouldn't have minded getting a few more problems so I could worry him some more.

"You're not really getting in the right spirit for California," he said.

"But the pinnacle of existence in California is going to the mall. I don't approve of California."

"I went to Yugoslavia. I didn't approve of it."

"But you don't have to live there. There's something I've gotten addicted to out here and it's very sad."

"Liquor?"

"No, nothing like that."

"Horseracing?"

"No, that wouldn't be sad. That would be healthy. Out in the fresh air at least. That's the California way. It would be exotic. The racetracks are beautiful here."

"Bingo?"

"That would be sad."

He agreed.

"What is it then?"

"The mall. I go to the mall and look at shoes all afternoon. How can I live with myself? I'm dumbing down in California. The pinnacle of my entire existence is the mall."

"I think a person who looks at shoes all day is fascinating. Shoes represent movement."

It was dear of him.

"I have headaches that can only be cured by going to a mall. I find myself browsing through resort wear. At one time I had a certain promise, but it hasn't been fulfilled."

"I couldn't love anyone who had never met with the commodity of self-doubt that you show, the dark side that you see. It's what attracts me to you." He went on, "You tend to see it even more when you're in this condition. I told you you would have another child in California. You can't appreciate yet what it will mean to you. You're only at the beginning."

How did he even know about it? We hadn't spoken of it.

"But in the middle of the journey of our life."

"The coward dies many deaths, the brave man but one. A pretty thought."

He had his finger on the pulse of many things. He had his

finger on the pulse of California. He had a quest to cover every square inch of L.A. to understand it.

Monrovia, Arcadia, El Monte and Sierra Madre; he drove a long route with Albert out of Hollywood and Los Feliz to the outlying towns, the leaves rustling in the cool blue Alpine-seeming air.

"Eternity is a long time, Miss Ford. Almost as long as it takes to get back from Glendale."

Which he knew because Albert had driven him there yesterday.

It was an uneasy exile on my part, but not on his, for he was the quintessential American despite being English. To me an Englishman in California, like a Yankee in the South, is an uneasy and ironic thing. But not to him.

He had his finger on the pulse of my past and present history and condition which I had never revealed to him or anyone else. He seemed a little old and seedy in his jodhpurs and you caught an air of decay. But it was an intriguing decay. I caught an air of it sitting beside him in the car, when he reached for me.

When I realized I was falling in love with Mr. Lieberman—bathrobe, depression, decrepitude and all—it was, appropriate to California, in a car. It started with an abstract worry, and accelerated into my heart crashing around in my chest, and I later felt it late at night in bed with Mac. I felt Mr. Lieberman was a man between us, and it panicked me. I don't mean to say it was dangerous. All men are dangerous until you get married. But of course after that they are lethal.

32

When we arrived at the hotel I was heartsick. "Can I ask you just one question?" I said.

"Just one."

"Would you like to get a cup of coffee?"

"Sure."

"Good. I like coffee," I said, and burst into tears.

"Forget the coffee," he said gruffly. He tried to reach for me again. It was shocking. And yet it seemed as if I had brought it on myself. I've never known myself to be a cad before. I was married, pregnant with my third child, possessor of an inexorable code of honor and an overwhelming dedication to my husband that persisted in the face of many and long absences in strange places and alien environments. But there was that subterranean connection between me and this man beside me reaching for me, who had roughly drawn me to his heart, who seemed to be disintegrating in various ways, the grief-crazed recent widower of an overwhelmingly beloved wife. He carried the memory of an older world, whether he would admit it or not, for it kept passing before my eyes when I was with him. I seemed to carry his memories of an older world. The L'Ambasciatori in Rome with doormen in old striped satin waistcoats. The former residence of King Leopold of Belgium at the Riviera, the Villa Les Cedres, the finest private garden in the world. From there across the seas to the last frontier, in one day from the palms framing the base of the Hollywood Hills to the magnificent or hypnotizing sea. You know it's love when you subside into a dream, but a faithful one, or with entire faith. Strange excesses and reserves of hope in your heart. He tried to kiss me. I think he succeeded. I kept thinking of what Edwardian mothers used to tell their daughters on their wedding nights: Lie back and think of England.

33

The next morning I got a call from him asking me to come to his suite to say good-bye. I found that during the night all his effects—mostly consisting of vast amounts of gadgetry—had been miraculously transported from the Alexandria so that his old suite and his new one were interchangeable. I found him ensconced in his robe. The international atomic clocks were still emitting their faint Morse code as from the beacon of the empire or mankind. Perhaps they reminded him that there was a world out there, beyond the overpowering palm trees and light, which I think overpowered most people in California. They forgot there was an older, antique, dying world out there across the seas that a dignity and merit far beyond mere light and palms could encompass. Or maybe that is what the Englishman unconsciously represents in California. The main difference between the old world and the new is that in the old one you are chastened, humbled by the vast weight of the ancient civilizations preceding you, whereas in the new world you are not, and therefore obsessed with your own well-being and strange antimortality treatments because you can see only that far, the surroundings only show that much.

You got the feeling he'd been up all night, with his gadgets and atomic clocks and his entourage. He worked from his hotel suites, without a formal office in L.A. He had all the latest computer and laser equipment for international communication and had no need of going out. As for the robe, it had the same effect on me as ever. He was beginning to look somewhat seedy in it.

I once went to a spa in Palm Springs; as I perused their brochure I noticed that everyone was constantly walking around in their robe. When I called to make the reservation the receptionist said heatedly, "Be sure to bring your robe." "Why can't I just use the robes at your spa?" I inquired. "We find that most people are more comfortable in their own *robe*." The emphasis was definitely on remaining in your bathrobe for as long as humanly possible. When I got there I found a collection of people looking distinctly under the weather, as if they had just been beaten up. It's always the way in southern California. It's supposed to be a health resort but everyone always looks very seedy. The more spas you go to the seedier you look.

"I was out at four in the morning looking for asterisms," he said.

"Asterisms?"

"You didn't see the meteor shower?"

Everyone was constantly talking about meteor showers in California.

I could just picture him, white-haired, gentle, going to seed, out in the garden all night looking for asterisms.

"It appears I had some energy to kill, Miss Ford."

There was the electrifying sorrow in his blue eyes.

"Maybe you can now stop calling me Miss Ford."

"Will you come and visit me again?" he asked rather

132

wistfully, but directly, staring me down. I expect he would never call me Fleming. I would not dare call him Harry even still.

We were standing at the French doors looking out into the courtyard where there was a pool. Some guy in a peignoir came charging out of his room on the second floor and headed for the spa. I've never seen so many varieties of robes before, that's for sure. It must be like ancient Rome, the spa craze here.

"Is the pool heated?" Mr. Lieberman asked the fellow before he plunged in.

"No and it's very invigorating!"

"I haven't felt like that in years, Miss Ford," said Mr. Lieberman.

"Like what? Like this guy in the peignoir?"

"Like last night." He looked at me thoughtfully.

He checked his altimeters. As if the man in the peignoir with the high energy might have affected the altitude. The altimeters were lined up in a row on the coffee table next to his many atomic clocks. A black box attached by a wire to the clock with the U.S. frequency was emitting a series of high-pitched beeps alternating with static. There were maps covering every square inch of Los Angeles and California, including obscure geological maps that could not be procured in any ordinary store, and technical charts, and files on local sites. I would venture to say he had a massive need for organization.

"Am I disturbing you?" I asked.

"Do I find you disturbing? Yes. Come back soon and disturb me some more."

How fascinating to feel those slow apprising blue eyes on me. There was something familiar in the depths of those mild and skeptical blue eyes.

"Would you visit me again in L.A.?" he repeated.

I thought it over. "It might be somewhat immoral. When?"

"I'll let you know."

At this point the visit was over. However I tried to prolong it. But it was hard to draw him out. In his day you were raised to be polite, ask questions, look outward instead of in, talk about what interested the other fellow—all of which made his appearances seem brief and enigmatic.

But between us an uneasy love had seemed to bloom. He must try to move on from his grief, to a new world of hope. I did not realize then that I had given him that hope.

I piped up with my spiel about the mall and such. Then he started reading my mind again.

"Don't worry, Miss Ford. It's just another feature of your condition. In your condition one likes to shop. Your brain scientifically decreases in size during pregnancy. No doubt this is the last time for you," he went on. "Try to appreciate it. Remember that. You will be nostalgic later."

He had no children himself and I then felt a cad to feature mine. Adelaide had children from her first marriage. Unlikely as it would seem to me, they did not cotton to Mr. Lieberman—they resented the divorce—and he had no contact with them, though I'm quite certain he would have wished to.

He said he would be willing to meet with Mac during my next visit if it was convenient to discuss the Trans-California Pipeline. He would have Albert take me to the train station. I felt like a young girl who leads a man on, I felt like a cad.

It was elegant of him to help me. That someone like him would pay me any mind meant the world to me. That he represented what I pined for while I was out West—culture and civilization and wit. That life had stirred, as if he had caused it. But despite what I felt for him, I could not be blithe to Mac. I was not a blithe frivolous creature, despite my interest in resort wear. I was not arbitrary and cruel and infirm of purpose, and was not unacquainted with honor.

But a man inflicts you with his desire. Once you get inflicted or infected with it then you go to pieces. It's like setting off a time bomb.

I would see him again in the guise of Mac's boss and savior. I would see him in the desert. If not for his involvement in Mac's enterprise, his prospective rescue of it, if not for that I think we would have fled—fled the West, fled the premises, abandoned the enterprise.

"'I'm a romantic, Miss Ford. I hear voices crying in the night and I go see what's the matter.'"

I was stunned.

"It's a quote. From Raymond Chandler. For California."

It seemed undeniable now that Mr. Lieberman would come to our aid. A certain optimism, a certain grandiosity, was suggested by the vision of the international tycoon.

34

Albert was driving the dark blue limousine again in his guise of chauffeur. But Albert performed many functions. He ironed the shirts, he mopped the floor, he monitored our conversations, he told you his life story. He was always around and heard everything that went on and in due time he came to admonish me. He rifled through drawers and repainted the terrace and changed the lightbulbs. His life appeared to be a catalogue of crisis, rife with attraction to tragic incident, and you wondered how he could perform his official functions with all the crises going on. But he and I had a curious bond.

I wasn't late so I asked if he wanted to take Sunset Boulevard instead of the freeways. I don't like the freeways.

Albert announced that his daughter-in-law was in labor; she had toxemia, she had no potassium, she had no magnesium, she had no phosphorus, she had gained more than seventy pounds, she was obese. Her house was being fumigated that day so they would have to come home with the baby to Albert's house. It was killing him.

I made the appropriate comments. "You don't say." "Wow." "That's tough." "Hmmm . . ."

He rambled on about how horrible Lucille's second delivery was, how they had to break his granddaughter's clavicle when she was born to get her out because they screwed it up, how he prayed God to give him only one child but instead he had seven. He had the personality of a madman, even aside from his penchant for crisis.

My brain grew scar tissue over the conversation as we rolled through Beverly Hills and the outlandish vegetation raging in the incessant sun. In spots with lush vegetation it's bearable because of all the shade, but in business districts and the famously hideous strip malls that go on forever it is completely unbearable and baking. That is its local color, though.

Some parts remind me of a place that is home, being green and having a settled and substantial air. The hills always glittering toward West Hollywood, the quiet green streets and old houses. Old meaning circa 1940. That's old for Hollywood. There is the occasional relic of the twenties. That seems like the vanished haunting of an ancient civilization.

While at the wheel Albert recited a relentless catalog of his thwarted dreams.

I continued my stream of rejoinders. "Is that right." "Wow." "Uh-huh. Mmm . . ."

"My sore throat is killing me," he continued. "Inflamed tonsils. I have a terrible fever. Here, feel my head." He craned around.

I meekly felt his head. But his head was cool as shade.

"You have a lot on your mind," he said enigmatically, pulling up to Union Station.

He got out of the car to fetch my suitcase. He shook my hand and again held it a little too long. He gazed into my eyes.

"We have to keep meeting for Harry's sake," said Albert.

I was stunned.

"Harry is fragile," he went on.

Harry? But I'm sure he didn't call him Harry to his face. Albert was out of hand. His natural tendency to get out of hand was probably exacerbated by Mr. Lieberman's clipped formality, and he had finally found someone—me—that he could get out of hand with.

Fragile? I guess so, but what about his ability to walk from Hollywood to Santa Monica? Or his ability to walk from Fifth Ave. and Eighty-fifth to Wall Street every day? Or his ability to stay up all night looking for asterisms? But fragile, yes, after all. Fragile nevertheless.

Albert could see I was stunned.

"You're not going to tell him I said this or nuthin?" He lapsed into a crude locution he had never used before. It was depressing.

"No."

"Good, because some people are like that. I'm only saying it for his sake."

For some strange reason I believed him. Just as some people are handsome no matter how old and craggy they become, I felt that no matter how many weird personality

137

tics and disgusting ailments Albert displayed, he had a good heart.

But Albert told you more than you wanted to hear. It was a betrayal, somehow.

Suddenly I decided to join in with the confessions. "Mr. Lieberman is searching for something," I confided to Albert. "He's looking for—"

"He's looking for trouble," said Albert, reverting to his dangerous mode, propped up against the limo, brooding.

35

It's much better when you expect trouble than when trouble comes unexpectedly. I had expected trouble even before I went up to L.A. It was true that I seemed to have a vast angelic adoration for Mr. Lieberman. But it is said that when things seem most angelic, the demoniac is just around the corner.

It got cloudy as I walked to the train. I was treasuring the cool overcast sky, the respite from the blazing sun on the ride down the coast. I was betting it would be blazing away once the train hit San Juan Capistrano and the sea, the first environs of Esperanza. It was thus that as the three palms signifying Costa Verde rolled into view, my prediction turned out to be stunningly accurate.

I have an apocalyptic book written in 1913, before the Great Divide, when the century was innocent, obsessively documenting the weather. It is by an American professor who constructed a map based on his theory that human energy was distributed throughout the world according to the climate. His map agreed with the history of civilization. The decadent countries, as he called them, were too hot. Thus the decadence. The climate of New York, Paris, and London, not surprisingly, was the one most conducive to human achievement, a climate in which the temperature averages 38 degrees in winter and 64 in summer, with a lot of storms and variability. People do not work well when the conditions remain constant; it causes monotony, in turn apathy.

But I guess Esperanza is the kind of place, like certain towns in Florida, that looks doomed when it rains or is overcast. A mariachi band, for instance, has a doomed quality in a storm.

Take it from me.

Going to L.A. from Esperanza you were not used to sleaze or to turmoil—or to humanity. Then you saw sleaze again on Sunset Boulevard and you knew you were in a world city that had the total picture.

There's a certain rivalry between L.A. and Esperanza. Esperanzans think they've escaped from the hideous crime-ridden stress-laden metropolis to a zone of pure and pristine beauty. Bake sales, skateboards, subdivisions, heartwarming neighborhoods called Driftwood where you can leave your doors unlocked. The Chamber of Commerce calls it An Island in the Sea of Stress. But where's the stress, I'd like to know? In L.A., where they not only have traffic gridlock and road rage, but frequently planes land on the freeway if they're in trouble. That blocks a few lanes for a while.

Coming back on the train you pass a certain demarcation point, where from the vast decaying urban outskirts of the metropolis you cross to the Esperanza environs and suddenly everything is quiet and calm and pure, just the hills and mountains and the sea, no more urban decay, and it's supposed to elate you. But it doesn't elate me. I miss the teeming humanity. Often in the past the Sunset Strip had seemed depressing, too sleazy even for me, but I didn't feel that with Mr. Lieberman. I felt it was swell, massive, thrilling—with the big California landscape, long vistas and the hills in the distance.

There is always that moment, captured so exactly by the visiting Englishman, when the sun, which is so overbearing, finally becomes daunted at twilight and then the vast landscape is thrilling. Even Hollywood didn't look bad. A relic of the twentieth century. History tends to be blotted out in Esperanza so you can't examine it. Like decay.

So when I came back on the train leaving the patina of civilization behind, and I got to the pristine blue sea and calm untroubled environs of Esperanza, my heart sank.

After an hour along the coast and sea, the train, nearing home, went through the bald barren hills. Maybe Mac would succeed in making the bald hills bloom and maybe it wouldn't seem so desolate. Maybe it would seem like an uncanny paradise with green agricultural fields and pleasing ranches and citrus groves. But maybe the bald hills weren't meant to bloom. They seemed implacable.

"This is the end of the line," announced the conductor of the train. He went through the aisles. "Esperanza. The end of the line," he repeated. The next stop would be Tijuana if the train went on. But this is the end of the line for America.

The last frontier.

36

Mac was out in his Hawaiian shirt and Bermuda shorts cutting everyone's grass and trimming their hedges—a guy who just likes to fix things so much that he just fixes everyone's things all the time on the whole block. I didn't ask him to meet the train—the trains were too unreliable. There could have been suicides. There could have been a spot of rain. There could have been a cloud.

"Mom! Mom! Boopsie's in South America!"

"How wonderful, dear."

The little boy across the street was imparting detailed knowledge to my son involving the art of spitting. My daughter was light-worlds away from spitting now. Only South America—to which Boopsie had fled—could possibly interest her. Still the little boy across the street continued desperately trying to pull my daughter back into the forgotten world of spitting, which was no longer exercising its vast allure, while alternately learning not to throw knives with my son. In the not so distant future my daughter would be writing idealistic letters to the President, which as she would note with indignation, went unanswered; while my son would simply crush the opposition with his armies. It's a gender thing. Spitting, however, does sometimes transcend gender.

Take it from me.

And so life went back to normal. I ate wheatgrass, antioxidants, and bee pollen. Everyone raved about environmental aggressions. I went to obscure and insensible gardening society meetings.

I studied the Events Section for the week in the local paper, trying to get New Perspectives:

Cascading Mums
Trail Cleanup
Cacti, Succulents, and Bizarre Trees
Moose Starvation
Chilean Wildfires
The Crescent Moon Returns

I studied the ads for Wellness items: Seeing the Human Aura; Toltec Wisdom; Penetrate Coexisting Realities; Transformational Counseling; Radical Sanity; Pleiadian Lightwork; Past Life Regression.

As usual I could see straight through my bedroom windows into the bedroom windows of the misfit neighbor, who was splayed out in an armchair asleep with his mouth hanging open like something out of *Death in Venice*.

I would attempt to penetrate his reality through Radical Sanity.

But first I would take a Fango Bath. ("Nourishing volcanic ash and soothing pine needle extract draws out toxins from the body.")

37

A sense of guilt did not elude me. Yet I felt a transcendence in the matter. In the matter of Mr. Lieberman. It was a thing apart from mundane reality and ordinary duty. But no one is exempt from the obligations of ordinary decency. Nothing too out of the ordinary had happened yet. I would pursue my regular purposes. And therein lies the malaise: in the ordinary duties of life. The malaise is in something far milder than sin.

Mr. Lieberman called me on the telephone to see that I got home all right. He sent a note or two with the heraldic mottos. His calls were stalwart and relieved the heart of wondering. Life was a paradise on earth. When it had to do with Mr. Lieberman, an ordinary sense of purpose turned into something more apocalyptic. I kept thinking of him in his office bedroom, with his hair all messed up, and wired with electronic equipment, his gadgetry.

I retreated to my office in the garage to contemplate the galaxies and seek to understand the central mystery of our finite existence. But I had no New Perspectives with which to reconcile my purpose and my treachery.

Life continued on. The misfit neighbor wandered around the street looking dazed. I got my hair cut, causing a sensation in the village. The misfit neighbor's four-foot-long iguana escaped, and he left a note to say that if I saw it I should bring it back. I had to seek iguana therapy for the next four hours. If I saw a four-foot iguana in my house I would consider ending it all. Perhaps iguanas are not carnivorous, but then again, four feet is twice the size of my children and more than two-thirds the size of myself. You have to admit it would be startling to run across one in the bedroom.

The iguana was named Puff, apparently. The talk of the neighborhood was Puff and his demented escape. Actually that is inaccurate. I was the only one who talked about it. It did not seem to faze anyone else. Iguanas, monitors, beavers, hyenas, you name it, it's probably down there—in the canyon. Not to mention the misfit neighbor, who sometimes drives his motorcycle in it, or hacks away at it with his golf club.

Actually I noticed a subtle change in the misfit neighbor. Added to his collection of reptiles and bloodthirsty dogs was now a small overwrought cairn terrier named Missy. I knew because he was out calling her plaintively at all hours in the canyon. He had better be plaintive. There's no telling what's in the canyon. And whatever it is, I'm sure it would love to make a meal of a small cairn terrier.

In fact Missy developed a dysfunctional relationship with a porcupine. She got quilled and had to have emergency surgery. She was heavily anesthetized, for when she came home she was stoned and weaved around the front lawn like a drunk for several hours.

After dozing in his *Death in Venice* mode all afternoon, the misfit neighbor became alert at two in the morning, and started playing loud records of bossa nova music. Missy was revitalized and started yelping hysterically. The coyotes chimed in like deranged maniacs in the canyon. Everyone on the block was awakened.

Gradually the din subsided, although Missy could still be heard yelping hysterically deep in the canyon.

I joined a Club. A swim and tennis club, mainly so the children could take swimming lessons. The Club is in a neighborhood called Vacation Village, which, as the name connotes, is basically for people who were at one time so tortured that they had an overwhelming need to put on polyester tourist outfits and relax by the pool all day at motels overlooking the freeway. Ironically, Vacation Village is situated directly overlooking the freeway. Yet this is the most ancient part of town, site of the original mission, the arrival point of the Franciscans and previously the Spanish explorers. In the palm-laden hills above the freeway you can sense, if you try very hard, the ancient history of the place, and try to visualize it. You kind of squint your eyes a lot and try to conjure it in your mind's eye.

While giving his sales pitch the manager of the Club soon devolved or deteriorated into telling me in a long involved way that he could have been somebody, if he had stayed with Bally's, and how his career went off track. Basically, he concluded, he has now been stuck in this dump for fifteen years, plus his wife left him. Another career slump.

After this glowing report, while plummeting ever lower in social status, I joined up. If I want glamour, I'll go to Hollywood—to keep another rendezvous with Mr. Lieberman.

The sun blazed away and no rains came. At night I gazed at the avenue of proud palms outside my bedroom window raging toward the harbor under the stars. The adventures of Little Sal endlessly played out in their limited way. We analyzed my son's imaginary friend, the ubiquitous Miles. Miles is out for revenge. That's one of the few things we know about him. It was fun being with my darlings; though at the same time it also drives you berserk. You're like a trapped, hunted animal, is the thing. You have to gain clearance if you want to go for a walk. And if no other adult is around you're pinned down.

One other adult was in fact around but he was watching *Home Run Derby*.

"Mac, sometimes I think you're cracking."

"Don't worry, I'm taking several herbal medications right now."

"Don't kid me."

"I've enrolled in the Relationship Training Institute."

"Mac."

"They suggest hospitalization."

It takes an optimist to want to make the bald hills bloom. What about the desperate game of marriage? Maybe he was optimistic there too—about making our marriage bloom. In one way it bloomed. We had a deep bond; I was skeptical and matronly and brisk, as one must be in domesticity. Whether an atmosphere of mild exasperation could escalate into something far worse, "the atrophy endemic to all fruitful marriages," whether the oath was inviolable—these questions pursued me.

But Mac was in his own malaise. A dark wood where the straight way was lost, at forty. A congenital emotional void? Obsessed with his generator—he had invested in a new generator for the desert site. Obsessed with his septic tank—he had invested in ditto for same. Incessantly rewiring the floor lamps or conducting experiments in the garage. Glued to *Home Run Derby*.

It was all part of his crack-up.

The mellifluously boring sounds of *Home Run Derby* emanated from the living room. The sharp crack of a bat against a ball. The silences of the taciturn Gil Hodges. The desperate enthusiasm of the announcer.

"How about some type of human interaction?" I suggested to Mac.

He thought it over.

"It's too late in the day for human interaction," he said.

"How about one half hour of human interaction every night after dinner then?" I asked.

"Maybe on Sunday."

"It *is* Sunday."

"And look—we're having unscheduled human interaction right now."

I gave up. But no. I would try again.

"Mac, you know how in Montana they have those fires raging out of control?"

"No."

He knew. He was just being perverse.

"Well, most of the northwest U.S. is consumed by flames. The government caused it by fighting each fire to suppress it right away. That's what will become of you and your emotions if you don't express them soon."

"How is it you know all this? About suppressing the fires."

"The Russians told me. They know about things like that. They know about things like genetically engineered corn."

"The Russians?"

"You know, the nuclear physicists. Josie's friend's parents."

"Oh, yes. It's all flooding back to me now. Atomic particles. Am I right? I keep getting it confused with the screeching violins."

He stopped.

"And how are your atomic particles coming along this afternoon?" he asked.

"I don't know. Fine."

"You seem to think I'm cracking. But I could say the same of you."

We made a pair. I had long ago reached the stage of pregnancy where I could only think about the battlefields of World War I; he in turn watched a man hitting balls in an empty stadium.

I had yet to break the news to Mac about the pregnancy. Maybe he knew. Maybe he didn't. I might have barely just begun to show. I assured myself I would tell him tomorrow. Meanwhile I put a lot of cataclysmic books about World War I around to give him a hint.

In an article in a women's magazine about how to save your marriage I read about a forty-three-year-old wife who makes her marriage work by devoting herself to her hobby: collecting antique buttons, which her husband duly supports, billing and cooing over each antique button she brings home. In turn, her husband (who likes to have "middle of the night meaning of life conversations") has a passion for painting military miniatures. He too is happy that his wife is so supportive. She compliments him about his military miniatures and is tolerant of his insecurities about them. If she says "That's nice" and then he asks her thirty times what she means by that, she still copes and is supportive. Aside from the epiphany that he could paint his military miniatures *onto* her antique buttons, thus achieving a certain further union in the matter, it occurred to me that these people have the secret of life. They do not have one foot in life and the other out somewhere in the galaxies, like me, worrying about their atomic particles. These people are not constantly fretting over their mortality. No. They're far too busy having ridiculous hobbies, and they have the secret of life. Crazed dedication to some harmless eccentric pursuit.

Mac was a man who had spent a lifetime shouldering the human responsibility while being ceaselessly gallant and closing off his own doors to achieve that end. So it may be that now he was cracking. He was a man of action. Men of action sometimes need to retrench and refuel by watching televised sports. Other men might listen to opera while watching the martins skimming in. *Home Run Derby* is not as poetic. But maybe it is. Maybe there is more to it.

I seemed to see two guys competing in a desolate arena, as per *Home Run Derby*. One was relatively young and strapping, dark and handsome, the possessor of my long love. The other was a white-haired gent, courtly and windblown and stoic, and I seemed to feel for him a vast Cartesian adoration. A man of seventy can never compare to a man your own age, your peer.

That was the trouble here. Mac's reaction to Mr. Lieberman's interest in the water plate was not completely as ecstatic as you might expect. He seemed to think it was a little suspect. Maybe it injured his pride somehow.

But all this changed dramatically when they met, as I noticed when Mr. Lieberman paid an unexpected visit.

38

A fascinating fog rolled in at twilight—fascinating, of course, because any change in the weather here is so rare. But an El Niño was predicted for the end of the century. Tropical nights in Norway, scorching days in France, snow in the Loire Valley in early May—these were but a small part of the somewhat demented conditions predicted. Stagnation would occur in Russia. Paris would have nights balmier than those in New York City. Unusual droughts would come to England, causing protests. "Mediterranean days and tropical nights are not what forged the British character," wrote a columnist for the *London Evening Standard* in outrage.

But the most violent results of the entire world seemed to zero in directly on Esperanza, where torrential rains, fires, earthquakes, and volcanic eruptions were planned. Elsewhere the results would be fairly benign. A little stagnation never hurt anybody. Tropical nights are not too hard to bear.

Whereas in Esperanza panic had set in: many articles appeared in the local paper telling you how to cope. "Plot your escape in detail, setting up a plan with family members to reunite in a remote location if you are separated. Decide in advance what you will quickly pack if your home is in the direct path of the danger."

Then there was the concept that I would be delivering a baby in the middle of this unnamed danger, possibly a volcanic eruption. Or in the middle of a monsoon. I kept getting the El Niño confused with the new baby, for the name El Niño is taken to mean The Baby. I kept getting it confused with *My* Baby. Both were predicted for January.

But when it came to pass, and you were scared out of your wits and had battened down the hatches and prepared for torrential monsoons, then when the El Niño finally came it was cloudy for about three days and the sky was an interesting slate color.

Esperanza exists on a climatic fault line. It has something to do with Pacific winds in relationship to the Equator.

Winter does eventually set in, at about the end of November. There is a chill when it gets dark. A chill means about sixty degrees, which is not chilly, but you're chilled to the bone because you're used to the inexorable sun. The population becomes incredibly diseased. An endless sequence of lingering diseases infects the populace throughout the winter season—people say it doesn't get cold enough to kill the germs. Hacking coughs, exotic viruses, hideous flus, tubercular wracks.

We don't have jackets or coats, for we put them away, we stored them in the basement in mothballs, as we didn't really need them here, but maybe that's wrong and we do. Otherwise we wouldn't be so incredibly diseased all winter, maybe.

Just when you have finally come to accept the pleasing healing desert sun, it fades somewhat. In winter the palms look a little sad sometimes, and the light has lost its glare, but what was ordinarily unbearable (the glare) becomes the subject now of nostalgia. The lack of glare seems out of character. The place has lost its quiddity.

Nostalgia works in the relentless continuum, always for the thing just past.

Now I even pine for the painful and exhausting Family Fun Day excursions we generally take on Sundays to massive children's emporiums in Esperanza. Which is odd, because until you've been to the Wienerschnitzel (a fast food emporium featuring the veal cutlet) in the baking sun at FunTown, you have not yet reached the portal of hell. But my bitterness to California begins to fade, for the human soul adjusts. I pine for the jacaranda trees in the hot still Esperanzan afternoons, the bougainvillea winding from the balconies. I wanted to arrest time; it was passing too quickly. Obsessed by nostalgia and wishing to go back. I had an obsession to compare the different houses I had lived in, since I've moved around a lot in Esperanza. That seems to be the way in California.

The house I lived in first here won my heart. Nothing was quite right about it yet it won my heart—the garden with no shade, the guest room that felt like you were in a boat because of how the wind came blowing through from the harbor. The living rooms we hardly used, for my furniture, which had graced an old New York apartment on Riverside Drive where the rooms were as big as ballrooms, didn't really fit into a California bungalow. The place was small and close. You felt as if you were about to walk off a ledge and fall into the palm trees.

I am nostalgic for even what seemed hideous at the time—my daughter's cough at night when she had colds that wracked my heart and every time she coughed it was a knife stab in my heart. A rare thunderstorm that caused horrified panic and dread, with the fuses blowing out in the kitchen from the one ancient box.

Time speeds up and you are nostalgic for the most recent past—the hideous moment when we were realphabetizing the bookshelves and I had a sick nauseous dizzy spell and realized I was pregnant again. The hideous moment before that when I almost blacked out in my office from a deep dizziness that was the first sign of the new pregnancy unbeknownst to me at the time, my atomic particles careening off into another's soul. The hideous moment when I smoked one cigarette and had to take to my bed out of nausea for a month, thus knowing for sure; watching *Tarzan* in the afternoon in bed while the stage set became one with the backdrop of my life in Esperanza.

Much seemed hideous at the time but now I pine for it, overcome always by nostalgia. In the future I have no doubt that I will pine for it even more. After all in pregnancy you may be more alive, being twice alive; since doubtless this would be the last time for me to attain that condition, in future I will be free to romanticize it like all things that are past for good.

Like my former hate for California that I knew would one day change to love. Driving home from the children's school with basic brain swirl, enraptured by the beauty, the blue sky, the opaque green-blue harbor, knowing well my bitterness would fade, for the human soul adjusts. I knew that we were meant to part, Esperanza and I. This knowledge formed the basis of my new nostalgia for it.

39

The offices of the Trans-California Pipeline were near the Presidio, where the old Mexican town used to be. The buildings were meant to resemble adobe or Mediterranean plazas, interspersed with cafés where mariachi bands played. The office was small; no one was ever there save for two secretaries, and Mac when he was in town. The main work was done in the field—the Mojave—where a team of geologists and engineers attempted to locate the water plate. The office was decorated with a historical mural depicting the original Mexican settlement at the spot: a few clapboard houses in a vast desert stretching to the sea.

The two secretaries in the office were pregnant. One secretary previous to these two had just gone off on her maternity leave. We had a Mexican maid who also became pregnant while working for us. We employed a blond-haired California nanny while I worked in my office at home and she too became pregnant after a few months with us. Now I of course was pregnant too. It kind of made you wonder about Mac.

The engineers in the field would sometimes come in and crack jokes about Mac's unsuccessful drilling efforts in the desert compared to the startling state of the office personnel.

When I got back from L.A. I noticed he was gazing lecherously at my cleavage. It of course had grown due to the pregnancy. "Yes, I know, my cleavage, it's very embarrassing," I said, trying to cover it up.

"Don't take this the wrong way, Fleming dear, but have you put on weight?" he asked me.

So the time came to tell him the news. His reaction came as a shock. He was like a man who keeps a grand old Rolls in the garage and every once in a while breaks it out and takes it for a ride. When I told him, he got that expression: an occasion to break out the Rolls. He went around fixing everything with his bare hands for the rest of the day, from the plumbing to the rafters. Our son helped him with his Home Improvement projects in the garage. "My boy, my boy," said Mac.

On that distant day in Fort Defiance I'd found the man who would put up with me. I know it was a function of his love for me to have taken the news about the pregnancy so well. But we soon lapsed back into our accustomed ways. Maybe the new life oppressed him after all. We lapsed into our mutual neglect. Or maybe there was a shadow cast in his path, a figure barring his way, who seemed more solicitous than he. Though both would build an empire in a wasteland, try to make the desert bloom.

Sunday rolled around. I wished I could be visiting the sick, a noble undertaking. But I don't know too many people in Esperanza and none of them are sick. At least not physically. Sick in the head is open to interpretation.

"Mac, I love you, but—"

"Same, Fleming dear."

We did not often forget our Alabama manners, but maybe we were too polite.

His eyes strayed back to the fascinating foul balls of *Home Run Derby*.

But one thing did capture his attention. A tall white-haired man was sitting on my stoop smoking a cigarette and pointing out the bird of paradise to a chauffeur parked at the curb in a limo. He had an air about him. Then the doorbell rang, and standing on the step looking bemused was this tall man wearing jodhpurs. The tall man roughly drew me to his heart. It was Mr. Lieberman on the Sunday afternoon in August—as if arrived to rescue us from our malaise.

"My dear, my dear," he said. He crushed me to his heart.

40

"I've brought you some gifts, Miss Ford."

"Fleming. Please."

He produced a small sumptuous leather diary embossed with titles:

Weather
Altitude
Temperature
Index
Notes

"How very useful. Just what I need."

He also gave me a vertical file and a leather catalog for notes that snapped shut. It had outer compartments and pockets for more notes on cards that fit precisely into their slots. These organizational/index-type items satisfied my vast Germanic need for order.

He seemed a bit more decrepit than when I had seen him last, but then there is nothing I love like decrepitude in a man. I noticed he gave off an aroma of tobacco and alcohol. But I like that in a man. Then there were the jodhpurs—the Cecil B. DeMille look.

I introduced him to Mac—"Mr. MacMoreland" to him, of course. The formality business was getting a little weird, especially for California. Mac took a liking to him. We shared that bond. We shared many bonds, even if the straight way was lost. Mac seemed infatuated by him. It reminded me of Castro's meeting with the Pope: Mac showing solicitude for the older man's slow step, Mac standing by getting him things, worrying over his welfare. All this despite—or because of?—the bathrobe and the meetings in the hotel bedroom that soon were a matter of course. Mr. Lieberman seemed the more inscrutable partner in the relationship, benignly accepting Mac's attentions.

My heart started crashing around in my chest. The coffee table was piled high with books antithetical to California and the last frontier that I had amassed before my visit to him in L.A.—the *Almanach de Gotha, British Lords, Heraldry Today, Debrett's Peerage*. I had since learned that Mr. Lieberman was not interested in such subjects, but before my visit to him I had thought I would prepare myself in case he was. Now it embarrassed me to see them in his presence. We were standing near the coffee table and Mac had gone upstairs to get our prospectus. The children were with their blond-haired California nanny at the park. I felt heartsick.

Then he reached for me again. Again it was shocking. I would put him off. But I began to realize that at some point I would have to give in.

You might imagine that an Englishman so far from home would be morally flawed in some way. But I judge not. I was the morally flawed one.

41

What was the reality and what was the vision? The only reality was in his handsome devastated face. It dawned on me he probably had had affairs after all. Adelaide used to say, "You think he's handsome now? You should have seen him thirty years ago." I didn't need to see him thirty years ago. I was more drawn to the devastation and the loss than to the perfect handsome youth. It was too late for compliments on either side: You've never looked handsomer. Nor you.

I only got the merest second's look into his dazzling blue eyes, his desperate blue eyes, before the visions came. The Mediterranean a refreshing shade of pale green and robin's egg blue, with green-and-white striped couches in the bar. Jaunty outside cafés looking on the darkening green-blue sea, striped awnings, low palms, gardens. A calm before a storm.

You would think that an experience like I had with him in L.A. would make you run for cover. But one heads straight for the same danger again.

Five minutes ago I had been making oyster stew for Mac. Mac for whom I am droll and skeptical and matronly. For whom I am detached and independent so as not to oppress him. We cherished a strong circumspect loyalty. He would not, I think, betray me. Is this how I repay him?

But if I could relieve Mr. Lieberman's burdened heart from its loss, maybe it would transcend conventional morality. Or would it? One deception can be traded for another.

Mr. Lieberman had a sensitivity to despair, I think. A man used to vicissitudes is not easily dejected, and in some odd way I think that was the story of his life. I could sense that even when ten years ago I used to see him striding along West End Avenue so crisply. In his dapper black suit, his old-fashioned suspenders, and overstarched white shirt like a southerner, and that furrow in his brow that reminded me of *War and Peace*. That furrow in your brow—it's driving me mad. Was that the moment of destiny? People come dragging up a dusty road into your life twenty years too late, and you are by then living in some remote outpost of the world, but they come dragging up a dusty road to see you, having come to you at last.

I was taking an ambiguous moral position. What was my moral position? I stood outside myself, amazed to observe the curious magnetism between us, the one bereaved and frail, the other married and pregnant, as always knowing it was more my fault than his. I only got the merest look at the increasing furrow in his brow before he regained his sangfroid. His crispness and sweetness and gallantry. What manner of man could be so gallant when he himself was in a position of infinite pathos, on his own dark journey?

There was a sound of someone coughing violently outside. I went over to the window. Albert was not far behind.

Suddenly I found myself cornered by a large middle-aged man in a loud suit. He started telling me about his medical problems. My brain grew scar tissue over the memory of the conversation and I staggered off toward the kitchen.

He came after me, going on about his terrible medical procedures. Then he cornered me in the laundry room.

"Don't come to me when your heart gets broken," said Albert.

42

It was decided we would show Mr. Lieberman around. Albert drove and we guided them on a tour of Esperanza. Mr. Lieberman observed that it had a certain intensity of blandness that was bound to be disquieting to the frequent visitor. I said it was also disquieting to the habitual resident. No sleaze, no decay, no vast disgust impugns the Esperanza landscape.

We drove through the incredibly ritzy Rancho Santa Rosa. The gauche unapproachable mansions are carved into the desert hills whose eucalyptus groves and bougainvillea are intensely irrigated, among the marble columns and barbaric bathrooms that are the size of living rooms. It is a sort of glorified subdivision. A millionaire's subdivision. You hear a lot about the American Dream out here. You hear a lot about the need for frontiers. Americans here have gotten their piece of the pie: they live in paradise and it's close to the mall. The changeless beauty is sometimes surreal, day in, day out, the swaying palms and exquisite sky. All that changeless beauty makes you—numb.

California changes you forever. Everything is so clean in this part of California, so new, but perfectly burnished to look handsome, so antiseptic, that it makes either Fort Defiance or New York look like a dying twilight empire. It makes the old South and the East Coast look like a florid, ornate, and decaying world, as ancient as Rome.

Mr. Lieberman mentioned that he and Adelaide had thought of Esperanza as a possible retreat. I couldn't feature it. The only possible area I could have imagined for them might in fact be Rancho Santa Rosa where the Hollywood stars retired, stars from the vintage of Pickfair, stars from the old Cecil B. DeMille biblical pictures. The old stars. The real stars. But it was a curiously soulless place, even with the old stars, which had pretty much dwindled down to Victor Mature, wandering around the well-watered eucalyptus groves at cafés and bars. You would have to have done pretty well to end up in Rancho Santa Rosa, which was incredibly ritzy. You wouldn't end up there if you were down on your luck or had been reduced to selling hot dogs outside of the Paramount lot. It had no humanity.

He was also considering La Dolcita, another ritzy town on the coast, which he said reminded him of Biarritz, a resemblance that is indeed in the nature of the coastline and a certain air about the place. Like Biarritz it had not "retained its quiddity." All those places in the environs of Esperanza had no history standing past the inception of the movie business, the 1920s, and few pieces of architecture from even that vintage had been preserved. Maybe that is what he sought, to blot everything out. But when everything is obliterated like that, the mind goes along with it. So does the heart.

Next thing he would be living in a subdivision carved into the bald hills called Driftwood.

"Who *are* these people?" I wondered.

"I think they're people who use the word 'gorgeous' a lot," said Mac.

The environs are gorgeous (I use the word 'gorgeous' a lot) but there is a curiously soulless quality. You get the feeling that the subtext is: I live in paradise, but my life is meaningless. You just don't get the air of cultivation that you sometimes do in L.A.—though you also don't get the massive chaos of a vast metropolis. You do get the obsession with gardening—so Mr. Lieberman was happy.

The oldest California fan palms had been grown from seed at the ferry landing in Esperanza. The largest date palms in California were in the Esperanza mission. So I could see his attraction to Esperanza after all. It has a lot of palm trees. It has the oldest palm trees.

We went to dinner at the U.S. Grant. It was old world for Esperanza, with a gilt sign saying MEN ONLY UNTIL 3 P.M., and white-haired diners in dinner jackets and even one aged Hollywood comedian in a tuxedo. Driving downtown was truly beautiful—the hills, the azure harbor, the old architecture. A palm tree shading a sign for the Agua Caliente Racetrack in Tijuana.

At dinner we discussed the prospectus. Mr. Lieberman's investment was contingent on his lawyers' due diligence of Mac's operation and his books, and an inspection of the drilling site not far from Death Valley, the hottest place on earth.

It was now August. August would be pushing it in Death Valley. We would wait until September, although frankly September would be pushing it in Death Valley too. But it would have to be. We could not afford to wait.

So the inspection was planned, and it seemed as if Mr. Lieberman had swept in glamorously to drop the bombshell that he was going to save the company.

What came to be Mr. Lieberman's massive investment was justified by the accountant's projections that once the water was actually delivered, the company would generate tens of millions per year in revenues for fifty years from the Mexican government and the Southern California Water Commission. Based on his faith in the projections he authorized the loan of a hundred million to start with if the company would put two-thirds of its stock in trust as collateral.

He would raise the amount through bank loans based on his personal guarantee. He also requested three seats on the board, together with the presidency. So the responsibility shifted over to him.

He suggested taking the company public to raise another one hundred million, which could be done through his influence on Wall Street. He and Mac would go on a road show—stopping in twenty-one cities in fifteen days to give their pitch to sell the shares.

The two hundred million would cover the entirety of costs for drilling and exploration and construction, the company would be in the black, then the huge revenues would accrue.

Mac would finally be able to set up Accounts Receivable—a department notably lacking so far.

It was late; Mr. Lieberman would stay the night. He would stay at the U.S. Grant, the downtown hotel containing the restaurant that was one of the oldest spots in town. As he made arrangements at the reception desk for his usual vast suite, I loitered at the valet parking lot with Albert, whose responsibility it would be to achieve the miraculous transformation of his effects to make each hotel they stayed at seem like home, installing Mr. Lieberman's electronic equipment and atomic clocks, his gadgetry, so that he could oversee his business interests and negotiate his bank loans and perform the work of an international tycoon.

Mac and Mr. Lieberman retired to the bar to smoke cigars and cement their own curious bond. There came to be a personal bond between the two that I found somewhat puzzling, though I shouldn't wonder, since I had a personal bond with him too. But this did not prevent my heart from crashing around in my chest late at night in bed, as if Mr. Lieberman was a wedge between us.

I would picture his daily life in L.A., working in hotel

suites in his bathrobe with his gadgets and computerized equipment, sometimes receiving business visitors also in the robe and even now in the bedroom, searching for asterisms at four in the morning, going for long drives that Englishmen like to take in California, analyzing the traffic on Wilshire, chauffeured by Albert, obsessively visiting gardens and later the desert.

The next night we went to the opera. It was magnificent. The most notable difference from New York was the dress code: you could dress like a cowboy. There would not be men lounging in tuxedoes in the boxes as you'd see in New York. A Wild West opera house.

Well, we're in the horse latitudes—that's the desert. Actually the desert is growing on me. As to the men in my life, I would attempt to preserve a sense of detachment.

43

Before he left the U.S. Grant I asked Mr. Lieberman to come by our house to say good-bye. I spent the morning madly cleaning. The children were still learning not to throw knives but had not yet succeeded in fully grasping it; they were at the playground so the danger was averted. Having children does give you a certain sangfroid.

Albert was wearing the usual loud suit and Mr. Lieberman the jodhpurs. Albert's full name was Alberto Moravio de Estalbo—conjuring the Zorro age of California.

I showed Mr. Lieberman the events listed for the week in Esperanza:

Marauding Swine
Brazilian Inundations
Thai Smoke Hazard
Sea Lion Kill

The marauding rampage of nature reigns supreme.

"And why do they list events happening in Brazil and Thailand?" he asked.

"We don't have much change in the weather here so the focus is on weather traumas in other areas of the world so we can gloat over how we don't have them. If you visit Esperanza from back east in winter everyone will talk gloatingly about the storms taking place in your hometown, and you will wonder how or why they know about it. The reason is the same. The weather reports keep track of it because there is no weather here to report."

You kind of wonder how the local news here can even have a weather segment since it's the same every day. But they do. First they show various angelic pictures of sunshine. Then they tend to go off on apocalyptic tangents about the perfect ideal, the most pleasant place on the planet to be, something about the marine layer. Then they generally spend the bulk of the time on weather traumas in other areas of the world. Other areas of the world that are actually having weather.

One day there was a spot of rain. The city was plainly Gripped by Crisis. Everyone kept talking about it obsessively. The weatherman warned in a dire note as if he were introducing nuclear annihilation, "It's a little chilly," panic-stricken. The next day there were huge articles on Rain in the paper, with diagrams and charts.

"Wouldn't they *want* rain here?" asked Mr. Lieberman.

"It's not that they don't *want* rain. They don't *understand* rain. You know how back east, say along the Hudson, there's an air of gnarled sorrow?" I asked. "Well, they don't have that here. They don't want that here."

Little wonder that I keep obsessively studying my book by the crazed weather professor, attempting to discover the crux of our changeless paradise and its impact on the human soul. The crazed weather professor guy says that there are more nervous disorders in this region. He says there are more suicides. He connects this with the constant favorable temperatures. A uniformity of climate—day in, day out the same—is the greatest danger to human achievement, he believes. But then, he associates a high rate of insanity on both the Atlantic and Pacific coasts and says that in the Tropics it's even worse. And the far North is equally bad—people who stay in the Arctic too long lose ambition and energy. He's always careening around the map with his ceaseless weather obsession.

Sometimes in an archway shaded by a banana tree or in a dark courtyard, I have visions of the Tropics. That's where my heart lies. But it is an illusion: it is not really tropical here. The weather guy notes a lingering doubt about the persistence of human energy in southern California, due to the constant loveliness.

I try to resist but I get brainwashed. Wandering through the Mexican courtyards with the mariachi bands, 70 degrees in January. Walking in the 70-degree sun among the swaying palms in February to the cafés with Venetian blinds. There comes a time, back east, when you have to stop wearing shorts. This time usually comes in October. A hard bracing winter is moving in and physically you could not wear shorts during it. Now my dearest wish is to see if I can wear shorts 365 days a year. And not only that but I want energy work, healing training, and intercranial sacral manipulation. I wear magnets. I eat shark cartilage. I need hugs. I'm a quack.

I had procured aromatherapy oil from my facialist. It was meant to be used on the skin of the face. After lathering it on and hoping for a miraculous recovery from the effects of the desert sun on my forty-year-old visage, I noticed a threatening warning at the bottom of the label: ROTATE, DO NOT RUB. I showed this label to Mr. Lieberman.

"Troubling," he commented.

For the hair we have many tonics and potions as well. At first you get in the spirit and buy expensive volumizers at esoteric spas. Then you realize you can actually get the same benefit from any product in the grocery store containing alcohol. Usually I just cruise the aisles looking for things that say Flammable. Because alcohol makes your hair have volume, actually.

We discussed crushed grape seed facials with antioxidants. He loved that type of thing.

"I need to exfoliate," I said. "I desperately need to exfoliate."

He gallantly said I looked fine.

"Would you like to take a walk?" I asked.

"Sure."

"Good. I like walking," I said, and burst into tears.

This was his cue to take me in his arms. Why was I such a cad?

"Forget the walking," he said gruffly.

It is true that he had a certain electrifying presence, despite the decrepitude and the jodhpurs. But perhaps that is always the way with the powerful.

"Let's rethink the walking," I said.

We walked to one of the cafés. It was exotic: everything was very still in the hot sunny afternoon in the remote outpost, the jacaranda trees lining the street, the Parisian bistro accordion music, the ceiling fans at the cafés, the old California bungalows.

In the same year that our house was built before the First World War, the crazed weather guy wrote his book; C. B. DeMille arrived in Hollywood, which was then known for cattle ranching, lemon groves, and an ostrich farm; the British Empire still ruled the waves; the Beverly Hills Hotel was built; Lord Northwood was elevated to the peerage; and Tarzan was created by Edgar Rice Burroughs, with some of his exploits being written in a California bungalow in Esperanza not far from ours.

The bungalow was invented in India. British colonials stationed in remote outposts in the nineteenth century and early twentieth before World War I adopted it. A posting to the colonies meant a chance for advancement just as well as setting off to America, the land of opportunity. So the bungalow came to California. In either setting it represented the concept of life in remote and untamed places, but with an element of coziness like home; in other words, in the bungalow you could still: lie back and think of England.

We went across the bridge to Santa Maria. Albert drove. Fruitarians (they only eat fruit) sought us there as we sat on a bench by the sea. They gave us reflexology foot massages. Mr. Lieberman loved it, of course. It may be more exhilarating when you come from a dying land with ancient history where they have radio programs droning on endlessly about etiquette and protocol for the Horse Guards at Buckingham Palace, to just have Fruitarians come up to you on the beach. How a people so old and historical with reminders of the world wars everywhere and broken hearts might be happy just to forget, as over here they leave all that behind, the history and the broken hearts.

It was somewhat breathtaking at the cove on the sea at first but soon became too baking and overbearing, and I was quite overcome. Only mad dogs and Englishmen go out in the noonday sun.

But eventually the day turned to twilight and dusk and it was cool near the sea.

Albert walked a few paces behind us like an Edwardian chaperone.

I was stricken with melancholy to look at Mr. Lieberman's handsome face.

He had a sportsman's air—like a southern man, as though he were about to go off duck hunting—with his jodhpurs and his flannel shirt. Looking at his handsome weary face was like reading an old book on a train using stolen time. Stolen time is all the dearer.

He lit a cigar. Then he lit another.

"I've never seen anyone smoke two cigars at once," I said.

"Live and learn, kid."

Every once in a while he would ask Albert a question:

"Temperature, please." Then Albert would consult a gadget.

"Altitude, please." Then Albert would consult the altimeter.

The touching thing, the compelling thing about him, was this: his loneliness. His complete solitude. He had no one. He had had Adelaide and that was it. A childhood, a youth, a lifetime, and one real attachment. I thought at first maybe it was his not having children. Then I thought people who have children don't get the luxury of this compelling solitude. Instead they have to be brisk and keep early hours to conform to schedules and procure food on a regular basis and be reassuring. They can't really fall apart. They must provide a basis of stability. They can't have nervous breakdowns and glamorous affairs. Or can they? No, they can't yearn for something else.

They can't dawdle at cafés at twilight. They can't pine for the Alabama moon. ("Oh moon of Alabama / We now must say good-bye.") They don't sit under ceiling fans in lonely hotel rooms waiting for the phone to ring, knowing it won't. Even if they did they are never really alone. Life is confined by parameters of strict and inviolable responsibility. That's the season of life they are in.

But when I think of the world's most towering figures, my parents, I can only aspire. Far more love and stability must I yet provide to compare to them.

Mr. Lieberman had grown up in a house full of servants. He did not have that towering figure to revere, to witness the spectacle of the love he bore. His father had not been strong enough to withstand the temptations of his massive inheritance. So he puttered around the Riviera and flitted aimlessly among resorts, sharpening his unparalleled grasp of the feuds and rivalries festering among the royal family; he occupied that world of swank of which Lord Northwood had been the unlikely inventor. Mr. Lieberman was relegated to a world of servants and boarding schools. Now his closest companion was his chauffeur. He had a succession of adoring housekeepers and secretaries, plus Albert. Was it the helplessness engendered by the lifetime of servants that hastened the alacrity with which they sprang to his aid?

"Parties are a strain for me, Miss Ford," he said calmly.

"Are we having a party?" I suppose we were.

When not being grilled on the meteorological conditions, Albert seemed restless.

"Would you like to make a rest stop?" asked Mr. Lieberman.

Albert shook his head.

"I think I'll make one," said Mr. Lieberman. He walked off toward the old Balboa Hotel whose white wood Victorian turrets and spires rose against the blue night. The sky glows at night in Esperanza.

The minute Mr. Lieberman was gone Albert started raving about how when he was a boy he worked in a carrot field and then at night he had to take care of his sister's kids and his fingers would bleed from the carrot field.

"You've had a life of toil," I noted.

"But this is the best job I've ever had," he uttered devoutly. He stared out at the sea.

"Reminds me of Guam," he began.

"Guam?"

"I was born in a typhoon. In Guam."

I asked how he came to be born in Guam, but he went off on a tangent about the citrus crop in California. He fell immediately silent when Mr. Lieberman came back. They were an odd couple.

"He's a nice fellow really. Just a little nervous," Mr. Lieberman remarked when Albert fell out of hearing. "Jumpy. Kind of like you, Miss Ford." He looked at me thoughtfully. We walked along the sidewalk by the beach, looking at the curiously bright blue-green sea.

"Would you visit me in L.A. next week?" he proposed.

"That might be somewhat immoral. What time?"

"So you will come. Next week."

"I'll see."

"How is your condition coming along?" he asked.

"Do you mean my shopping addiction condition or my pregnancy?"

"I imagine the one presupposes the other."

I spoke about my quest for ceaseless moisturizers for my midlife crisis.

"It's good to have a quest," he said supportively.

He asked me if I needed anything for my condition that he might procure. "Pickles. Bath salts. Lotions. That sort of thing. You might have cravings."

I did have cravings. I craved Eggs Sardou, carbonated beverages, and Mr. Lieberman.

We returned to my garden, with its crazed appearance due

170

to the madcap efforts of my botanist. *"Delphinium exalta-tum,"* pronounced Mr. Lieberman, guiding me among the pots. "Its name indicates its nature."

Certain flowers would prefer to be farther north; if nurtured they will exist but they are incurably nostalgic for their native climate. So the heart has its climate. Some prefer repose, some crisis. Some society, some solitude.

Some show great tenacity of life but irregularity of purpose.

I sat in my carefully orchestrated lawn furniture. I had procured lawn furniture that makes a statement: "Here I am in paradise in southern California, so maybe I can stop thinking about decline and death every five minutes."

Naturally it didn't work. I thought about decline and death every two minutes.

I apologized for my earlier breakdown. He said if I didn't have breakdowns he could never feel at home with me. My breakdowns transported him back to Alabama, associating it with Adelaide and her eccentric southern family, he said.

Tactful.

"Her family was very neurotic. I miss that. Life is very boring without that."

He paced around the garden with his hands behind his back. Then he sat beside me and put one arm around me. He took my face in his other hand and held it for about five minutes looking at me from the side, as if he were studying the sight for a portrait. I went into a reverie: Europe, a man in a tuxedo, opera music, a lifetime.

There was a risk here, that you could poison your life. It is a type of risk that blunt instinct tells you not to take. But then I suppose I am a coward. I am too much a coward to go to those dark places and take such risks.

I wished it were all just my fond acquaintance with him, that having a turn with him in the garden would just be a pleasant memory in my heart rather than any anguish.

But this was not to be. I did not know what I wanted from him. Being older he had a certain virility to me, a certain complete lack of youngness, which intrigued me. That he was nearer the end gave him a glorious philosophical bravery that I sought for. This may be why Europe seemed to me his element, or why I kept having visions of it when with him. Because to be in an ancient cool dark passageway by the statue of Molière in Paris, by the garden of the Palais Royale, near to the Bourse, with opera crashing through your head, then you have a long glimpse of posterity, that the world does not end.

Of course he had the reverse point of view, having come from the old world, across the strait from Africa to Baghdad in his family's remotest past, to the Continent and England and back to the Riviera and the pleasure lakes of Europe, until the last of the line longed only for the newest thing without the weight of history—on the blue sea at twilight among the palms at the opposite edge of the world.

It was time for him to go.

"How is your Index of Life coming along?" I asked.

He mentioned that for a time, now past, he went to Scotland, for cool climates claimed his heart. He was obsessed with fjords. Much earlier of course, in better times, it had been the Riviera. But then he became obsessed with Scottish glens. He was working it all out in his Index. He had hired a series of professors to tutor him in obscure subjects related to his quest—to fill him in on esoteric types of topiary and other horticultural topics. He had had a mental crisis in Italy in 1950, he revealed, and he was dealing with that next. Then on to trees, music, and cigars.

His Index reminded me of Montaigne: his object was to portray himself; his opinions were confined by the extent of his vision, his knowledge was confined by the extent of his learning. So it would be a staunch record of his personality.

172

An index of his life. To go off into your own little world like that I applaud. Whatever it takes to make life tolerable. In him you could plainly find a man who had decided to devote himself to other things than the sorrows that would have otherwise consumed him.

I should start my own Index of Life:

1) Addictions
    a) Refreshing addictions—horseracing
    b) Sad addictions—bingo
    c) Adorable addictions—horseracing

A theme seems to be developing in my Index of Life: I should take up horseracing.

I could make an Index of Life out of the local cultural events:

Rare Rhino Sightings
Mozambique Floods
Greenland Ice Thinning
Parliamentary Discipline

Not sure how that last got in. Shades of the British Empire?

Albert was brooding by the limo, staring at us darkly. We said our good-byes.

Only later did I notice on my desk a card from Mr. Lieberman, after I had seen him off, written in his old-world style in the third person: "Mr. Lieberman sends kind regards and hopes that you may with pleasure remember in future this day."

I lay back and thought of England.

44

Something seemed to change after he left. The house was like a boat with the views of the green-blue sea in certain rooms. The gardenias bloomed in my garden, as if he had ordained it, though ordinarily they require a more sultry climate involving rain and shade. But they bloomed away in the baking sun. A profusion of nightingales sang outside my bedroom window.

However, something was still very wrong. The next morning I found myself at the mall browsing through resort wear in search of the perfect Bermuda shorts. I was obsessed with Bermuda shorts. I possessed a detailed knowledge of Capri pants. I used to spend a lot of time alone, quietly seeking. Not quietly seeking Bermuda shorts, mind you. Quietly seeking knowledge and meaning. Now I spend a lot of time seeking sunglasses.

I chatted with the other mothers when picking up our kids from school. Many of them were scientists. They discover molecules. You wouldn't catch them at the mall. They were busy with their biotechnical research. California has a lot of that. One of the fathers was a geneticist whose entire life was devoted to working with corn. He refused to work with anything but corn, and he refused to apply his knowledge to humanity. He would only do pure research. He used to work with yeast, but that was all over. He and yeast had parted ways, and not kindly, it appeared. Now his whole life was corn.

Many of these were Russian physicists. One such sought me out.

"I know who you are," she said in her thick accent. "I know what you do. And I know what your husband is doing in the desert," making it sound as if it were a spy conference in Geneva.

"And what is it you do?"

"We are scientists. We discover molecules."

The weather changed. It was August but the temperature stayed in the 60s, refusing to ever hit 70. It made the harbor look more nautical. It made the air seem sweet. Retired admirals in Santa Maria yearned for a cocktail at 3 P.M. in the gray afternoons that softened the constant blinding light they could never escape.

Nostalgia overcame me, as did the knowledge of my disloyalty to the green Atlantic. The longer I remain on the blue Pacific, the more certain I am that it would come to thrill me. Where's my loyalty?

The mood on the napalm front remained quietly hopeful. NAPALM MAY FINALLY BE DESTROYED IN MISSISSIPPI ran the latest lead.

Well, of all the unmitigated gall. Mississippi. My dear Mississippi.

But Mississippi would not go quietly. So the saga soldiered on. As if any state in the union is going to meekly embrace our napalm. "Oh yes, fine, I'll take it. I'm just a decadent, decaying, uneducated state anyway so why don't I just destroy your napalm for you. And while we're at it why don't you just add in your nuclear waste products."

I went on to study the local events for the week:

Stork Rampages
Pine Needle Basketry Course
Bee Skep Collection

45

There was a fair in August. It was like an Oklahoma State Fair type of thing. It was filled with booths and activities like

What It's Like to Be a Human Cannonball
Hormel's Best Spam Recipe Contest
Using Kitchen Scraps
Team Penning and Hog Tie

There were fifty million gardening lectures. So I went to a meeting of the Esperanza Bromeliad Society.

While walking later in the neighborhood among the bungalows with Josie, my daughter, we met a British person. He was an elderly white-haired gent, and was walking his dog. When exchanging pleasantries I detected his accent.

"What is a British person doing so far from home?" I asked.

His name was Cecil. That was perfect for a British person. Virtually all British people are named Cecil.

He was from Sussex, once long ago, but had been in Esperanza for fifty years. He missed the weather in England, ironically. That was the only thing he said that he missed.

"But what about civilization and history and ancient things, compared to this last frontier with everything new?" I asked.

He said it's a part of you when you're from there and you don't really notice it.

I asked him if British people pine for the British Empire.

He said they do. To some it was a world they lost. This would be wrenching.

Cecil left me in the lurch, however. My next question, "What exactly do you miss about it?" went unanswered, as before I could pose it he took his departure.

So I wonder what Cecil misses about the British Empire. Ruling the waves? Wearing white tie and tails every night? Going to hear speeches in Parliament after midnight? Hanging around with your valet?

Unless I find Cecil again I may never know. I don't think Mr. Lieberman missed the British Empire. He was too democratic. But my response to the new world was to become obsessed with the old one. The contrast between the Wild West, the constant blinding light you can never escape, versus Edwardian England and grace and civility. Forms of etiquette are often missing in California. If you can hang on to them it's like having your dance steps. Sometimes you lead and sometimes you follow, but you know where to go.

But I was haunted by a line in a British novel where the hero is on a boat going out to one of the colonies between the world wars. The British Empire was not entirely squashed at that point. He notices a pretty woman, the wife of some colonial governor. He remarks on her beauty. Then: "She would not keep that skin long in Burma."

Back to the facialist.

There are quite a few British people floating around southern California. It's very curious. I had reached the stage of pregnancy where I could only watch the movie *Lawrence of Arabia* over and over, to think about the pivotal moment when the empires were poised on the brink of a precipice about to crash in. "The English have a great hunger for desolate places," says King Faisal. "I fear they hunger for Arabia."

Now they hunger for California.

46

I sought for New Perspectives, while fighting off the encroaching reign of nature looming in the canyon. "Raptor Watch" was listed as one of the weekly events in the paper, after all. You might want to do some yoga after warding off raptors and iguanas in the backyard. You might want to check in with your visceral manipulator. At home my reverie of Wellness was interrupted by Chip. Chip is a small stuffed dog or mammal of some kind—it's hard to tell which—belonging to my son, who has to bear the brunt of my children's hostilities. I'll hear screaming and beating going on and will make inquiries as to who is bearing the brunt of this cruel treatment. Then there's a long answer about how it's Chip, it's only Chip, or Chip can handle it. Or I'll hear the sounds of someone being brutally massacred on the stairs. "Stop that. How can you be so mean."

"Well, it's just Chip. It's only CHIP!!!"

Poor Chip. He bears the brunt of much.

We watched *101 Dalmatians*. Minus Chip. Chip is in the hospital with multiple bone fractures. I fixed the elaborate lunch that was requested, the entirety of which was of course thrown on the floor. We went out and I walked amid beauty while the kids ran around. I nurtured my phobias. We stopped at El Pico, the Mexican dive fairly near. Mariachi music among the palms.

In the afternoons we picked up my daughter from her ritzy day camp. Chip lay limply on his bed of pain.

"What did you do at camp today?" I asked.

"I found a pinecone," she admitted.

"What is the name of the counselor again?" I inquired.

"Mrs. Furious."

"Hmm. Do you know what 'furious' means?"

"Yep."

"What?"

"Not telling."

I had a monthly checkup for the pregnancy. I was attempting to choose the obstetrician who would deliver the baby. There was a woman I liked, but she would not likely do the delivery. She didn't work Mondays, she didn't work Thursdays, she didn't work weekends. So it looked as if I would be getting a stranger for the delivery. After all, I am a stranger here.

I consulted another obstetrician. She kicked me out. She pawned me off on the high-tech high-risk guys in La Dolcita. High risk due to my age—over forty. The doctors here are too stern and puritanical for me. You have to be sort of a nut, have a certain daring, have a personality, to be a tad less puritanical. The doctors here are not used to seeing someone who is crusty and gruff; they're used to paragons of self-sacrifice. I came from a vice-ridden part of the country. I had my first two babies in New York amid a careening chaos, yet I felt secure there, with a doctor who had a personality who yelled at his kids on the speaker phone while examining me and allowed me to smoke a few cigarettes and had mercy. But here the obstetricians have no mercy, and they have no personality.

So I ended up at the high-tech high-risk guys in La Dolcita to handle my pregnancy and delivery. The area of the hospital looked like a bleak Antonioni movie, with soulless modern skyscrapers amid a scrappy landscape of scruffy hills with chaparral.

But there was a courtyard within that had giant palm trees and bougainvillea groves and a café with Roman umbrellas.

I overheard some ladies chatting.

"I need something to nurture. But I don't want it to have fleas."

White fly disease raged away in the hibiscus.

47

My high risk doctor had an incredible British nurse. She was unpuritanical. She kept saying how they used to give alcohol drip for preterm labor, and phenobarbital drip for something else, and everyone smoked through their pregnancies and we were all still here.

"Does that mean I can take phenobarbital?" I asked.

She plainly was fond of a cocktail, for she kept raving about how they can't expect you not to drink.

British people are pretty decadent, I think. Thank God someone is. Maybe it's the loss of the empire. If you haven't lost your empire yet, you have to be all uptight and puritanical. Whereas if you've lost your empire, anything goes. Like Cervantes, a failed writer in his late fifties before *Don Quixote*: "come to that fateful pass when failure reverses itself and confers a freedom all its own."

I asked the unpuritanical British nurse about the delivery. I was terrified that the people in Esperanza would act like pioneers during my delivery and refuse me painkillers. But the unpuritanical British nurse gave me hope. I always ask from the very beginning how many painkillers they are planning to administer during the delivery. The British nurse sounded as if she drank her way through hers. In New York they gave me as many painkillers as I wanted. I was very surprised at how calm everything was—from the movies you expect to be on a stretcher careening down a hall with sirens and flashing lights and people getting hysterical.

But in fact you just calmly hang out for hours on end once they give you the painkillers, chatting quietly with your husband, planning your life, drinking white wine with your arms linked. I learned to bring a book for my next delivery, being as you have about twelve hours to meditate. I read *A Handful of Dust* during my second delivery. That is a fond memory I don't wish to fade. But I was still worried about how it would go in Esperanza, where I was a stranger, and it was the Wild West. And then there was my age. My next meeting with my maker might not go as well.

48

"Mac, what do you think of mortality?" I asked.

"Make a list of things you want to get done before the end," he said from under the kitchen sink where he was fixing the plumbing.

That was Mac. Ever the pragmatist. Note: Get prestressed

concrete. Reshore the retaining wall. Refinance the mortgage—before the end.

It was one of the many things I loved in him. Homeowner's insurance, sandblasting, renovating a kitchen with his bare hands—these things were Mac's domain. In his domain it must be reassuring to know that there is an answer at the end of the road. He would be perfectly happy spending a decade analyzing sediment. At least I have the comfort of being married to someone who still does have the answers, or knows that he can arrive at them with mathematical certainty.

As a boy he had been mischievous. In grade school he was sent to the principal's office almost every day. The principal was a large black man named Mr. Yarborough. Spending so much time together they got to be close friends. You would see Mr. Yarborough walking through the grounds with Mac, his arm around Mac's shoulder. Pretty soon Mr. Yarborough wouldn't wait for Mac to get sent to his office and would simply go to Mac's classroom at a certain hour and pick him up; then they'd take their man-to-man walks around the grounds. Pretty soon they were inseparable. That was what became of a person trying to discipline Mac.

My childhood friend Butter Wilson came to visit. She was reminiscing. "It was sad," she said of the Palais Jamais in Morocco where she went with her first love. "It was really sad," she said of the street where I was married when the awning was still up on the church the week after my wedding. From that green day, still remembered in its glamour and ineffability, time would always speed. It would speed from that moment when Mac stood in the hall in his suit and tie with his briefcase and I saw his goodness. When one did not possess him there was a less heavenly bond to bear. It was his gallantry that had determined that our course would be together.

It takes a certain type of person to shoulder the human

responsibility in that way, just as it takes a certain type of person, a magnificent one, to tend to an invalid, to sit vigilantly by the bedside. That's the kind of person you want to have around. But they don't come that way very often.

So in return I let go of Mac to travel where he must and not interfere with his dreams. He would do the same for me. Therefore it worked out that I would take my next trip to L.A. when Mac returned. It worked out that we would travel separately so one of us could stay with the children to be on the safe side. It worked out that I would hang out in L.A. with another man.

Before I left I studied the Events list in the local paper to see what I would miss:

Dolphin Deaths
Chinese Whirlwind
Ongoing Rumblings
Tempting Fate

Somehow that last one seemed to apply.

49

Some nameless momentum carried me back to L.A. It was the inexorable attraction to that other man. In the taxi the views from the freeway looked like some strange Mediterranean coast, with the thin palms ranging in scrappy rows at the base of the parched hills.

It was still amazing to see in the heart of Hollywood

one mere block off Sunset Boulevard the old bungalows and occasional orange grove left over from when it was paradise; even on those blocks it still is. It is to me. I get it now, I understand the paradise. Or maybe a place is a paradise if you love someone in it.

I stayed at the Alexandria again. In the European garden the old yellow neon sign shaped like a shield seemed impossibly old and ancient and intriguing even though it was probably just from the forties. The sign was turning brown with age and kind of falling into the palm trees, which gave me a thrill.

In the *New York Times* that day there was a story about Los Angeles touching on the repute of the Alexandria. Mr. Lieberman was quoted on the subject of the hotel, since he had been staying there for a month. He was quoted as saying that it was very benign. He was quoted as saying that he lived in New York. He gave the impression, as he was described lounging by a window looking out, that his plans to leave were not fully formed. He was photographed in his bathrobe standing on a balcony aimlessly ruminating. He looked more philosophical than your average industrialist, who would perhaps be wearing a suit and tie. He was asked how long he was planning to stay. He said he had some business in the region and some business in L.A. He did not reveal what it was.

From my room there was a thrilling view down Sunset winding to the hills. As thrilling, even more, as my old view that wound up Broadway in New York. Humanity raged away in it. I tried to identify each house in the hills, fading palazzos in huge gardens; then the hills turned to green mountains with no houses, sometimes sunlit, in the Wild West landscape. Beyond would be the San Gabriel wilderness and the Mojave Desert.

As I sat in the garden a mysterious black limousine pulled

up at the side entrance. A solicitous chauffeur walked around to the back door and peered in to conduct a whispering conference with a head of white hair that would appear to belong to some demented celebrity who of course turned out to be Mr. Lieberman.

He emerged from the car and looked fragile. He looked shaken and unwell. One had the sense after all of him as a widower finding his way. He had only come out west to trace the steps that he had meant to follow of his wife. He had only come out to Los Angeles from that vantage point of the old world in his heart, the one in which he was meeting Adelaide at the Alexandria.

We were the only ones in the impossibly beautiful garden.

He insisted on escorting me to my room, which developed into a long afternoon. But then why else had I gone there save to be with him? I was a cad. He was kind of kneeling beside me as if in a supplicating position. He would have certainly stayed all day had I not kicked him out, which I did partly to observe a conventional sense of propriety. In New York no one would notice if you hung out with some guy all day, and in the South no one would care. Eccentric behavior is the norm or at least the delight of the South. But in Esperanza there is a sense of the proprieties that may come from the midwestern influence—state fairs with Spam recipes and the like: you can't just hang out with guys who are not your husband.

The proprieties are weird. But then I wouldn't like it either if Mac hung around with some girl all day. I'm just lucky he never would, he's not that type of guy. It would be incredibly annoying if he did. I did not believe that Mr. Lieberman would do it had Adelaide lived. He was bereft. His heart had gone haywire.

During Adelaide's illness he had arranged for nurses around the clock. He took the situation under control. He was able to hold together and still retain his crisp British elegance. At that time he had had an implacable schedule, an inexorable routine, for the fulfillment of his daily work. This he did not desert. He was taking care of the woman he helplessly adored. He thought she would recover. But she did not, and his former reality had deserted him now.

I remember when I saw them at the Biltmore in Florida, the last time I ever saw Adelaide. After dinner I was loitering in the lobby and ran into Mr. Lieberman. We exchanged pleasantries and he hurried off, saying "I have a sick wife, I can't stay to chat," and in his gray-and-white striped seersucker suit and white bucks and pepper-and-salt hair he looked dapper indeed.

"I'm sorry," I had called to his retreating figure—I was always calling out to his retreating figure. "I'm sorry you are going through a rough time."

"I never promised you a rose garden, kid."

Now he seemed to have lost some of his former crispness, with his anchor to reality gone. In a way he was the perfect California person because they were always agonizing over which reality was theirs and what level of reality they were on and adjusting to their new reality. But then so am I. If I see the word 'wellness,' I'm interested. I'm *very* interested. Count me in.

He said he had been to an esoteric spa not far from Costa Verde, and had tried out some esoteric treatments—"transfrictional work"—something about trigger points.

"Did it make you feel funny?"

"I feel funny all the time."

"What was the schedule there?"

"First there was tongue shaving."

"Tongue shaving?"

"There's a lot of tongue shaving out here."

"What's it for?"

"Bacteria."

"And then what."

"Numerous lectures on enzyme biology."

"What the heck is that? It sounds kind of disgusting."

"Oh, it is. Let me just put it this way. Your diet is toxic, Miss Ford."

"I know. I should eat wheatgrass. And then what?"

"Fango baths and transfrictional work."

"So you liked it?"

"Well, you can't smoke cigars. That's bad. It interferes with my personal growth. And they want you to have personal growth. It's a conflict."

I was stricken with sorrow to look at his handsome face. His California garb had for some reason been abandoned. He was back in his Alabama seersucker. He still towered over me. I myself was wearing maternity clothes at this point. But I was wearing elaborately calibrated maternity clothes from the handsomely burnished mall.

"Very fetching, Miss Ford," he commented, looking me up and down.

How fascinating to feel those slow apprising blue eyes on me. He took my hand. I could not figure out what we wanted from each other. I had not thought it was a prurient matter. He had a disarming shyness. He still held my hand.

"Maybe you'd better go," I said.

"Do I disgust you?" he asked.

"No, it's not that; it's the proprieties," I said. I was tired of being a cad. Mac would claim to be a man not prey to jealousy—ever calm and rational, studying sediment, rewiring the floor lamps, repairing a child's broken toy. But surely it would be annoying to Mac if I hung around with some other guy all day for hours on end.

So Mr. Lieberman stood up and prepared to take his departure.

"Meet me in the garden tonight," he said. "Would you?"

"That would be too highly immoral," I said. "About what time?"

"Before dinner for a drink."

There was a knock on the door. It proved to be Albert. I let him in and he stood beside us, doffing his cap.

"The banks are calling, Mr. L.," he said.

Albert was uncharacteristically stiff and embarrassed. He retired to Mr. Lieberman's suite with uncharacteristic tact.

My position was strictly and inviolably confined by my standards of honor. However, my position wavered.

I found it surprising that he would be interested in a fading forty-year-old the way he might be in, say, a blooming twenty-eight. One blooms till forty especially if at forty, one goes to the blistering desert.

Mr. Lieberman did not appear to have inviolable standards of conduct. But then he was free. It is easier for the free person to forget the other's ties.

"So you will meet me? Tonight."

"I am confined by certain inviolable parameters of responsibility and conduct, harassed by toil and bound by care," I announced. "What time did you say?"

"Fleming."

Stop the presses. He called me Fleming. Just like that. Or was it a slip? No. It was not a slip.

It was my cue to cry. But then he called me darling.

Darling. Darling Fleming.

I wouldn't break a promise. I wouldn't break a vow. Sure domesticity can be boring and you don't want to stay at the hearth every second. But that's it. End of story.

"What about extenuating circumstances?" he asked.

"Like what?"

"Are you lit from within by Mac's love?"

"Lit from within?"

"By his love."

"Put it this way. He's the most adorable man this side of the Rockies."

"I'd like to be adorable."

"Don't worry. You are."

Like when he kept hanging around in his bathrobe looking natural and suave—probably like Fred Astaire looked in his bathrobe. There had to be both gaiety and decline to create his air of gallantry and courage.

We went downstairs together. We walked a few blocks on Sunset. The conversation rambled on to the usual topic, our malaise.

"Do you ever have a sense of mild unease?" I asked.

"I can't imagine *not* having it," he answered.

A pair of phobic cosmopolites rode down Sunset in an outmoded car—you get that type of people in L.A. Who knows their history? They could well be Englishmen, or just old-time types from another era who got stuck there to the end.

"By the way. Do you miss the British Empire?" I asked.

"I have no use for it myself but I can understand how some might."

"What exactly is it they would miss about it?"

"Spit and polish. Standards. Pomp and circumstance."

Maybe British people have an ancestral adaptation to their antecedents: for instance an explorer mentality and an empire mentality—you thus tend to find them in remote outposts and sunny climes like California. And with them they have been known to bring the cynicism and self-doubt that was born on the battlefields of Europe. It's in their blood.

He turned to go. As I watched his retreating figure—I was always watching his retreating figure—he turned back to say there was another mountain we must climb. It was nearby. My delicate condition might forbid climbing it, he noted. But I must see it.

We went back toward the hills, among the palazzos and a few seemingly ancient white clapboard bungalows hidden in the palm groves, until we came to an iron gate. Through that gate I beheld vast mountains in the blazing sun with dusty trails, eucalyptus groves, and pepper trees, right in the middle of Hollywood. It was a massive beauty you succumbed to, made more massive, I think, by the patina of civilization all around it. You think about the old reality back east that always seemed so promising. But the question is, are there mountains to climb every day? I mean that quite literally. Back east you could presumably embark upon a walk. But it would be a flat road. There would not be mountains to climb in the middle of town. California is a respite from the East. But which is better, the respite or the old reality?

"I find it endearing that you have held on to your hate for the West, Miss Ford, but you have to admit that it's hard to hold on to it when you see this."

It was hard, it is true, to hold on to your hate while walking up a mountain in the middle of a vast metropolitan cosmopolis. The hills were green and the sweet sun shone. You were in a dream.

"There's the Cecil B. DeMille sunset," he pointed out. True enough, the rays of light shone down apocalyptically through some gathering clouds on to the vast hills and canyons.

A sign was posted to beware of rattlesnakes. Some young people walked their dogs. Tortured disheveled young people like the ones who kept straggling out to the café in the garden of the Alexandria.

The young people seem very debauched. But then young people are always debauched. But then how debauched can you be while walking up a mountain. You see the basic stages of life in L.A.—the young, the decadent, the ambitious, the exiled. You also hear a lot of Russian spoken among the people climbing up this mountain. In Hollywood there are many Russian exiles, people even farther from their home than I, from what is familiar, and they struggle to adjust, climbing the trail.

It was the same with Mr. Lieberman, standing on the dusty trail surrounded by the Wild West in his Alabama seersucker and bow tie. This is what I expected of him: the perfect Englishman with a cane and bowler hat and formality in the sunshine among the deck chairs. That is not, on the face of it, what I got. That is not the image he liked to present of himself. He wanted to be the perfect American, shun the old world, declare his independence. If you're independent the old dominion doesn't have to thwart you. He figured this out when he left the old world for New York. It takes a lifetime, for example, to recover from a childhood and youth in the Tropics. Take it from me. Maybe it's the same from the damp drenched moors. Maybe I understood him better than he understood himself. We were both deprived of our moorings, the dignity of staying where you belonged, instead being imbued with the desire to flee. Instead being on the run.

Sometimes an early sorrow is the making of a man. Take Mr. Lieberman. He didn't really like England. But wherever he went it was still the England of his parents that he evermore recalled, as the paradise he lost. It was a well-known tradition in his generation to be sent away to school at around the age of seven. A well-known consequence of this was a certain calcification of the heart, the stiff upper lip said to constitute the soul of the British Empire.

Again I was having Proustian flashbacks to his life, a study of his nostalgias, and I had the strictest vision of the moment when he turned back at the gate to look at his parents one last time on the day that he was sent away. He felt the same thing for their image now at seventy as he had at seven. A limousine was waiting for him and a chauffeur—things had not changed much in the intervening sixty years. He had already said his good-byes but he turned around at the gate to fix a picture of his parents in his mind. There they stood in the door in what was to him their ineffable glamour. His gallantry was formed in that moment as he turned to catch his last vision of them, a kind of photographic memory in his heart, for he did not want to leave—no child of seven wants to leave—and he squared his shoulders and moved on.

Now he had the resilience of the palms he loved—they sway with the wind rather than remaining rigid so that they don't snap during hurricanes.

He was frankly incredibly handsome, with a head of white hair, electrifying blue eyes, and the skeptical look in his eyes and demeanor.

"Watch your step," he added. We were halfway up the mountain. "Maybe you should rest. Or we should stop."

"Did you ever have a midlife crisis?" I asked him.

"I didn't have time for that. I had too much to do."

He stopped.

"I am not insensible to female fascination, Miss Ford."

So it was still Miss Ford.

This was his cue to roughly draw me to his heart. He did.

"We are standing on the edge of a precipice, my dear." Poised on the brink of a precipice about to crash in. Like the empires before World War I. And literally—on my beloved green mountain in the middle of Hollywood.

If a place can be defined by a person, or inextricably

linked to one, that place for me is Los Angeles and that man oddly enough was Mr. Lieberman.

Albert appeared out of nowhere and admonished us. He disappeared and returned with the car when we arrived back at the iron gate. Mr. Lieberman asked him to drop us off on Sunset Boulevard a few blocks from the hotel.

We parted outside of a sordid café.

"Call me tonight?"

"I'll meet you at eight."

He didn't look back. He seemed calm. Perhaps he would tell me of his early sorrows, which are the making of a man, or of losing an empire and a world of youth on the battle-fields of Europe, until the new world took over with gadgets and conveniences and American well-being on the last frontier.

I watched him walking down the street. He lit his cigar and seemed more dapper and less fragile than when he had emerged from the limousine some hours earlier. Perhaps I had distracted him. Late at night, I had the feeling, he must conduct some waking nightmares. But in the end he was never beaten down by whatever he had to endure. He was a man of ardent character, with a temper that no disappoint-ment could ultimately disturb; and life to him, for some strange reason, stranger than I know, was still a rhapsody— the elations of youth despite his age, perhaps.

A man used to vicissitudes is not easily dejected. His broad-shouldered grace, the manner of his walk, his upright posture, somehow suggested that he was always going uphill. As if he had exalted heights to scale. He was in fact lit-erally often going uphill—climbing his mountains in the middle of town.

No one asks to lose his faith, in religion or anything else. It's just the way our century started out, losing any tendency to optimism on the battlefields of Europe. Spit and polish, standards, pomp and circumstance—these things went out and were replaced with gadgets and conveniences and American well-being, for me ending on the last frontier.

And so to the mall.

50

It's a thrill to be loose on the streets when you have all those kids. Usually they don't let you out at night. A mere walk at twilight becomes an ecstasy.

I went to the mall on a desperate and successful search for women's beauty products and then strolled through the garden at twilight to meet Mr. Lieberman. "In that latitude the midsummer days were long, midsummer nights only a short darkness between the long twilight that postponed the stars and the green dawn clarity." We had a drink at the café in the Italian wicker chairs at the far end of the garden, near the ancient-seeming neon sign falling through the palm trees.

I noticed another white-haired man coming toward me, somewhat unsteady on his feet. "Is that Fleming Ford?" he said.

It was Mr. Lieberman's sick friend, the Duke. His teeth still hadn't entirely grown in, and he did look pretty sick.

"Debris and wreckage," he said, "the story of my life. The shattered remains."

"He comes from a long line of hereditary degenerates," said Mr. Lieberman.

British people are so fascinatingly decadent. Their U.S.A.

is a vast sea of decadence. Is it them or is it us? I wonder. They tend to go to pieces here. Then again I tend to go to pieces here too.

The British lost their empire; the South lost the Civil War. Each has a close acquaintance with defeat. It makes them jaded and debauched and cynical.

The so-called Duke generally spent his time sitting tight at the Bel-Air or the Beverly Hills Hotel joking with the waitresses and playing the afternoon gin game in a cabana.

He too was a widower and Mr. Lieberman had made a point of having a "dinner party" consisting of himself and the sick Duke once a week. They were quaint. Soon it would look as if they had wandered in from another century. Things were still quaint in the twentieth century. You suspect they won't be quaint again, or for long. Most people wouldn't care for quaint anyway. Mac, for instance, would spurn the quaint. When Mac had to be in L.A. he stayed at a hotel that was literally underneath the 405—in the merge of the 405 and the 10. But I like that in a man—it's rugged. No-nonsense. He's a man of action. He doesn't have time for quaint.

"What is the correct time here?" asked the sick Duke.

"I'm fifteen seconds slow," said Mr. Lieberman—as if this vast discrepancy prevented him revealing the time. "My cesium clock loses a millionth of a second per century."

"Well, we can't have that. Your time is far too inaccurate."

The sick Duke wandered out but then he reappeared. He was disheveled and wearing Bermuda shorts and some type of slippers. He stopped to admire the hibiscus.

"Do you ever feel a little depression creeping up on you?" I asked the sick Duke in my poll on malaise.

"You say it so courteously—a dainty little depression sidling up. You should say am I living in an incredibly deep hole of depression all the time like a bulldozer rolling over me," he answered calmly. He kept saying everything was pointless. He himself had been kicked out of the House of Lords in Parliament.

He was a shining illustration of the book I was reading, *The Decay of the British Aristocracy*. According to the author, the British aristocracy had decayed because the aristocrats left their ancestral seats, owing to their desire to flee, for to keep their prestige and power they should stay at home and perform their local duties. The sick Duke's father had been born in Abyssinia and was part of the problem, for he obtained, so far from home, a lifelong craving for barbaric splendor, for savagery and the throb of drums. "All was drab, alas too drab, in England." For others it was the desire to flee from the trenches of World War I; but the aristocracy traveled because they were decaying. As the author of *The Decay of the British Aristocracy* says, "Decayed they undeniably are but by no means totally extinct"—like the sick Duke.

This book transformed all those places suffused with an air of old-world glamour such as the Riviera into a herald of debauchery and decay. Again it seemed to share a part with the South I knew. Our kingdom of debauchery.

The debauched British aristocrats fled not only to the Riviera but to California, such as the sick Duke who had lost almost everything by investing in a cattle ranch.

I piped up with my spiel, did he not miss his ancient shore? I asked the sick Duke, "Don't you miss ancient things?"

"Well, I've become one, you see. So I have that."

The conversation progressed from there to the afterlife. I asked the sick Duke what he thought.

He gave a long involved answer using the word "normative" a lot.

"The Muslims have belly dancers and pomegranates," said Mr. Lieberman, rather wistfully.

196

There were gliders and crashers, he remarked. Gliders were always kind of sickly and eventually slipped away, but crashers were abundantly healthy throughout life until a sudden end. The sick Duke appeared to be a glider.

A waiter came to take an order for drinks.

"The lady will have an Arnold Palmer," said Mr. Lieberman.

"What the heck is that?" I asked.

"You don't know?"

"I don't know."

"Iced tea and lemonade mixed up."

The sick Duke ordered champagne.

I really didn't know what to call the sick Duke. "Your Grace" seemed a bit much. I couldn't figure out what his actual name was. Mr. Lieberman called him Churchy, but I of course wouldn't. I assume it was a nickname for Churchill. "Mr. Churchill" would I'm sure be incorrect. Lord Churchill? My Lord? Your Majesty?

The sick Duke felt that various widows around town had their eye on him, and that he must be vigilant in eluding them. They barricaded him in the grocery store, he claimed. He was in constant battles with his family over money. There were lawsuits. It was like the war of the bad seeds. People in his family were in feuds that lasted seventy years; but then when they were on their deathbed, the brother that they hadn't spoken to in seventy years would suddenly show up and refuse to leave the sickroom.

The sick Duke wandered over to the terrace beyond the far end of the garden to admire the Moorish palaces and French châteaux of the neighborhood overhung with palm fronds.

"I don't get this guy Churchy," I said to Mr. Lieberman.

"I don't either," said his old friend with typical terseness.

"What's his general profile?"

"Unfavorable."

"He seems to drink a lot of champagne."

"I never knew he was drunk for fifteen years until one day I saw him sober."

"Did he know your wife?"

"Not only did he know my wife, he's a defeated suitor."

So they were old rivals.

"Really? And so the crumpled rival is consumed by jealousy?"

"He held up manfully. He's a defeated suitor but I'm not the one who defeated him. It was before my time."

After a while the sick Duke returned dressed for dinner. He had noticed an advertisement for a trip to Machu Picchu, a place in South America people in California were always going to that was known for its spiritual properties and resemblance to eternity. He and Mr. Lieberman of course were devotees of newfangled California spiritual cults and the like. They compared notes. Mr. Lieberman produced from his breast pocket a pamphlet about "Spiritual Dynamite" that expelled diabolic influences and involved spiritual issues stored in your energy field. The sick Duke kept talking about his Primordial Sounds Seminar. And to think how far away it all was from their old green land, their sceptered realm, etc.

"I really must be going, old boy. I have to go to my Primordial Sounds Seminar."

Their interest in these things seemed so incongruous to their general appearance. The old rivals were dressed for an English garden party—Mr. Lieberman in a white summer suit and pink shirt and green tie—the type of dramatic outfit once decreed by Adelaide—and the sick Duke now in a blue blazer with an esoteric club pin and the watery blue eyes of an old English explorer. I was in my element with the white-haired gents in the twilight garden. Mr. Lieberman smoked his cigar with his stern grace and reserve, and the usual curtain of glamour descended on the scene.

There was something very curious about him: it was as if he had to be old before he could be young. I don't doubt that at twenty he had been a heartthrob in his way, just as in a peculiar way he was one now. But at twenty he had probably been closed-off or confused by his colliding past and future and the great change of venue in his life. He had probably been old and traditional, building his financial empire. At thirty he was a devoted husband. Ditto till seventy. Now suddenly he could be a newfangled California person.

"I'm thinking of taking a workshop in Remote Viewing," he said, perhaps in his rivalry now with the sick Duke to see who could be more outlandish.

"What the heck is that?" I asked.

"Learning how to transcend time and space. You transport part of your body into another dimension."

"Which part?"

"I'm not sure. And then I might take a workshop on healing."

"Good. Then you can heal me."

"By the way, I've spoken to Michael."

"Who's Michael?"

"He's an entity from a mid-causal plane."

"Not someone you run into every day, I expect. What did he say?"

"He said you're the widow's dream."

Mr. Lieberman received a summons in the lobby and said good-bye to the sick Duke. "OK, Churchy, take it easy, kid," he said.

The sick Duke took me aside. "Do you find him any better?" he asked.

"I think he's improving."

"Harry is fragile," he said, joining the chorus.

This was true, I had learned.

"I understand he's been spending time with you. It's done him good. He does seem to be improving," he said. "You have that effect on him. I remember a day in the spring in New York when I saw him on the street. He hardly recognized me. He was adrift. Certainly not the case today." He stopped.

"Yes, I saw that look in New York too."

"California has done him good. But remember what I told you before. We may have to rein him in."

Then the Duke departed, little knowing it was I who needed to be reined in.

51

"I just want to sit here in the dark with you," Mr. Lieberman remarked when his sick friend had departed.

"That could be dangerous."

"We are dancing on the edge of a precipice, Miss Ford, as I told you," he said suddenly.

Miss Ford again.

"Then maybe you should stop calling me Miss Ford."

He smoked his cigar as if pondering this milestone anew.

Wisdom is a love of the good. But not even goodness is proof against human weakness. There was a wild contrast between the suitable and still young man who was the father of my children and the wildly unsuitable slightly seedy disintegrating much older man. I always preferred the old. The young are so callow. Mac was the only young one I ever saw capable of taking on the responsibility.

I used to wish for normality—someone who would follow me around in the garden asking questions wearing a seer-sucker suit. That's pretty much what I got, when he's around. But for "asking questions" substitute raking the leaves, mowing the lawn, refinancing the mortgage, reshoring the retaining wall, and taking the kids to massive and hideous children's emporiums called Funtastic Farm or ReptileLand. The poor man has a neon sign on his forehead saying HUSBAND. FATHER.

That night when we met at my father's house for the first time we stayed up all night talking, I have no recollection of what we said, but I only know I saw his soul and vice versa.

We understood each other, though it was not always spoken, and in fact the opposite was spoken, if we were pressed to speak. There was a time when we parted, before marriage. It stuns me that he used the same words as Mr. Lieberman did: he said we were standing on the edge of a precipice and he was scared to go off the edge. I said, Let's jump in. He said he wasn't sure. So I showed him the door. I was not sure that he would ever return. In fact he only returned when after extensive thought I recognized the lack of obligation involved in love. He wasn't obligated to love me. It's the old adage: the definition of love being that you love without expectation of a return.

His was not a worldly guiding character. We were equal. The worldly guiding character belongs to that of the older man. The towering figure cast in your path.

So keen a longing had I always felt for Mac and never for another. But then you train yourself in marriage not to long for another. I don't need religion to keep myself in line, I only need ethics. It doesn't take much to give me a thrill. Knowing a baby-sitter is coming gives me a thrill. I had never had a temptation to sin. Or is it that the attraction was never powerful enough—either to the man or to sin? This was my first temptation.

One of the sociological studies that I found in L.A. about the West quoted from an article in 1943: "All in all, one quarter of our population are in a state of flux, physically and psychologically. If you ask them where they expect to be five years from now, they shrug their shoulders. The question for some twenty to thirty million people is 'Where do we go from here?'"

I would have said precisely the same thing. That's what you feel out West even now. Maybe that's what you feel on a frontier. Maybe it's a psychological state, denoting the same question Mr. Lieberman and I had to ask ourselves: Where do we go from here? It was uncharted territory that lay ahead, at the edge of a country that borders another, at the limit of knowledge that I had always possessed.

Sometimes you must go through the wrenching difficulty of giving up something that is both beautiful and beloved. Whether I would give up my vast Cartesian adoration of Mr. Lieberman or my long love for Mac, I did not know, but in trying to appreciate the situation, I was consumed by remorse. One of these loves would involve a parting, or else how to be loyal to all?

52

On the train going back there was the rugged California landscape, green fields and orchards and the sunlit mountains, even at Anaheim and Irvine, so Orange County is not ruined after all. Or maybe my eyes were opened by my ever increasing love for the region and my adjustment by ordinary human nature to my new locale. I don't approve of Irvine, of course. They've bulldozed the last orange grove in Orange County. Now it's all one giant series of ultra-new burnished mini-malls. But they are handsomely burnished with a pleasing namelessness, a refreshing lack of personality if all you have to do is pass through. There were still green hills and ranches at Laguna. Lemon groves at Rancho Capistrano. Who needs the sea? I mean it was even better than the sea.

It's partly the damn human soul. Will adjust. Will forget? The light here is at first a complete shock; then you get used to it. Then you adapt: now I wouldn't go to the beach in the broad of day—only mad dogs and Englishmen would do that. You learn to take your walks at twilight. You realize that the air is pure and light, the temperature is cool at night. First you have to give up the old empire in your heart—the North and South—and surrender to the West.

As ever, though it had been overcast in L.A., once we hit the demarcation point—the climatic fault zone—at about San Juan Capistrano, all was clear and at Esperanza brilliant.

On the train I read *The Decay of the British Aristocracy*. I'm always careening through the desert and cowboy outposts reading *The Decay of the British Aristocracy*. It's so incongruous. But paradox is what keeps me going.

Then it was a mad whirlwind of chores at home. My house is a holocaust of Barbie. There is always something like Barbie's Computer that is permanently emitting tinny psychedelic music, with Barbie's voice saying "Wow, let's party" over and over driving you slowly insane. Or there is a tinny electronic tune of "Mary Had a Little Lamb" being played over and over throughout eternity from some but-

203

ton on a toy being accidentally pressed beneath a mound of stuff driving you slowly mad. There is a fifty-year-old man dressed up as a duck who arrives in a souped-up Corvette with scotch on his breath and demands to be paid in cash, amid small children who have a demonic need to rebel, a demonic mania for protest, which I should realize they inherit directly from their mother.

Each child brings a different chapter, the quest to instill basic knowledge such as to avoid destruction, that many more Cheerios to sweep up to achieve one's vast Germanic need for order, that many more women in full-length plaid dresses at snobby private schools to try to convince of your worthiness. I'm from high society in Fort Defiance, Alabama, but out here I'm strictly chopped liver. But I don't have to convince myself of my social standing. I just have to convince transplanted midwesterners in full-length plaid dresses.

As I watched my social status plummet disastrously by several levels, I noticed that the misfit neighbor was literally cutting down his entire garden, pruning his trees to extinction. I don't know why.

Mac was under the house redoing the electrical wiring. Later he invented a gadget in the garage for washing the windows, mixing concoctions and causing explosions like a mad chemist in his laboratory. He had struck up a friendship with the misfit neighbor, who was lured into the garage by Mac's madcap experiments. Now it seems Mac is the misfit neighbor's mentor, turning him into a king of Home Improvement. Next thing I know the misfit neighbor will have geraniums in window boxes and garden trellises. He will be a heartwarming fixer-upper guy, making his garden bloom again, while Missy (his dog) yelps adorably.

Speaking of geraniums, my botanist is going through a career change. A lot of people out here are in fiber optics. A lot of desperate people. Fiber optics seems to be what they

204

go into when their own career fails. Take my botanist. He's supposed to be this famed horticulturalist and his whole life is geraniums, and then you find out just last year he was in fiber optics. After the extravagant newspaper treatment and famed botanist bit, now suddenly it turns out he knows more about fiber optics than flowers.

What are fiber optics? you might ask. Let me give you a piece of advice. Don't ask a person in fiber optics what they are. He will go on for hours about wires and the speed of light.

Anyway, the whole world will be converted to it one day.

"How was your trip?" said Mac. "Did you keep track of your atomic particles?"

"I don't know. Yes. No. They're seeping out."

"And how was the international tycoon? He seems to be rather nuts about you."

If I could construct an equation of harmony, if I could adjust one cog in the mechanism in order to make it run smoothly, it would cease to highlight my treachery.

"Mac, we live on the Pacific Ocean. How about a haunting walk along the beach?"

"Does it have to be haunting?"

"Well, that's the whole point."

"What about your enmity to the Pacific Ocean? I thought it had no personality and was a scourge against the green Atlantic and all that."

"The Pacific is starting to grow on me."

"That's a step forward, I guess."

He stopped.

"We're having unscheduled human interaction," he commented.

"We are?"

"Yes. The ball is in your court."

"It is?"

"Sure. That's the whole thing with human interaction," he said. "It's all about whose court the ball is in. That's what you have to determine."

"But often our human interaction involves discussing details about your generator. Or your septic tank."

"We're still interacting, though."

"Could you please move aside? I'm trying to sweep up."

"Oh, excuse me. I wouldn't want to thwart your vast Germanic need for order."

I occasionally tagged along with Mac to his accountant's office, not a romantic spot, while they developed the budget—cost estimates and projected revenues for the Trans-California Pipeline—to comprise a prospectus for Mr. Lieberman's lawyers. Accountants are not always as boring as you would think. Actually I have often found that accountants are loaded with personality. Especially in New York. An accountant in New York is always a severely eccentric individual, completely harassed, with flyaway hair and a pathetic hole in the wall somewhere for an office the size of an elevator.

When I watched the accountant calculating the odds, it was possible to envision a more apocalyptic equation: based on your emotional composition, how much happiness or harmony you would find, what qualities you are drawn to in another, whether irreconcilable differences would arise. Duty, constancy, responsibility, malaise—these were written on the future. Gallantry had always been in Mac. He was lean and serious—though also being your archetypal droll southerner, he had a touch of the sublime. He would not be arbitrary and cruel and infirm of purpose. He would be constant, sober, and mild. Others perhaps must slide around in a sea of uncertainty and be infirm in their purpose. That was not for Mac. He aimed for the direct hit. It hadn't happened yet for the Trans-California Pipeline. But as to the result of our last romance in the desert, there the direct hit had been made.

53

I attended a lecture on Birds and Your Garden hosted by a federally licensed wildlife rehabilitator. It was delivered by a madcap hummingbird expert. His whole life was hummingbirds. I studied the list of local events:

West African Inundations
The Starry Sky at Night
Ethiopian Hyena Attack
Beach Volleyball

I studied the suicides in the local paper, of which there always appeared to be several a week. A man tried to hang himself from a telephone pole. Another sat calmly on the trolley tracks awaiting the end, which soon came.

The milk of human kindness does not, I think, flow freely in this region. If you're suicidal, everyone else is out playing beach volleyball.

But the Russians—parents of my daughter's friends—are always fabulously nice. They discover molecules and make vast gloomy sweeping statements. They couldn't be nicer yet their natural atmosphere is vast gloom. It's quite refreshing. At their houses they have fetid ponds for which they have procured an apparatus giving off dry ice to create a depressing vapor, to add atmosphere. One of them was a materials scientist. He discovers new materials. Perhaps he had discovered the swamp vapor arising from his fetid pond.

The Russians had no sense of time. They were always picking up my daughter for vast timeless Russian play dates. They had no idea that it was daylight saving time, they picked up Josie hours later than the appointed hour, they brought her home past nine at night.

One day we were at the Russians' house for a vast timeless children's birthday party.

I tried to ask the Russian material scientist about nostalgia. Did he miss his ancient land? I asked.

His glance wandered proudly to his fetid pond. When he looked at his fetid pond it was the only time his expression varied from vast gloom to fond bemusement. Especially when he turned on the apparatus that added the misting swamp vapor–type effect.

"Nostalgia, I think, is for people who have some trouble in their life, financial, moral . . . For me America is so wonderful that I am not nostalgic for my land. Nostalgia is for the sad."

In the darkened kitchen his wife cooked heavy inappropriate Russian meals for the summer's day, to the accompaniment of mournful Russian folksongs playing on a tape recorder. I told her that her husband had surprised me by disparaging nostalgia, which I found incredible for a Russian.

"He lies to himself," she confirmed, and glanced darkly at the fetid pond.

I quietly admired the dead garden and brown grass—reclaimed by the desert—in which the children frolicked timelessly.

"My land is crippled," mused her husband.

The Russians aren't cheery, unlike most California people. That's what I adore about them.

There was an article in the local newspaper about the Russians. Some didn't feel comfortable here and had to go back home because America had no *Weltschmerz,* it had no vast longing, it had no spiritual side. Unlike the Russians, who revel in their mystery and their timeless melancholy and their fetid ponds. If a California person had a fetid pond he would immediately call the plumber. Meanwhile he would avert his eyes.

I doubt that stress is something that the Russians bother with. *Angst* is one thing. Stress is entirely another. I doubt the Russians would find Esperanza very stressful. To them it's such a dream of paradise that they have to build a fetid pond to remind them of their moldering land; they have to have a vapor coming off the fetid pond to remind them of the mystery they left behind.

They're like British people, in a way, though more open with the *angst.* But both had a vast empire once, now in shambles, an ancient history of adversity to contemplate, giving them a broader perspective, making them less cheery than your average Californian. Maybe even than your average American. Maybe a man should not ask for happiness. Maybe the happy man is the stupid man. Or it may be that the happy man is the American.

What must the Russians feel when driving around the streets and areas that have names like Vacation World and FunTown among the palms and highways carved into the desert in the baking sun? Everything is strictly new. Gleaming with newness. Unlike their moldering land.

54

To be a writer, you must stand at the edge of the abyss and look in unflinching. Like the Russians. Though they stand at the edge of a fetid pond.

Soon after the publication of his first book, long before he was prime minister, Disraeli was overtaken by a singular disorder, marked by malaise and fits of giddiness. Once he fell into a trance for a week. The mysterious malady continued and he set out on travels to try to dispel it. He had a desire to flee. It comes to the problem we all must share, the constant longing for respite, whether from malady, drudgery, or reality. So the world stops, you get off, and immerse yourself in geraniums. Or hummingbirds. Or trying to make the desert bloom.

But my work did not go well. I had a desire to flee. I plotted my escape.

My family always seemed to be at the height of historical moments: in the antebellum South; inexplicably removed to New York during the Civil War; in the old world they constructed one of the great French châteaux, Azay le Rideau on the Loire. Maybe my family had this quality in common with Mr. Lieberman's. From Baghdad to the Jewish ghetto to the British peerage. In the 1920s his parents took a trip around the world by steamer and railroad, including Hollywood where they saw a Tarzan (whose father was a British lord) picture being shot. Maybe a taste of California was in Mr. Lieberman's blood through this ancestral antecedent.

I heard from him often. He moved to the California Club, a rare vestige of the quaint in downtown Los Angeles. He called from Santa Anita, where he had bet on a horse named Open to Reason. He located the largest tree in California (a Moreton Bay fig) in Pasadena. While he was at the L.A. Arboretum he saw a picture of the largest tree in California and went to the basement to interrogate the horticulturalists until they told him where it was. I pictured him strolling around the neighborhood with Cadillacs glinting in the madly blazing sun among the palms, or sitting on the gorgeous terrace overlooking the San Gabriel Mountains at the Ritz-Carlton. It could have been Lake Como, or Zaire. He called from Catalina, where he had an attack of happiness, he said—something about the way the sun was. Never underestimate what the sun means to the English.

He had told me to hold on to my dark vision. In many moments it is easy to let go of it and find yourself in paradise among the bougainvillea of incessant gardens in the sweet winter sun. It is hard not to let go of your dark vision for that.

"Don't become a booster, Miss Ford," he would say. But he didn't have a dark vision.

He frequented the Arboretum, where the old Tarzan pictures had been shot, conferring madly with the horticulturalists. He had an evening cocktail with the sick Duke in the garden of the Alexandria, which reminds you of the Caribbean. It always reminds you of something else. The Hollywood Hills remind you of the Amalfi Coast. The courtyards of cafés remind you of Mexico—the dappled shade, the birds hopping around, the barbaric sun. He took his massive walks around L.A., covering vast distances. Shadowed by Albert. He walked up entire mountains in the heart of town.

But in his mind he kept returning to the places of his youth on those occasions when his father had taken him somewhere—which prompted him to start an index of his memories before the Second War—that world of swank of which Lord Northwood had been the unlikely inventor.

He didn't invent high society, of course. He would not have been considered part of it by many. He never quitted the tents of his people or renounced his faith. He didn't invent decadence. He was hardly decadent. But in making his retreat in the Edwardian era at the green shuttered villas on Mediterranean coasts and Italian lakes he had oddly enough started a trend associated with debauchery on the Continent whose precedent had not been seen since Lord Byron.

I was awakened at night by a profusion of nightingales. I had a vision of a boy and his father at the Villa Serbelloni with its palm garden raging at the front, an orange palace with long corridors and green latticed shutters and bell-boys in red Venetian jackets. The L'Ambasciatori on Via Veneto, with footmen and doormen everywhere in slightly seedy old satin striped waistcoats. Even a dining table look-ing out at the exquisite view of the Bosphorus at the Malta Palace occupied by the paranoid sultan who lived there before World War I: his world was doomed, his empire soon to fall, amid this crushing beauty. I knew how he felt. You have all those atomic particles seeping out to create another soul, so you want to build things back up. You want to build an empire in your own soul.

Walking home along the village street, there was the beauty of the night, the avenue of palms beneath the stars. I might as well be in Malaysia or any outpost of an empire in the last century, hanging around with white-haired British colonials like the sick Duke and Mr. Lieberman at old clubs.

But I was brought back to reality by Mac's accountant.

Immediately after the road show we would meet with Mr. Lieberman at the drilling site near Death Valley.

55

There had been some consternation in New York about Mr. Lieberman's removal to the West Coast. Especially when he began to mortgage his companies there to borrow against those assets for his massive investment in the Mojave Desert. He had intended originally to stay for a month or a season. But of course the seasons never changed. And he did not reappear in New York.

He began to meet with lawyers and investment bankers in L.A. who would accompany him and Mac on the road show throughout the U.S. and Europe to raise money. A grueling schedule was drawn up—fourteen cities in fourteen days, meetings and presentations daily in each spot to pitch the company. He briefed the research analysts, he wooed his international banking contacts.

There was a trader in New York with whom he corresponded several times daily who executed his transactions. There was a tycoon in San Francisco who frequently invested in his deals. There was O'Hara, the Chicago magnate, though O'Hara had long since wanted out. Now he wanted back in. There was a coterie of people who invested with him knowing they would win more often than they'd lose. The tycoons were called in and met at ritzy restaurants in private rooms or sometimes at hotels in their California bathrobes. What they liked about him was that it wasn't backroom deals with Mr. Lieberman, the kind where if he did you a favor he would expect a lot in return. It was exactly the opposite of the way his father-in-law, Standard Ames, had done business in the South of the previous day.

But the attitude of the tycoons was: If Lieberman's in, I'm in.

He carried on business with extraordinary nonchalance, yet with shrewdness; in California he conducted meetings in a style he would never dream of using in New York. He judged the atmosphere. He judged correctly. Formality was not prized out west. He kept the courtesy of a suit and bow tie in San Francisco, but that wasn't the way in Los Angeles. He would conduct important interviews there wearing the bathrobe on a couch littered with books and papers in his hotel suite, as if fulfilling a type: the Hollywood mogul—and when the deal was cut and the interview was over, the other party would be astonished at the efficacy of the result.

An army of assistants and secretaries materialized in Mr. Lieberman's hotel suite in L.A.—his bankers, his boards, his team from New York. Lawyers and key financial people who would draw up the prospectus for the road show, the purchase agreements, the massive amount of documentation and presentation materials required. He had a commanding presence. Dreaming won't get you to Damascus, as the British general says in *Lawrence of Arabia,* but discipline will. I could see that he was an astute and disciplined manager of people, he treated everyone with equal respect—that impressed me—although he ran the show and I could see that it is a delicate matter to run people. When he led the business dealings their movements were fleet and swift; people treated him with veneration and some awe. Despite his humility and gracious treatment of his people he still struck the fear of God into them. Despite the bathrobe or the jodhpurs or the Alabama seersucker. It was energizing to study to meet his standard. But then that goes back to the appeal of etiquette—which is in fact a striving toward excellence.

Mac had gone back to the Mojave. Mr. Lieberman arranged to meet him there to visit the site before the formal inspection. Later I heard what transpired on that occasion. After Mac showed Mr. Lieberman and Albert around the drilling post, they repaired to the crap tables in Vegas— where Mac had tried to make payroll once or twice until the funds were raised. A rather pitiful introduction to the venture, but as it turned out, right up Mr. Lieberman's street. Who is more of a gambler than an entrepreneur?

In the desert you became nocturnal because the atmosphere is unendurable in the broad of day. You could see that as another reason why the desert is the perfect place for gambling.

Mac and Mr. Lieberman would be an odd pair in Vegas. I wonder what Mr. Lieberman would wear—the Alabama seersucker or the jodhpurs. Probably the jodhpurs. Albert might dress down in the heat. Then you could see his tattoos.

Vegas has lost some of the allure of the seedy and the failed since the whole town has been torn down and rebuilt. But if you want the seedy and the failed you need only travel to the outskirts or to any nearby town.

Nevada tends to be incredibly sordid because every gas station, convenience store, and stupendously uninviting cinder-block bar is a casino where depraved Wild West types are at the slot machines all day, in sad lounges attached to convenience stores cooped up in the broad of day. But what is worse, or at least what makes the Wild West types in sleazy lounges seem historically old-fashioned, are the antiseptic replicas of European capitals that rise dim-witted from the sand now in the heart of town.

If you pine for the old world in the new, don't go to Las Vegas. It will make a mockery of you.

215

56

It wasn't Mr. Lieberman's first trip to the desert. I think he covered every square inch of California. He hung out in Palm Springs. He careened around the region with Albert. Going east near the mountains, with winding roads and cowboy fences and old ranches and large palms under the glittering sun. He haunted the environs of Esperanza—the oleander and palm nurseries, ostrich farms and orange groves of Otay Canyon, a remote part of town. It is this drive that is the most beautiful one in Esperanza. He took it often. He came to the mountains, through which you must pass to reach the desert. The mountain towns, such as "beautiful downtown Dulzura," pop. 7, at the side of the road with a café and a papyrus grove, wove in with the desert towns down to the border. In the mountain towns there were a lot of cattle and horses and some real old-time ranchos. One was called Meanwhile Ranch (as in Meanwhile back at the ranch . . .), but most had the old Spanish names and crosses, and there was a small mission at the border town. He went up to Jawbone and Grapevine and Victorville. Sometimes there would be an oasis (like a mirage) of palms shimmering against the bald hills and rock-strewn mountains in the middle of this godforsaken desert, artificially irrigated for some godforsaken country club. Did he want to so transform the desert, down through the border towns to Mexico, into a string of gardenias and palm trees blooming away beneath the baking sun?

The early emigrant to the West with the irrigation obsession had maintained a "swank pioneer establishment" attended by desperadoes next to the town of Calipatria in what was later named the Imperial Valley—shades of the British Empire—after it had been transformed from a desolate wasteland to an agricultural paradise. He took control of the Colorado River through a system of levees and canals for the water to reach the desert through gravity. The whole enterprise took fifty years, but in the end this early settler did achieve the object of bringing the desert under cultivation. Palms and other semitropical trees, green fields, and date farms gave this area the appearance of a mystical oasis. Some sort of utopia. They're always looking for utopia out here.

So I could imagine Mac and Mr. Lieberman walking in the dark night at the site under the largest amount of stars that Mr. Lieberman had ever seen, discussing how to make the desert bloom. Of course the English have a mania for gardens. An Englishman—or a southerner for that matter—cannot do without the color green for long.

The desert is filled with places that have names like Mount Misery and the Funeral Mountains and Hell's Gate, not to mention Death Valley. It's so dry that perspiration evaporates instantaneously, and this is the danger toward dehydration, the signs of which are apathy, dizziness, delirium, and death. Actually the same symptoms sometimes set in in Esperanza if you don't drink gallons of water throughout the day. The atmosphere causes a bouquet of obscure sinus ailments and dry coughs. You have to use complicated moisturizers from esoteric spas. There is a way that a woman in her forties with three kids can look if she doesn't take extra precautions and even then she can look that way anyway.

I'm always driving around in the desert making myself sick, getting nauseous from dehydration and sinuous mountain turns. To me the desert is enervating and oppressive. Entirely forbidding. Huge mountains of bare rocks formed in volcanic upheavals or earthquakes and Paleolithic fault lines. The latter makes engineering projects like Mac's difficult. There's an earthquake every three minutes in Death Valley. You can't always feel them but they make it difficult to conceive of building anything there, even outside of the national park territory. This place is a geologist's dream. Sediment. Lava. The marine layer. The shifting of tectonic plates. Paleolithic faults.

Still, a Paleolithic fault is a Paleolithic fault, and you can't change that. The folly of deciding to build a huge metropolis in a desert—that's L.A.—was illustrated when Mulholland's Saint Francis Dam collapsed and hundreds were killed.

If you were a pioneer in the last century and you got to this region you would definitely say to yourself, This is not the place to build my house.

57

"The Nile Valley was in Paleolithic days simply a swamp," says my crazed weather professor. So I guess it was the same in the Mojave—simply an ocean, darling.

During World War II my crazed weather guy became more boring and tedious, devoting in a new volume entire chapters to subjects like "The Future of Air-Conditioning." But what is the same is that he is obsessed with the weather. "Great men may come and go," he says, empires may decline and fall, but what really matters is the weather.

For example, according to this guy, the South lost the Civil War because of the weather. The states above the Mason-Dixon line were more energetic and ingenious due to their invigorating climate.

World War II, he predicted—for his last book was written in 1944—would be won by the Americans because they have the best weather (the Americans being "men from optimum climatic zones"). "The organizing of so much power on the Allied side will take time; but however long it takes, the result is inevitable."

Right again.

He then goes into his massive penultimate chapter on "The Future of Air-Conditioning." But you can't air-condition the desert. And I'm not sure that you can make it bloom.

Though it would seem to violate the natural order of things, the source for making the desert bloom was theoretically an ancient aquifer from Paleolithic times when the Mojave was simply a swamp. It would hold what is known as fossil water, or ancient water, which would have been under there for thirty thousand years at a minimum, naturally purified of bacteria during that time. So it would be a natural ecological fact, not an artificial engineering feat to harness what poor rivers remained in the parched West. It would be a massive geological discovery.

Science is very big in California. It may not be as great for the humanities but it's great for geology and science nerds. It's great for sediment. Lava. Molecules. That type of thing.

The place is crawling with Nobel Prize winners in physics and mathematics. Science—yes. Humanity—no. At least that's my opinion, in the paradise of Esperanza.

58

The road show was not a success.

The road show began and ended in New York. The party consisted of Mr. Lieberman, Mac, and the bankers handling the deal. The second stop after New York was London. One of the fascinating things about London is that all the money is in Scotland. So don't even go to London, advised Mr. Lieberman. Go to Edinburgh. Spend a week in Edinburgh. But the bankers insisted on London, where there were a lot of Rolls-Royces and no money. Whereas Edinburgh bought half of the deal in one day.

A lunch in Paris was pointless. The French never buy. The next stop was Zurich. There's money in Zurich. You tend to be surprised in Zurich. But unfortunately Zurich did not surprise them.

They returned to America and next hit Chicago. A breakfast for a handful of investors. A lunch in Minneapolis. You don't expect to sell much. Midwesterners are very conservative. But expectations were high for Denver. Water, energy—they understand that in Denver. Denver was a potential home run. It's fast money there. They're kind of sloppy in Denver. That's why the money is fast. And that wasn't Mr. Lieberman's style.

Then to the West Coast. California is like England—

there's no real money in L.A. The only reason to include L.A. is for the Trust Company of the West. They never buy but if they do, they buy the whole deal. Steely stares greet the mention of Mexico.

San Francisco—that's where the money is. Fast technology investors. Like Denver. Again it wasn't Mr. Lieberman's cup of tea.

In the first week and a half of the road show you fine-tune your pitch. Now you're in the home stretch—getting serious: Houston. These people understand natural resources. Oil. Water. If it's in the ground and you're trying to get it out, they understand it in Houston.

Boston is the smartest money in the country. In Boston they lift up the hood and check the engine. In Boston if they like it, they buy big. In Boston there were eight meetings and then a return to New York for eight more. Then the bankers start calling all the accounts to get the orders: Are you in or are you out?

The deal didn't go well. Edinburgh bought 50 percent. The rest was barely covered and Mr. Lieberman had to put in the last 10 percent of the deal himself. Then it traded down to $5 a share on the first day. They had been hoping for at least $15. In this scenario ordinarily you would pull the deal. But in this case the need for funds precluded any choice but to take what was offered.

There was speculation about what role Mr. Lieberman did or did not play in the failure. This was not the kind of deal that would in any circumstances normally get done— too risky. So its failure could not necessarily be laid at Mr. Lieberman's door. Is he going to have the energy to dedicate to the venture? people might have wondered. It was his name alone that sold the deal at all.

Some had darker thoughts. That it was the diminishing star of the Lieberman family. That the Lieberman line had lost its luster. In Lord Northwood's day there had been a massive stake in the railroads linking the Austro-Hungarian Empire to Italy, the pioneer stake in electricity, even his backing of the fledgling picture business, hiring D. W. Griffith during World War I for the Cinematograph Committee of the War Office. Mr. Lieberman had had the vision to move forcefully into the U.S. markets, thus rectifying his grandfather's single strategic mistake in finance, and he had always felt the promise of California. He and his grandfather both did things on a grand scale. But as one of the Rothschild bankers had said of the Americans, "If their profits sometimes reach fantastic proportions, their failures cause deep catastrophes," which some felt was the looming danger over Mr. Lieberman's last venture.

When Churchill was First Lord of the Admiralty he understood how he would be treated when great ships were sunk and things went wrong. Mr. Lieberman quite understood how the CEO would be treated when a road show failed and the expectations for a stock price plummeted. But he would not throw up his hands in despair. He could not stand aside. The future's fortunes would be even worse without him.

That he accepted the blame was indicative of his courage.

Just as Neville Chamberlain stood aside for Churchill at the start of World War II—he didn't grasp the nature of the crisis—Mac knew when to let go. It is not a small feat to let go. It takes no small amount of courage. He stepped aside for Mr. Lieberman. It was Mr. Lieberman who would now preside over the failure, if it came to that, and continue to accept the blame. In British public schools, it's said, they taught you how to lose with grace.

I had a flash of nostalgia for the figure he had cut in New York. His tall commanding presence, an upright posture forever unbent, something ineffably jaunty in it despite his sorrows—a man from an earlier era, like British explorers before the First World War—Shackleton, Mallory, climbing their mountains. Those people were always climbing Mount Everest or exploring the Arctic and being incredibly stout-hearted and stoical as, mired in catastrophe, they failed to arrive at the hoped-for spot. Or like Raymond Chandler, another product of the British public school, who also set out for a far frontier: Los Angeles. Like them Mr. Lieberman seemed a fellow filled with solitude, he seemed a man alone in all things.

The tycoons had mysteriously reversed their positions, in a flurry of disloyalty. It was the first time they had been disloyal. It was also to be the last. Consequent to their return from the road show Mac said things would be very tense. He said the atmosphere would be very charged. It could be unpleasant, he said. It may be that the old strong-hearted gallant-hearted British stiff-upper-lip types knew how to lose with grace, but that's not to say the Americans do.

It was in this atmosphere that we all met in Death Valley at a hotel in Furnace Creek (so named by the pioneers when sighting a spring that emitted blasts of heat) for the inspection of Mac's site.

59

I flew to Vegas, where I was met by Mr. Lieberman. Albert drove us from there. Mac held down the fort at the site, shifting from his Neville Chamberlain role back to his Lawrence of Arabia mode, and would meet us later on at the hotel.

On the road to Death Valley there is a certain foreboding. After all the name of the place, for one thing, is not calculated to improve the mood. But the spirit of the place is actually belied by its name. You don't ordinarily associate bliss or beauty with Death Valley. You expect it to be the usual forbidding desert scene magnified ten thousand times.

But instead you are in for a shock. When I saw Death Valley it was as if I'd been initiated through a ring of fire. I get it now. I get California. Purple mountains' majesty and all that. I used to pine for Europe here, and the old world. But Death Valley is older than civilization, it is prehistoric and unchanged. It's better than the Amalfi coast, subduing you with its majesty as you drive through.

It's always sunny in Death Valley, ironically. There could be a driving rain in Las Vegas, there could be threatening storm clouds throughout Nevada, but once you come into Death Valley, the storm clouds dissipate and you feel like you are entering the gates of paradise.

You drive on through twisted layers of metamorphic rock, shot through with granitic stone, crumpled swirls of sedimentary layers—a strange prehistoric landscape.

A wasteland, and yet, you're euphoric.

The sunny atmosphere starts at Death Valley Junction, with an old mining camp consisting of a rambling whitewashed hacienda around a windblown dusty court with a piece of sagebrush bowling down the deserted street, a Wild West opera house, and a broken weather vane on top of the Death Valley View Hotel.

It's so godforsaken, so historical, and so pure that you are curiously elated. It may be called Death Valley, but the minute you get there you are subsumed by a vast and incongruous gaiety.

Albert had a different reaction. He went berserk. The desert appeared to drive him mad. We stopped for gas near the California line at about five in the afternoon. That hour does not yet technically constitute twilight in September. The heat outside the car admittedly was pretty bad. Albert asked the gas station attendant if it was hotter than this in August. The attendant began to formulate his answer but Albert slammed the door in his face—he could not endure to wait in the heat to hear the fellow talk.

Temperatures in the desert in September may sink from the 100s to the 90s. So it is rationally conceivable that a trip may be conducted in some comfort then.

Mr. Lieberman had opted for the jodhpurs. The Cecil B. DeMille look. With his safari shirt he was also wearing an ascot, which made him look curiously piteous. He was touchingly solicitous for my welfare. He forced me to remain in the air-conditioned car at all times, and later in the air-conditioned hotel, until evening when the temperatures always cool off. He held the door for me wherever we went. I had an image of him always holding doors for people. He stood up whenever a woman entered the room. It was my fifth month of pregnancy—the best month—but to be on the safe side this would be my last trip for a while. I would not want to deliver a baby in Death Valley. I would not want to deliver a baby in an emergency transport from Death Valley to Las Vegas, the closest point of civilization, not counting Pahrump, the next closest town. I would not like to deliver a baby in Pahrump, Nevada, really.

Little matters save life and death in my condition. That is one reason why prospecting the demise of the venture, the odds for recovery from the downward path we appeared to be on at this time, did not upset me as it normally would. You can't care as much about success and failure when nothing matters save life and death and trying to hold on to the child and carry it through. In the very late stages one can look forward to being on the other side, that moment of glimpsing

225

one's maker. A magnitude of hope begins to set in—you don't want to push your luck by hoping too early. Now it was growing late enough for hope. In the end there is always the infinite and sublime relief that the nine-month ordeal is over, for it is mentally harrowing to house another human being and grow and nurture her in what seems to be a decrepit and decaying body, trying to shield her from all the harms bombarding her, finally to see that she is safe out on her own, not living and growing inside of one in that mentally harrowing way. If I was meek and angelic and kind, then surely someone else would be kind in return—that is, the nurses and doctors, that is, my maker when I meet with him soon.

"Sometimes I wish I were a hydraulics engineer, Miss Ford." Mr. Lieberman interrupted my reverie, staring at the strange formations of the desert badlands as we drove along. Perhaps he felt the deep contentment conversely found in desolation, such as explorers felt at the South Pole.

"Romanticism is the distortion of the classical—when the symmetry is lost," he said, looking at the twisted shapes of rocks and slabs. We were driving through the desert on a two-lane blacktop looking at the strange purity of the vast slabs and shapes of rock, a lunar-seeming landscape, yet infused infinitely with sun.

"Sometimes I wish I were a geologist," he said, "so I could figure it all out."

The twilights are deeper out west. A vast gorgeousness occurs at that hour. The overpowering atmosphere deepens with the oncoming relief. Suddenly you pass a bend in the road and see an ocher-colored rambling hacienda in a palm oasis. It could be Jerusalem. That curious gaiety pervades the place. This was our hotel.

The hotel was built in the twenties. Inside the walls are painted a kind of pale yellow, the same color as the desert.

The screen doors open to the land, and wicker chairs line the balconies and porches, which are the same wheat color as the desert slabs.

The hotel clerk who welcomes you stands in wait at the pale yellow reception room with his screen doors open to the desert. He springs forward in welcoming you with an ecstatic air of glamour, as if a swing band is about to play—which in fact it is. There is a bandstand and old-time music that much befits the place.

You're in Death Valley and everything is suddenly incredibly upbeat.

When we arrived they were having a tea dance. An orchestra played outmoded violin jazz. I won't go so far as to say it was an oasis of cultivation—the few other guests wore shorts and cowboy hats, the food was bad, the decor was in mohair and rawhide—but there was a vibrant air, a happiness, suffusing the place.

The hotel used to close from May to October but now their busiest season is summer, when 90 percent of the business is Europeans who, rather demonically, want to see how hot it can get, and automotive engineers who like to see if certain things will explode at certain temperatures.

The welcoming clerk—a forty-four-year-old man from New York obsessed with the desert, who has more personality and knowledge than anyone else there except for the demonic automotive engineers, and who bears an uncanny resemblance to Burt Lancaster—tells you to take care that your car tires don't explode on the asphalt. Of course the demonic automotive engineers would be ecstatic if their car tires exploded on the asphalt.

I fell in love with the place.

Vegas is not for me. I'm not that crazy about the rest of the Mojave. But Death Valley, now that's another story.

The Burt Lancaster look-alike sidled up to deliver a message to me from Mac: he was delayed at the drilling site and I should not wait up.

60

When we went down to dinner the atmosphere of joy was even elevated, as if everything were vibrating with joy and emanating a vast fascination. A bistro in Paris, sun-drenched legionnaires marching toward the desert while early Stéphane Grappelli violin jazz plays at a North African café, a dusky voice like Marlene Dietrich from the tuxedo-clad orchestra leader who roved around the open dining room beneath the stars.

A few old cowboy couples and demonic automotive engineers slouched toward the dance floor. Albert loitered at the bar looking over at our table from time to time like a Mafia bodyguard. Disheveled stragglers congregated in the corners. Then the orchestra was for some reason replaced by a lone accordionist. This lone accordionist, however, was still vastly glamorous, if a little scruffy, playing old jazz numbers, a one-man Paris bistro.

"You know that book you're always reading, *The Decay of the British Aristocracy?*" said Mr. Lieberman. "Well, this dance floor reminds me of what it would look like if it were *really* decayed."

On the cover of *The Decay of the British Aristocracy* was a sepia photograph of women in 1930s evening gowns and men in white tie having cocktails on a gorgeous lawn. Oh, to be in a lovely world of white tie and cocktails and cigars. But this was close enough. For some reason I see now—be it midlife or motherhood—that life will never be otherwise really. Once it was white tie and cocktails and cigars. Now it is duties and responsibilities and cowboys. Once it was decadence, the last ensign of our fading empire. Now it is the finite span of life. Too late for decadence at this point.

Did Mr. Lieberman brood over the decline of his star? I wondered. It would not really be like him. But he did brood over Adelaide, his only anguish being that he lost her, the only woman he had ever loved. She traveled with him, and he could not really get over her, he was not that manner of man. To share in his dismay, or to dissipate it, I brought up my own troubles. I was not in the mood to lose my dignity in that moment, however. But I was sad, hearing his story. I couldn't comprehend the solitude of such a man. I sank in a bit of a quagmire. It was partly the pain of relations with Mac. It was partly the pain of worry always for the kids, including the one I carry. They for whom I must build the scaffold, as my mother did for me, on which they can then go forth and achieve something. They whom I must save from destruction. The inescapable fact of your gallantry in giving them life is not a consideration yet at this time—too early for hope until you see the result of your one brief moment of courage. Meanwhile there is the ever-present pain of self-loathing. Then Mr. Lieberman asked me to dance. Suddenly it turned out he was a great dancer, and I found that I had my head on his shoulder shedding some tears, and the accordion guy was playing an old jazz song called "Stars Fell on Alabama," with that suave old American jazz harmony, under the desert moon, and there descended a sudden relief from anguish. There was a kind of a Fred Astaire thing happening, with that resemblance Mr. Lieberman bore to him, and then his dancing ability, to lead you and sweep you around in his arms as if you had no weight—I am petite, even when five months pregnant—while he crooned the words of the song in the suave American syncopation:

Did it really happen
Was I really there
Was I really there with you?
We lived our little drama
We kissed in a field of white
And stars fell on Alabama last night.

It put me in a reverie. To give a moment's peace. Or maybe it was the way he danced. Then it transported us to a place we loved, Alabama, each for different reasons, for me because it was my native place which had a glamour blazoned on my heart; for him to remember Adelaide. Maybe she was watching over us, sending us a message from the other side, for it was such a rare and transcendent moment of release and beauty, when pain and anguish lift, and suddenly there is suavity and relief and happiness and hope.

"You're my last love, Fleming," he said.

What once has loved must love incessantly. That was the key. The heart is trained. The heart is in the habit. That was what drew him to me.

It would destroy me to break my word. It would break everything I have elaborately constructed to live by.

"But you have many more years for more loves . . . You'll find . . ."

"Sometimes I hardly know there's a world out there." He made a graceful gesture with his hand.

"Oh, not you, who covers every square inch of California . . ."

"Yes, that's my quest. It's good to have a quest."

It had always been a sort of privilege to be near him. I felt a reverence toward him. I had been instantaneously fascinated by him from the first. My paradise was peopled by two, and an old jazz song. He was standing there looking at me, holding my hand, his brows slightly knit, my heart at his feet. They don't take your heart unless they mean it, and unless they know you mean it. And they know well enough how to determine that. When you want to stick around but you are also dying to leave, then you know you are lost. The strong thing was that I loved him without reservation, his character as well as to be in his arms, and at last, at last I was there.

61

So I was on the edge of a precipice again, dancing. I was poised at the edge of a cliff like the empires about to crash in. A crisis was developing. It is in a crisis that you may unlock the secret of your heart. I tried to look at it from the outside. Would I like the girl who danced off the edge of that cliff, who had the satisfaction of achieving an actual sin, a sin I am too strong to commit? "There is very little sin in the depths of the malaise." This woman wouldn't be strong. But she would have a heart. It's plain at least she would be in an odd situation. You don't leave your husband when you're six months pregnant and have two other kids at home and know the measure of your husband's worth, though the towering figure is cast in your path. What mysterious, even mystical thing is it that holds two people together that way? Fear of losing him, fear as of God. The sinner knows God, it's said. God loves the sinner even more. But why?

I had those black and white scruples, but there was the dangerous issue of my awe and reverence for the older man, the towering figure, the white-haired gent—the basic figure of my heart. It was overpowering to be with this person. It included many visions of the world, a vast sense of promise while he lived, that anything was possible. I thought of it all, of my love for him, and his, remarkably, for me.

Mr. Lieberman was still standing as the suave song played, "Stars Fell on Alabama," though I retired to a chair. The song had me in a trance. I saw Mac walk onto the dance floor. Mr. Lieberman shook his hand.

"She's in the reverie chair," said Mr. Lieberman, pointing at me. "Would you mind not leaving me alone with this woman in future?" he said. I looked over at him through the stars falling. I felt austere. The air was cold and clear.

Later when I went back inside Albert was sitting at the bar with Mac. Albert was telling Mac about his diseases.

"I have a rare disease they can't diagnose," he said with obvious and ill-concealed pride.

He said he had collapsed in a parking lot only last week. People collapse in parking lots often here. A lot of things happen in parking lots here. What with all the cars. "It's my kidneys I'm worried about," he clarified.

"What is the finest type of whiskey?" Albert then asked.

"It depends if you want bourbon or scotch," said Mac. "Who's it for?"

"It's for me. I want to get soused," said Albert.

The lanterns and the exotic accordion music floated on the night down a trail of dying palms across the desert leading to the low-end ranch. They even have social classes in Death Valley, something they don't have much of in this region. You had two choices in Death Valley: the jubilating

232

hotel, or the low-end ranch; the ecstatic orchestra or a cowboy jukebox. It was like the difference between paradise and reality. The hotel was paradise; the ranch was reality.

"I'm going to the ranch," said Albert, which after complaining about a few ailments (pleurisy, gout), he did. But first he rebuked me. "Your husband is very gallant," he glared at me. "Forbearing," he added. Then he seemed to evaporate into the night.

Mac remained.

"What is it between you and Mr. Lieberman?" said Mac.

"I adore the guy. You do too."

"But you seem to be having some sort of flirtation."

"I live in a land of barbarians. Here at the quiet limit of the world. I don't come across that many people I can relate to."

"I'm still asking the original question."

There are two types of people in the world, I was thinking. One will take whatever crumbs are offered, when it comes to love. The other is more stern and would refuse crumbs, in favor of the whole pie. All or nothing.

I kind of like the first type better. Someone has that much love for you, they would take crumbs. You can always sense it when you are confronted with a person of this type. They're all fellow souls and feel at home when they find themselves in one another's company.

Sometimes they are innocents. Sometime they are moral arbiters who can be counted on to make a distinction between black and white, disdaining gray.

"The Victorians needed heroes as an addict needs heroin." I know what that means. I need heroes and the way I worship them is a drug I get high on every day of my life. Picture a god, standing astride the earth. That was your father in Alabama.

"Are you happy here, Fleming?" Mac demanded.

233

"The human soul adjusts. Mine's adjusting."

"Harry is fragile." The chorus. "You're strong. I'm wondering if he is strong enough to withstand your flirtation."

"I thought he was so cosmopolitan that he had established a certain distance at dangerous times to quarantine himself against the perils of such things."

"But here we are stranded together in the desert. It's not so cosmopolitan here."

"Maybe he needs my help. The man is bereaved. The man is a grieving widower. And what about you? I don't know where I stand with you. Jealousy doesn't even enter in for you. It takes courage to lose with grace, but who is the loser here? If I lost you the inordinate thing I would seek for is dignity."

I remember the night Mac left Fort Defiance to take his job in New York. He left before I did. The gin and tonic bottles and lemons and limes lined up so neatly, in readiness, on the gallery, and the empty chairs, at four in the morning. It was after one of those wild drives to New Orleans in the middle of the night. The Gulf Coast was a shambles, the sleazy motels, the ignorance, the plantation of Jefferson Davis that always seemed like something you should leave behind, the retreat of a failure, a rather ignominious failure, though the place was beautiful and once, when not lined by sleazy motels, with sleazy casinos one day to follow, more beautiful still. Obscure ignominy was the mood.

Then, as now, I got up to leave. What drives two people apart? I'm not sure an affair is what drives them apart. It may be something deeper, that one doesn't love as much as the other does.

An unpromising revelation. But why unpromising when it is something to recognize failure, see the truth, and then one can strive to make a change?

I still had Proustian flashbacks to the night we first met:

a light coming on in the heart, some type of awakening from my circumscribed existence to a larger world, for then he took me out of the small one of Fort Defiance, wearing a seersucker suit, the one I had envisioned. It was a matter of the soul, since when you have between you the conception of children, there seems in fact the hand of God involved. I felt it even then, when we first met: the inescapable fact of his gallantry—as Albert had noted.

"But I know you, Fleming. I know what you're capable of. I know what you're not capable of."

Then I was walking down the hall alone and when I passed Mr. Lieberman's room I heard him singing. A million times were worth that moment, standing in the hall, rooted to the spot, hearing him striding around his room and singing—"Let me be the first one to kiss you good morning and the last one to kiss you good night"—in that Fred Astaire old-time voice, with lilts—with Death Valley outside so vastly. Reverberating through the night to the stars more visible in the vast landscape of the galaxies than I had ever seen before. At the end of the horizon. With Fred Astaire and the secret of life. I read an article in the newspaper about a woman who suffered from mental depression, and Fred Astaire was the only thing that gave her hope. I stood transfixed in the hall as he was coming out to get some ice and gazed at him so longingly that he crushed me to his heart, as he so often had. He was upright and crisp and manly, as if he too had the secret of life. It was humility. The humble shall be exalted. His embrace had a tacit, impassive grace.

"You grace your surroundings, Miss Ford."

I think he had me confused with the relief of the night and the dance. It was he who had the grace.

"Grace comes easily when there are no other duties to perform or be harassed by."

"I'm harassing you. And you still have grace."

"You couldn't possibly harass me. Tell me about the battlefields of World War One."

"I wasn't born then, you know. You have me confused with an older relic."

But he did seem frail to me in his Alabama seersucker and white bucks, if dapper.

"You asked me once if I ever had a midlife crisis. I told you I didn't have time for that. Fleming, you must have surmised. You know my story. Now my crisis is you."

I held on tightly in our embrace, and some tears were shed, looking at the vast desert at the end of the hall. I held on tightly to him that way for some time. I felt his heart beat wildly in its fragile cage.

He put his hand on the side of my face; his expression was wistful, but gruff.

"But don't worry, kid. I've fixed things. You're going to be fine."

I retreated to the hallway and said good night, and he looked at me for a moment as though he had forgotten some question he wanted to ask, or as though staring at this girl for the first time in utter perplexity. Pondering the odds, standing at the edge of his precipice. He looked at the girl standing in the hall and thought that she seemed to be receding in a crowd, or walking down a solitary corridor, across the years between them.

It was uniquely pathetic. There was a feeling I could not repel, that I would never see him again outside of Death Valley, "this camp of trouble, of forlorn hope, on the edge of a desert stretching out before us like a small sea, with no hope for relief except at the end of a struggle which seemed almost hopeless," though to me it had been so jubilant, and so overpowering.

The next day was the inspection, which I did not attend, and later I returned to Esperanza with Mac. Mr. Lieberman and Albert drove off down the two-lane blacktop in the middle of the desert, a beautiful desolation, in the opposite direction.

62

After that Mr. Lieberman disappeared for a few weeks. Someone saw him at a spa in Palm Springs looking very run-down. Mac didn't hear from him either.

"Maybe this old Count you're always talking about knows where he is," suggested Mac.

"No, no. He's not an old Count. He's a sick Duke. And I don't know where he is either. I could try the hotels. Do you think they have him registered under his title?" I could never figure out what his actual name was. I think his title was styled as the Duke of Churchill. But then Churchill was not his actual name. It was like a Trollope novel: people in the know refer to Lord Silverbridge as Silverbridge, as if that were his first name, but it's not. Yet people don't refer to the Duke of Omnium as Omnium. I couldn't figure it out. When Lord Maltravers marries Mrs. Best-Chestwyn he becomes the Viscount Metroland. You can't keep it straight.

The sick Duke was no slouch either, in reality, or at least his family wasn't, being of some branch of the Westminsters, who owned Mayfair, Belgravia, and Pimlico. However, as it was said of one of his relatives, his life was "shamelessly, successfully and simultaneously devoted to self-indulgence and self-destruction, and he achieved more distinction in each of these fields than most men achieve in any." It was said that when this relative expired it was the only time that his behavior could be characterized as gallant.

I would have followed them anywhere, the sick Duke and Mr. Lieberman, wandering out of the century against the untoward backdrop of this cowboy outpost. The paradox was what kept me going—one culture transplanted to another, like the quixotic attempt to create Barsetshire on the Equator in the old empire, or even the sight of a seersucker suit in New York. Thus it was I had followed the seersucker suit out of New York.

I remember the sick Duke once telling me that Mr. Lieberman hated clubs. Never went to them. Hated the exclusion. It was difficult to resign from them, however. He did resign from some that he hated most of all. The California Club would be different. It was strictly business, I believe. So I tried him there but to no avail.

Then the water was discovered at the desert site one evening in October, when it came up gushing like an oil well.

Within hours Mr. Lieberman was on the scene, as I heard from Mac. So he had spies about.

A few days later he sent me a copy of his Index of Life, with a note saying that he knew I would meet the coming event with the grit and determination for which southern women have been known. It was written on a card with his heraldic crest, and underneath a poem was quoted: "Thou art the same through change of times, through frozen zones and burning climes; / From the equator to the pole, the same kind angel through the whole."

So I waited for my time to come.

63

Fall is not coming to Esperanza, by the way. You will not find fall depicted on the local weather segment of the news nor in the local atmosphere.

Yet I've gotten so obsessed with the weather that every day I generally turn first to the weather page in the *New York Times,* the one where they have three careening paragraphs madly summarizing the weather throughout the nation, usually encompassing an esoteric weather theme like "Atmospheric Memory" (the tendency for unlikely events to recur in the same area). Everyone is terminally obsessed with the weather in Esperanza. Walking down the street you'll overhear passersby discussing the marine layer, saltwater basins, tangential winds—using technical terms as if they were trained meteorologists. I suffer from fright when witnessing the world weather traumas that comprise the local news. Even two hours north in L.A. they're always having some disaster or other with the fires and the mudslides, etc. But in Esperanza things are always calm.

Sometimes I'm not in the mood for mariachi music, though. But that's tough. Because there's always mariachi music. Escape to the El Cortez, a Mexican dive near the Presidio with the kids.

In the twilight it is always more beautiful than in the broad of day. In the evening it is idyllic. The café was perched on a canyon. Everything was green, for some people even water the canyon and have elaborate gardens down there, and their palm trees are greener than others.

"Do you come here a lot?" asked a man standing near.

"Incessantly," I said and swilled my lovely nonalcoholic beverage.

For such are my old haunts—Mexican violins and sleazy cafés, which are not that sleazy in the gorgeous weather.

How delightful to be in a nonplace, where you know no one, have no friends, no past, no history. The weight of the past, of the generations, which was once to me so dear, compared to California seems a heavy weight to bear. This is how California changes you forever. It blots everything else out.

Next thing I'll want to go surfing, and live in a subdivision called Driftwood.

I look longingly at the shiny new lodgings just carved into the bald hills called *Extended Stay America*. Such a light weight to bear. Maybe I'll stick around for a while. Maybe I'll extend my stay. Maybe I won't. I'll just spring up like a weed here and there.

At the café I thought I saw Mr. Lieberman—looking beleaguered and troubled and romantic—inexpressibly fascinating—walking forcefully past. My heart leapt. I got up to follow, went searching down the halls. I could have sworn I saw him. Perhaps I had willed him into existence. There was no sign of him now.

I took the kids to LegoLand, the demented creation of a vast maniac. Detailed re-creations of San Francisco, New York, and New Orleans all made ingeniously out of Legos, everything in the entire place made out of Legos—the rides, the statues, the grass—no matter how obsessively intricate. The CEO of Lego has gone around the bend, obviously.

We watched down-on-their-luck actors who have to have

jobs doing the children's show in FunTown at LegoLand. They're not headed for Hollywood. They're headed for Orlando. They're headed for more children's shows. They're headed for dressing up like a duck and reeking of scotch to perform at birthday parties.

The light is very disorienting at LegoLand. The sun, the glare—it's the freak-out sun thing with the violins screeching. My brain swirled. I had a desire to flee. It's the Wild West everywhere—the bald hills, the desert, the mountains, the vast landscape. It doesn't get cold but there's a chill at night, but it is impossible to get a coat in California. Everyone wears T-shirts throughout the winter, even though at least at night there is a definite chill on. But no one would ever be caught dead wearing a coat. They're cowboys. They're tough. It's the Wild West.

That night was my first earthquake. I was awakened at about three in the morning by the armoire rocking side to side for what seemed like minutes but was more likely seconds. It came from the Mojave Desert, this earthquake, and taking place in a region without much habitation there were no injuries.

Mac was out there. He called to say they were all right.

The next day the local weather segment had something to report. People riddled with brain swirl were interviewed in their Hawaiian shirts, saying "I'd rather be in earthquake weather than in a blizzard back east." I agreed with them! The baking blazing sun was dear in winter amid the old wood mansions and the giant palm trees in the hills on the azure Pacific. An attack of happiness. The way the sun was.

A Santa Ana blew through as I walked with Josie while the coyotes howled in the canyon in the broad of day.

"Where is the nearest mailbox?" I asked the Federal Express girl where I was sending off some New Perspectives to my editor. I finally had some.

241

"Eleven palm trees down the road," she pointed.

"Another day in paradise," said the man standing behind me.

The sun shone brightly on the palms, all eleven of them.

64

Three months passed. Still I didn't see Mr. Lieberman again. Which was odd, but then, an impasse had been reached, at Death Valley. He had established a moral position.

The so-called rainy season came. But no apocalyptic catastrophes or biblical inundations appeared imminent. So as I waited for my time to come I was reassured. Volcanic eruptions did not arise. The famed thin green flash made a nightly appearance. Something about the horizon in collusion with the sunset.

The sky turned an interesting slate color. The azaleas bloomed in my garden. The grip of nostalgia tightened its hold. I was incurably nostalgic for each house, each season, each phase of life represented since I'd been here.

At La Dolcita I missed the thick sheaf of palm fronds outside my hotel window at Santa Maria, the vodka tonic capital of the world—retired admirals—when Mac first brought me out to visit Esperanza and the quiet hot town with the atmosphere of a resort, and we had lunch on the Italian patio among the Roman umbrellas in what seemed like the Mediterranean sun and walked along the ocean and the Pacific grew on me. Not at first glance a comforting sea, it being so vast and barbaric—the cliffs, the beaches are not gentle—but over time it became beautiful.

My human nature was so lowly, my nostalgia for the thing just past so relentless, that I repined for my first days here when I was forty, a stranger in California, and companionless except for a debauched botanist. I would pine for my career slump and my old haunts in the sudden palmy garden of the Mexican town. In a certain way it seemed exhilarating, looking back. That's the thing about looking back. What seemed hideous at the time looks very fond in retrospect. And being a failure in Santa Maria, the vodka tonic capital of the world, was different than being a failure in New York. It was a good place to be a failure in, among the retired admirals in a dusty border town with some military bases in the blazing sun of the endless evenings on the sea, the alien atmosphere of a resort. Being a failure among retired admirals, washed-up starlets, down-on-their-luck actors who are reduced to doing the birthday shows at Fun-Town, and fifty-year-old men dressed up as a duck to perform at children's parties, cash only, is actually less excruciating than being a success. I will then review the sloping street I live on now, its view to the twilight and old Craftsman bungalows, the boulevard of tall palms outside our bedroom window.

It is not for the far past that one is nostalgic—the drives along the Gulf Coast to Dauphin Island and Biloxi, childhood—it is for six months ago: the house I lived in then that won my heart, the garden with no shade, where driving home you always saw the glimpse of the blue sea and the harbor baking away between the swaying palms or at night lit up entrancingly, and your heart stopped with its beauty. I no longer have nostalgia for the farther past, remoter spots, but only for the canyons and coyotes that I lived with last.

Only for incessant mariachi music at Mexican cafés. For Albert pruning in the hotel garden, having swept the porch, raving on about his kidneys. Zorro in polyester. Zorro with a lot of personality problems.

The tendency to bask in nostalgia goes to the root of existence. Here is what I recollect when I walk past my previous houses and neighborhoods: innocence and hope. That is why nostalgia so allures. You think a past time was more innocent and that then you had more hope. Sometimes it's as if a wave comes over you that remembers hope—you can't always quite recall if it was a place that hope resided in, New York maybe, or a certain house, with its air of promise and ambition, or just some more innocent state.

A complicated cocktail of college girls helped me with the kids and I attempted to send in my New Perspectives to the paper, while I waited for my time to come. It was strange having your husband absent during the late stages of a pregnancy, but I had adjusted to my new position as pioneer woman in the late stages of a pregnancy in the Wild West. Or at least the modern version of it: when I drove past *Extended Stay America,* the residence inn unburdened and untroubled by the weight of history or aesthetics, situated on the freeway, it was refreshing and alluring to me now even as a home. How exhilarating to be so in flux that you might extend your stay, or you might not. How cozy it becomes to hear the roar of engines on a sleek new freeway in the night, Americans careening toward their temporary homes.

Here we have no abiding city.

The whole night glows—some esoteric meteorological condition pertaining to the paradisiac beauty of the place. Unless, of course, suddenly at the last minute you find out there's a radioactive nuclear waste dump just down the road that's making the place glow all night.

I was looking at real estate brochures about the latest millionaire subdivisions carved into the bald hills. "Relive the romance of Italy! Authentic Tuscan Villas offer a privileged and luxurious old world lifestyle . . . Timeless setting of serenity . . . 18th-century chandeliers and built-in 10-foot television and surround sound systems . . ."

I know how much they enjoyed timeless ten-foot televisions and surround systems in eighteenth-century Tuscany.

We used to go out to dinner on Saturday night in New York at the French bistro on Fifty-first Street. Sometimes we went to an Italian trattoria on Fifty-seventh Street, a vast cold avenue lined by skyscrapers. I used to think, It's not exactly homey here, on Fifty-seventh Street. But I do think *Extended Stay America* is homey—bare stark stucco in bland nameless neutral color, the whole place carved into the bald hill above the freeway five minutes ago, as yet unplanted, with a garden of raw dirt. Yet I find it homey. And I am not nostalgic for New York, but only for my remove to Esperanza, at the quiet limit of the world—because it was so shocking. This is an advance against nostalgia. Nostalgia is only a way of treasuring life itself, wishing to go back, thus to prolong it— life.

I heard that Mr. Lieberman had returned to England for a time, to the depressing seaside resorts that had never played a part in his own youth there. What did he search for on his dark journey? I wondered. He languished on the Yorkshire Dales. But the Yorkshire Dales are not noted to allure in December.

Then I heard that he was back in Pasadena. The mornings were glorious, an exalted paradise, the San Gabriel Mountains framing the palms below, the pure blue sky and sun. The air of a resort, the air of respite. If you had a desire to flee, here was the correct place to flee to. Yet that which was so paradisiacal at dawn by noon becomes unbearable until evening, far too much respite for the soul to bear. The soul needs a little gray sometimes. The soul needs to toil in darkness at times.

So he careened from coast to coast and continent to continent. Now very near, roving around his beloved California. He stopped at resorts in Palm Springs and Anza-Borrego. On the first day of October at seven o'clock in the evening it was still so hot that it was beyond simple endurance to stand outside. Ditto on the first day of November.

Someone heard he was in love again—what once has loved must love incessantly, the heart is trained, the heart is in the habit—and saw him at Palm Springs, sitting at one of those outside cafés where a fine mist of water sprays from a sprinkler system to refresh the patrons in the desert heat.

The Santa Anas raged.

I studied the list of local events for the week:

Overwintering American Redstarts
Tropical Cyclones
Australian Heat Wave
Loyal to the End

Then came a note from him with the address "Darling Fleming." He said he had regained his joy in living. He enclosed an article on the forty-five varieties of palms he grew on his place in Florida. He signed it "Harry."

It was more than a fond dream. It was my reality.

65

There is nothing quite like reading books about World War I to make you feel fortunate. I wouldn't mind reading books about World War I all day. One conclusion I've reached after reading a number of books about World War I is that I think it would be heroic to be a deserter.

It is to be supposed that a British person who lived through both world wars and the Depression would have a worldview similar to that expressed by Dr. Johnson: "In human life there is everywhere much to be endured and little to be enjoyed." Or maybe it is just a British attribute or personality trait. It is plain to see that for someone holding this attitude, America and especially California would be distasteful. Suffering, not pleasure, was their constant, whereas California represents the opposite point of view, to seek ceaselessly for personal well-being.

For example, everyone keeps trying to get you to buy a boat. They keep hanging around in their bathrobe and telling you you should get a boat. Sometimes they try to sell you *their* boat. The great point is you should go boating a lot. I keep thinking maybe they were at one time so tortured they needed to escape to a life of boating—on the smoothest sea, under the perfect sun. It's catching, of course. The human soul adjusts.

I used to think it was all so weird, and what's so terrible about a little rain, and how can you react to the sameness of the perfect conditions every day, but now my transformation is complete. Forgot my sunglasses today—big mistake—yet I reveled in the broad unending sun. It is amazing how the human soul adjusts. White tie and tails? The clamor of empire? Just give me a canyon and a vast bald hill. I'd feel at home.

Maybe it was the pregnancy. For one day you hit that phase of pregnancy where you feel ecstatic. You look around and say, How could I not have noticed that this place is rapturous? This balcony to the giant palms and bungalows and harbor. Its forms of beauty. The gorgeous hamlet and its actual shade, the ravishing view at the front porch of the old Craftsman houses, all from the early century, and the quietude, which the coyotes yelping only make more picturesque—in the smashing palm-laden twilight.

The drive is rather quaint through Homeville, Normalville, and Normal Heights to Starlight, each with its old-fashioned neon sign emblazoning the name of the neighborhood hung between the palm trees across the flat boulevard, with the sun being destructive of all you have known and believed, and the mountains coming up in the background at Starlight. Some rare old neighborhoods toward the desert are kind of raunchy, kind of seedy, kind of like they've seen better days in the fifties, kind of gutsy, with Mediterranean-style porticoes and broken neon signs on the main street, and an old-time theater and everything falling apart and baking in the sun like Palermo.

Maybe a man should not ask for happiness. Maybe the happy man is the stupid man. Or it may be the happy man is the American.

Everyone looked like Mr. Lieberman—white-haired and old and intriguing.

66

The baby was born (all went well). That's one thing we got out of California. Mr. Lieberman was right. It could only have happened here. Never amid the ambition and catastrophes and winters of New York. So I now hold California greatly dear. The baby made even the most hardened criminals and depressed cynics glad. There was something mystical about her. But Mr. Lieberman was not around to see it.

I thought of him in the delivery room, I thought of him first off after the baby was born. I tried to call him from the hospital. I tried the Alexandria, I tried the Ritz-Carlton in Pasadena, the Bel-Air and the California Club and the small hotel in Santa Monica on the sea. But it turned out he was at a spa not far from Costa Verde. I thought I would see him again, but I didn't. To my unending dismay, he died of a sudden heart attack there some days later.

Life and death coincided for us. He was not around to see the new life he had done so much in fact to nurture. There was a sign from him on what I later realized must have been the night he died. The gardenias bloomed wildly in my garden, and their scent overpowered the air. The baby (Adelaide) cried so I brought her in my bed and Fred Astaire was singing in an old movie on TV. She and I were lying side by side as I held her dear and close; it was before I knew. The music was as glamorous as ever, and ineffably sweet, and there was a ring of fate around her, a greatness Esperanza

249

gave to me that New York would not have, my California miracle. Odd that we, who forty-one years separate, should have that sublime bond, and how she was destined to exist, sensing her opportunity, since her parents' times together to conceive her were so rare. The proud palms raged down the boulevard outside my bedroom window in the night, as Fred Astaire in black and white sang suavely on, with the lifting of a weight of grief, the dark syncopation, our gift to the old world: jazz.

Before the obituary appeared in the *New York Times*, it was Albert who told me the news. He called from the spa not far from Costa Verde where Mr. Lieberman had been taking one of his esoteric California cures. Albert was in pieces, and had been called on to make all arrangements, for which he sought my aid. There was no next of kin. The sick Duke called in the obituary to the *New York Times*:

> . . . Daring career in finance that spanned the century . . . Brought the storied banking name to the U.S. . . . . Leaves a legacy of water in the desert to quench the thirst of the West . . . End of the line for a man, a family, and an era . . . Leaves no survivors but endows, as he had in life, an astonishing array of charitable and educational institutions . . .

I went to New York for the memorial service some weeks later. New York with the kids was, as ever, sometimes hard, obliterating even my remorse. There was a catastrophe day: subways closed, no buses, no taxis, gridlocked traffic, and stranded in midtown with a three-year-old. That type of thing. But on a breezy afternoon amid the humanity I took Josie to a Broadway matinee. It was very Busby Berkeley, with people dressed up as spoons and knives and forks and tablecloths doing elaborate production numbers. Dressing up like a spoon every day of your life for six years (that's how long it had been running) with punctilious dedication strikes me as most endearing. The costumes were extremely elaborate. People who sing and dance in Busby Berkeley–type spectacles every day for six years trudging backstage to smoke a cigarette while all dressed up as a spoon are very dear. In fact they show a spirit of excellence.

Everyone in New York looked hauntingly familiar as when after a long absence you return to what was once home. You would run into people you knew at the Oyster Bar and have a communion with them and everything was colloquial and promising and kind of old world. I kept thinking it was more promising in New York, that someone would care. It was never promising of that out west. That was perhaps what made Mr. Lieberman so striking.

As Norman Douglas said, "What is life but a search for a friend?" Or a love. Same thing.

The air in New York was more clear and normal and stern and serious than in Esperanza. For whatever the reason, the contrast and the human malaise: it was ecstatically beautiful in New York. Winter was a dashing thing back east, while walking around New York in your overcoat and wool scarf in the gray suave days. You conquered the place when you were young. It was suave and gleaming and old and you had come and seen and conquered. There was the deep thrill of seeing something old—which you do not often get in California—ancient architraves and dormer windows giving off the keen emotion of the vision of another time.

Dark memories pursued me at each corner, where I met his spirit, which accompanied me and which always I addressed as Darling. The Beaux Arts buildings glittered in the brilliant air. There was storminess at twilight, clarity at noon, undreamt-of weather changes in one day. Everyone on the street looked like they were thinking about something. You don't get that on the other coast. Humanity raged away while in Esperanza there was only solitude, reclusion, and disgust. But if we had fled the West I would not have got the baby. I would not have had the guts. Only amid the bougainvillea and the blue sea and the calm could I have had the guts.

The memorial was held in a church on Park Avenue. It was attended by philanthropists and politicians, tycoons—the tycoons who had mysteriously reversed their positions in a flurry of disloyalty and were now sorry, government officials, the powerful. To most of the people there it came out of the blue, as had his remove to the West Coast, and it was a death of senseless abruptness to them. But not to me. So I became one of those people who cannot tolerate otherwise than thinking that there is an eternal consciousness.

I saw the sick Duke, disheveled as ever, wearing some sort of monogrammed slippers with his suit. But he could never fill the place of Harry. It wasn't at all the same. The sick Duke had inherited a place in the world. There is a type of man who would have felt the joy of heaven once he got in—the outsider looking in wistfully, enraptured. That wasn't Harry. He could care less about that glamour world and had more of a pride in his own and earned place. But he was in a curious position. He was in with the in crowd, but owing to his pride and his acceptance of his more humble origins, he left it behind. The sign for Cipriani at Grand Central reminded me of that favored world he had been taken into by his father and had left behind.

I could never see Hollywood again but through his eyes. I could tell exactly what it once was like, despite its reputed present ruination, a North African air, some Moorish architecture, the maddening sun, the vast palms and pepper trees. Even Hollywood has to me that storied and substantial air that you would get in Vienna or Budapest or any great cosmopolitan city. But then you would be walking up the hills among the palazzos and Craftsman bungalows so mysteriously hidden behind the thick foliage, until suddenly an iron gate opens to—the Wild West. Vast mountains and bald hills in the blazing sun with dusty trails, cowboy fences, eucalyptus groves. You walk up a huge mountain and see the entire city beneath you, this raging Wild West wilderness in the middle of a great cosmopolitan metropolis. I was astounded in wonder and in joy for the duration of the day he took me on that endless trail; and had kept looking back to try to fix it in my mind, at the base a jungle, a palm oasis, then looking up to the vast hills and mountains, then back down to the mysterious palazzos. There would be no more mountains to climb with him. But I would climb them still. He showed me where they were. The heights to scale would seem less exalted without the courtliness and fascination of his personality. For he was also a heartthrob. It was more than a fond dream. It was my reality. What gets me is that he didn't make it out of the twentieth century.

God, I miss the twentieth century.

FICTION LEMANN
Lemann, Nancy.
Malaise :a novel /

OCEE LIBRARY

Atlanta-Fulton Public Library